# HIGH
# COTTON
# AND
# MAGNOLIAS

# HIGH COTTON AND MAGNOLIAS

a novel

# KATIE HART SMITH

*To Hannah,*

*Many Blessings!*

*Katie Hart Smith*

Deeds Publishing | Atlanta

Published by Deeds Publishing in Athens, GA
www.deedspublishing.com

Printed in The United States of America

Cover by Mark Babcock
Text layout by Ashley Clarke

Library of Congress Cataloging-in-Publications data is available upon request.

ISBN 978-1-947309-79-1

Books are available in quantity for promotional or premium use. For information, email info@deedspublishing.com.

First Edition, 2019

10 9 8 7 6 5 4 3 2 1

Lovingly, for my parents

# Acknowledgements

I would like to thank the following:

First and foremost, to my adoring husband, Jeff, for his unwavering love and support, always.

To Georgia's Former First Lady, Sandra Deal, who has unselfishly given her heart to the State of Georgia, supporting literacy, and who served with passion and grace to inspire the lives of those she touches. I'm forever appreciative of your lovely notes of encouragement for the Sacred Heart series, the trilogy, a time capsule preserving Georgia's history and iconic places.

To those medical professionals who have or are currently dedicated to the healing arts in service to their communities around the world.

To the readers, I thank you for embarking on this fictional literary journey with me. I encourage you to visit the historic landmarks described throughout the Sacred Heart series with a sense of wonder, adventure, and imagination.

To my maternal grandma, "Gigi," who, despite family objections, bravely broke the chains of poverty, followed her heart, and pursued her dreams to become a registered nurse in 1927. She forever changed our family's lineage. Gigi was the inspiration for the Sacred Heart series. We honor her legacy and memory at Georgia Gwinnett College, Department of Health Sciences, School of Nursing, "History of Nursing" exhibit, where her story of being a first-generation graduate inspires future generations of nursing students.

"Give every day the chance to become the most beautiful day of your life"

*Mark Twain*

Alexander Street

Alexander Hall

Ambulance

Barn/Garage/Storage

A Wing

Alan
Edward
Clyde
Leus

Tx Room
Maternity
Waiting Room

Nursery
Peds
E
E

Concierge

Gray Tunnel

Goode Tunnel

Spring Street

Pharm

B Wing
OR Suites

Med/Surg
ED

Greene Tunnel

S.H. Nursing School

A.H. Nursing School

Ambulance

**SACRED HEART HOSPITAL GROUNDS**

# 1

*Dear Diary,*

*Today is day #1 of writing in this silly book and day #402 out of 1,095 days left of nursing school at Sacred Heart Hospital. My Nursing Superintendent, Lena Hartman, gave me this beautiful blue diary, complete with a gold lock and key, as a birthday gift last year on Christmas Day. It has taken me nearly five months to pick up this darn thing and write something clever in it. I've not had the urge to write about myself and feel more comfortable charting about my patient's surgical wound site and bowel and bladder habits instead. Nurse Hartman suggested that it would be good for me to put my feelings on paper. She told me that my stories will serve as a reminder of all that I have and will accomplish and be a gift to the generations that will come after me. Nurse Hartman and I have a close bond. I've shared things about my past; she knows things about my family that not many people know. So, I guess, I'll use a few of these blank pages to sum up the past nineteen years.*

Addie dropped down a line and placed the grey-lead, new-

1

ly-sharpened pencil point on the paper. *Crunch!* Tiny bits of graphite crumbled off the end of the pencil. Addie blew them on the floor and wiped the remnants away. *Name: Addie Rose Engel. Date of birth: December 25, 1895. Age: 19. Birthplace: Hope, Georgia. Parents: Dead. Sister: Dead. Brother. Dead. Best friends:* Addie stopped, refusing to be sucked back into those dark days, and found sanity in levity, writing, *They are among the living and named Opal Alexander and Roberta "Bertie" Jones. Boyfriends: #1- Garrett Darling, my childhood friend who is now a fireman for Firehouse #6 in the Fourth Ward. He lives in his aunt's house that was given to me in her last will and testament when she passed, an unexpected inheritance after serving as her nursemaid after my parents died.*

Addie remembered Nurse Hartman telling her, 'Write your entries like you are talking with one of your best friends.' Opting to be honest and conversational with her new hard-bound friend, Addie chose to give her diary a nickname and added, *Oh, Blue, I forgot to mention that Sacred Heart's pediatrician, Dr. Randall Springer, also resides in that house. He was my original renter, relocating to Atlanta from Children's Hospital of Philadelphia, and needed a place to stay. The good Lord smiled on me when I found out I was accepted to nursing school and I needed to figure out what to do with the house. Dr. Springer came into the picture at the most opportune time. I think he's sweet on me, too. That's what Opal and Bertie keep telling me. I just tell them they are crazy. However, from time to time when he and I are working side by side at the hospital, I find myself getting flushed and flustered; my mind wanders to amorous thoughts of him.*

Addie returned to the top of the page where it read *Dear Di-*

*ary* and erased the word *Diary*, replacing it with *Blue*. She turned the page, paused for a moment, and shifted on her dorm bed. Addie reached for her necklace, twisting the gold heart-shaped pendant between her right index finger and thumb. She kissed and released it. Putting her pencil back to the paper, she scribed, *Favorite memories: 1) Maw's sweet kisses on my cheeks. My sister Sissy's laughter, and my brother Ben and his incessant teasing. I miss Paw, the good version of him. 2) Sneaking kisses with Garrett. (If I were to get caught, I could possibly be expelled from nursing school and I failed to mention Garrett gave me a gold heart-shaped pendant necklace for my birthday last year at the Alexander's Christmas party. It took me quite by surprise!) 3) Assisting in the delivery of a baby boy named Judson Davis Miller on a stormy night with the help of my nursing classmates.*

She stopped writing and tapped her pencil on the bottom row of her teeth. *What should I write about next? Nurse Hartman would want me to write something big and grand. She's big on goals. She says, "A life without goals is a directionless and lost life. It's random and reactive, like trying to catch drops of water falling from the sky." I've never had to think beyond the borders of Hope, Georgia. Life was so tragically simple before I came to Atlanta. All I've known is the red clay dirt under my feet, staring at the foothills and wondering what's beyond the thick pine forests. These past two years in the city have opened my eyes and I find myself thinking and talking about subject matters that were once foreign to me. I stare up at the moon in a star-speckled night sky, curious about all of the people around the world who are doing the very same thing, and I ask God for favor and direction.* Addie toggled her pencil in the air. Struck by an idea, she resumed journaling. *Life goals: 1) Make a difference in this world by being the best nurse and person I can be; 2) Help others; 3) Travel the world; 4) Find a place that I can call "home" amongst the high cotton and magnolias; and 5) Marry the love of my life and have a family of my own.* Addie drew a tiny star, heart, and a flower to fill the line's remaining space.

An inch and a half of blank space remained on the page. Addie gazed out of the second-floor window at the walking-garden below. The azalea bushes were in full bloom, boasting shades of pink, red, and white. Addie fidgeted with the top button of her nightgown, before concluding her entry. *Favorite Bible quote: Again, Jesus spoke to them saying, "I am the light of the world; he who follows me will not walk in darkness, but will have the light of life." (John 8:12). (It reminds me of what Maw use to tell me, to walk in the light and shy away from the temptations of the demons in the dark). Favorite quote: "The two most important days in your life are the day you are born and the day you find out why." – Mark Twain. Dear Lord above, I'm still trying to figure all that out....*

Addie felt someone's hot breath on her neck. She slammed the book shut as she whipped around. Her cheeks rosied and chest flushed.

Deborah stepped back; her dark eyes narrowed. She mocked, "Dear Diary."

Addie said, through gritted teeth, "What the heck is the matter with you, Deborah? How dare you sneak up on me and invade my privacy like that." Addie tucked Blue underneath the pink silk kimono that was crumpled in a pile next to her on the bed.

Deborah reared back and cackled, her speech rapid. "I didn't get any further than that. After all, I don't need a diary to tell my secrets to. That's for insecure people. I'm not insecure. I'll have you know that I am the best!" Deborah touched the center of her chest. "I, Nurse Owens, am the best nurse in our nursing class!" Deborah flung her red kimono open, revealing her naked form underneath, and spun around, saying, "I am my patients' guardian angel."

"Angel?"

Deborah stopped twirling and looked out the window up at the partly-cloudy sky. Combing her hands through her dark curls, she stretched her arms above her head. "I'm a bird. Watch me fly. Do you like birds? I bet you don't. Do you like my red kimono? I have a red one, a blue one, and a white one. How many do you have?"

"I…" Addie tried to interject, realized it was futile, and continued to watch Deborah in her one-way conversation.

Deborah turned away from the window and began studying the books on the white bookshelf at the end of the room. "Best we get ready. Nurse Hartman posted a notice on the bulletin board in the stair hallway that we have to help get this dorm ready for the new cohort of nursing students coming in two weeks." She sauntered over and adjusted the gold fireplace screen. "They arrive on Monday the twenty-fourth. Twenty-four. Did you know I'll be twenty-four in four more years? I'm older than you." Deborah stuck her tongue out at Addie as she dropped her kimono to the floor and sashayed into the communal bathroom. She nearly collided with Opal, who was toweling her strawberry-blond hair dry.

"Hey! Watch where you're going and quit parading around here in the nude!" Opal reprimanded.

Addie and Opal exchanged wide-eyed expressions. Addie raised her right hand beside her head and twirled her index finger in circles.

Opal walked over and covered Addie's head with her white towel, tucking her head inside their make-shift tent. "Sometimes, I think her butter has slipped off her biscuit," Opal whispered. The girls giggled.

Opal hastily removed the towel and turned to find Deborah standing and glaring at them from the foot of Addie's white iron bed. Opal screamed.

Startled too, Addie reacted. "Holy crap!"

A ray of sunlight cascaded over Deborah, casting her larger-than-life shadow on the heart-of-pine floor. A cloud passed; her silhouette vanished.

### SATURDAY MORNING, FIFTH WARD

Alan Waxman flipped open the morning edition of the *Atlanta Dispatch*. The headline read *Lusitania Sunk: Americans Among the Dead*. Alan read through the article, a recounting of how the Germans had torpedoed the British ocean liner without warning off the coast of Ireland yesterday, killing thousands of innocent victims. The story outlined Germany's most recent and egregious acts, including the sinking of the first American petroleum tanker, SS *Gulflight*, in the Mediterranean near Sicily last Saturday and how poison gas was used for the first time on the Western Front against Allied troops last month.

"Dear God, in heaven." Alan tapped his slippered foot nervously on the navy rug four times, and then patted his right thigh four times. Setting down the paper, he rubbed his forehead and then moved his hand across his balding head. Alan was still having a difficult time erasing the images in his mind from the April article's account of the horrific gas attack. A Canadian nurse described being "helpless" as she rendered aid to the French and Canadian soldiers who were affected by a green toxic cloud in The Second Battle of Ypress. Over 5,000 canisters of chlorine gas had been released along the stretch of "No-Man's Land" in northern Belgium. The paper had no problem printing the medical personnel's account, word for word: *We felt helpless. The soldiers were alert and aware that they were dying. They were choking and suffocating on their own secretions. Eyes and faces were eaten away by the gas. We couldn't touch them. There was nothing we could do to provide comfort to our soldiers. They experienced their own hell on earth. What kind of world have we become?*

"Goodness! What a ghastly way to die," Alan muttered as he reached for his coffee cup. Eager to brighten the mood of the morning, he took a big swig of lukewarm liquid, grimaced, and replaced the cup in the blue saucer. He picked the paper back up and skimmed the stories of the day, including one about the installation of new county police call boxes. He thought that was a good idea, since not everyone had a telephone in their home. Flipping to the *Sports* section, an advertisement by A.G. Spalding and Company promoting their new light-weight, kangaroo leather baseball shoes for seven dollars caught his eye and reminded him to check the schedule for the Atlanta Crackers. He briefly scanned a short article recounting the baseball scores for Thursday, May 6th for the National League teams, the New

York Giants, and the Boston Braves, and the American League matchup between the Boston Red Sox, who lost to the New York Yankees. The story highlighted a first career home run for the Red Sox pitcher, a player named Babe Ruth.

Alan loved watching the Crackers play ball, finding sanctuary at the "Poncey." He enjoyed keeping score, tallying hits, runs, and strikeouts in his scorecard booklet. It provided him a reprieve from his accounting duties at Sacred Heart Hospital.

He continued to shuffle through the pages. The words printed in black on the white newspaper were beginning to jumble. He felt like the stories were all screaming for his attention – for him to feel, act, laugh, cry. His hands began to shake. Growing anxious and overwhelmed, he slammed the paper shut, rolled it up, and tied it with a piece of twine that he had retrieved from his bathrobe pocket. "There you go, nice and neat."

Alan got up and tossed it in a brass bucket that sat next to the fireplace, half-filled with rolled-up issues of the *Atlanta Dispatch*.

*Ding. Dong.*

"Coming!" Alan pulled on the lapels of his black cotton bathrobe and secured his sash in an effort to not expose his nether regions as he walked from the dining room in the back of the house to the front door. He opened the grand oak door. "Yes?"

"Good morning, Mr. Waxman. I've got mail for you." The postman tipped his hat and reached into his brown leather bag, pulling out three letters.

"Thank you, Percy." Alan took the letters. "Have a pleasant morning."

"You, too, sir." Percy tipped his hat again, turned, and strolled down the stone walkway.

Alan closed the door and flipped through the letters as he stood in the foyer. The last white envelope caught his attention. The return address read *Eastern State Penitentiary*. Alan ascended the stairs, took a left at the landing, and entered his home office. He took a seat behind his desk, set the other mail down, and opened the last envelope. As he unfolded the rank-smelling note, bits of short brown hair fell out while some fragments remained stuck to the words written in blood: *YOU TOOK MY BABY!*

Alan hastily refolded the letter and stuffed it back in the envelope. He slid the chocolate brown leather desk pad to the side, pulled out a tiny gold key from underneath, and unlocked the desk's left bottom drawer. He pulled out a red wooden box, opened it, and placed the envelope amongst nineteen others. Alan took a deep breath and exhaled in four short increments as he replaced the box, turned the key, and placed it back under the pad.

# 2

"Thank the good Lord above! How I love to see the newspaper's myopic focus on the war overseas replaced with the latest headlines about spring baseball." Dr. John Williams, Sacred Heart's Medical Director, held the paper high above his head as he entered the conference room on the second floor of the hospital for the leadership meeting. He tossed it in front of Alan, who was already seated next to Nurse Lena Hartman at the large table.

"Thanks! You know how to make my Monday mornings brighter." Alan picked up the early morning edition of the *Atlanta Dispatch* and skimmed the article. He raised a question to the group: "Do you think the Crackers will get the chance to play the Boston Braves?"

Edward Alexander II, the hospital's founder, seated at the head of the table, rocked back in his chair and was first to speak. "Boy! That would be an incredible match up, the Crackers versus the reigning World Series champions! Talk about an underdog gone wild. The Braves really pulled themselves up their bootstraps, moving from last place to first with the upset of a lifetime over Philly. It's no wonder they were dubbed the 'Miracle Team'!" Edward slammed his hand down on the table as he spoke. The white bone china coffee cups rattled in the saucers, hand-painted gold rims and handles glinting in the morning light.

Oliver Louis, Chief Operating Officer of Alexander Hall—Sacred Heart's sister hospital for Negros—eagerly chimed in, "Hell, the Braves even lacked a home field advantage and had to rent Fenway from the Red Sox in order to have a place to play." He rubbed his hand over his smooth head as he spoke, blue eyes peering over glasses.

Lena wasn't going to let the men have the last word. "Maybe someone will have a grand idea and relocate the Braves to Atlanta. After all, I think it has a nice ring to it, don't you? The Atlanta Braves?"

Clyde Posey glared at Lena and asked, "What could you possibly know about baseball?"

Lena found Sacred Heart's Chief Operating Officer irritating. Without hesitating, she responded, "I'll have you know I've hopped on the streetcar to see my fair share of games at Brisbane Park and now take the trolley to the Poncey, where Alan and I catch a game together every now and again." She decided to toy with the rest of the men at the table. "I am especially fond of the Magnolia tree in deep center field. The fact that we're the only baseball team that has rules that allow balls landing in a tree to remain in play is priceless."

Clyde waggled his finger between Lena and Alan. "Really? I had no idea that either of you knew anything about sports, or that you two were an item."

Alan's face flushed. He snapped, "We're not. We're just

friends. I don't see women as predatory conquests like you do, Clyde." He picked up his coffee cup and grumbled under his breath, "Or men...."

Fearing Clyde overheard Alan's prickly remark, Lena scooted her chair back and shot up. "Gentlemen, if you please, let's get our meeting started. I've got a busy schedule and I know that Dr. Williams has a full day of surgical patients awaiting him."

Having overheard Alan and wondering if Clyde did, too, Edward erased the smile from his face. "You're right, Nurse Hartman." Realizing she was purposefully redirecting Clyde's attention away from Alan and still standing, he motioned for her to take her seat. She obliged. "We've got a lot to review this morning. I want to start off the meeting by saying how much I appreciate each and every one of you. You have been here from the inception of the hospital and your input is vital so that we maintain our strategic direction as we care for Georgians. With that said, we're going to be encountering some more competition for patients, both young and old."

"How so?" Clyde inquired flippantly.

Dr. Williams interjected, "I'm sure you've heard about Mr. Asa Chandler's "Million Dollar" letter he wrote to the Educational Commission of the Southern Methodist Church last year, offering to donate one million dollars and seventy-five acres of land in the Druid Hills community to move Emory College from Oxford and create a university."

Clyde shook his head and stared blankly at Dr. Williams.

Shelby Maddox, the fair-haired pharmacist, spoke directly to Clyde. "Where have you been? It was written about in all the papers."

Alan began to say something under his breath, but Lena slid her left foot out and nudged his boot. He fell silent.

Edward picked up the conversation where Dr. Williams left off. "Atlanta Medical College has transferred their holdings to the university, solidifying Emory's School of Medicine. Their medical school will be one we want to have a great relationship with, in the event they need to partner with area hospitals in addition to their sister hospital, Wesley Memorial, for clinical rotations and the like."

Clyde sat up and used his hands to smooth down the side of his slicked-back black hair. "Fair enough, but what does that have to do with our young patients?" Reaching for the napkin in his lap, he wiped his hands, leaving the crumpled cloth beside his breakfast plate.

Alan watched Clyde like a hawk. He gagged quietly and swallowed hard when he saw oily stains from Clyde's hair tonic on the napkin, immediately losing his appetite. He set his fork down. His light and fluffy scrambled cheese eggs, sausage links, and biscuit, culinary creations made by Maybelle Reed, grew cold.

Edward sipped from his coffee cup and then wiped his thick, greying mustache and beard with his hand, before adding, "I've also been hearing about a new hospital at my Masonic meetings for indigent pediatric patients. It's slated to open later this fall in a donated home in the Decatur area. It's going to be called Scottish Rite Convalescent Home for Crippled Children, serving Emory's Wesley Hospital and Piedmont's Hospital."

Lena nodded her head. "I've heard from colleagues that Dr. Michael Hoke will be the Medical Director."

Dr. Williams finished chewing a bit of his warm buttermilk biscuit and brushed a few stray crumbs off his red and white paisley tie. "I heard that, too. He's a fine choice. I ran into him last month at a physician's educational meeting. He believes the institution is necessary and that it will eventually amount to a big thing in years to come. I concurred with his assessment and believe that pediatric patients deserve to receive the best care in specialized hospitals delivered by professionals who are educated in ailments and conditions of the sick child. The practice of pediatric medicine is completely different from that of adult medicine." He took out his pocket watch, noting the time. "Edward, I've only got five more minutes before my first surgical case this morning, which is going to be a real humdinger for me and my colleagues."

"What do you have?" Clyde was curious, finding unusual cases intriguing.

"We're going to remove a tapeworm from the colon of a formerly obese woman. Her anemic state, dementia, and seventy-eight-pound weight loss was a real head scratcher until she confessed to ingesting diet pills that she had ordered from an advertisement in a magazine." John pulled out a dark green glass bottle from his lab coat pocket, put his thumb over the cork, and shook it. "See these here? These pills contain the cysts of beef tapeworms. Once swallowed, the tapeworm grows inside the intestines and absorbs the nutrients in the food, thereby allowing the individual to eat what they want and lose weight."

The blood drained from Alan's face. Beads of sweat popped up on his forehead and upper lip. Using the back of his blue serge suit sleeve, he dabbed his lip four times.

Observing Alan's pallor, Edward rolled his right hand to urge Dr. Williams to move things along. "So, what medical-surgical updates do you have for us?"

"Last month, we conducted sixty-three unique surgical cases, sixty-seven surgical procedures, and there were...." He lowered his voice to a whisper. "There were twenty-five deaths."

"Jesus! Why was Sacred Heart's mortality rate so high? Our numbers typically are in the teens."

Dr. Williams referred to his notes. "The top causes were pellagra, Bright's Disease, which is a condition that causes chronic inflammation of the kidneys, tuberculosis, pneumonia, and work-related accidents." He shrugged his shoulders, saying defensively, "People die. Chalk it up to being a bad month."

Edward reached out and touched Dr. Williams's forearm. "You are doing a fine job here. Death rate statistics aren't a reflection on the competency of your medical staff, so don't take them personally. Please, go and attend to your first case."

Without further utterance, Dr. Williams grabbed his black leather medical bag off the floor as he got up from the table, shoved the diet pill bottle inside it, and walked out of the room.

"Let's continue to keep moving this meeting along." Edward made check marks by entries on his agenda. His pen stopped at the last items on the list. "Oh, and by the way, I've not been surprised by any shocking headline leaks about this hospital for quite some time. With that said, please stay vigilant. If you suspect an internal gossip, please keep me apprised. I prefer to stay ahead of the headlines, not behind them."

Alan flipped through his meticulous records, which captured names, times, dates, and meeting minutes, referring back to the following notations: *Monday, August 17, 1914: Moira Goldberg, Concierge. Lied about phone call. Overheard her saying how she loves being called 'Miss Sunshine.'* He flipped back a few more pages. *Wednesday, May 20, 1914: the grand opening and ribbon cutting ceremony for Sacred Heart Hospital. Moira Goldberg, Concierge. Overheard her on a phone call asking, "Is it sunny out? Of course not, it's very cloudy right now." She promptly hung up the receiver. Weather note: Cloudless, sunny day.*

Edward continued, "For the sake of time, I'm going to table discussions about Alexander Hall and the Sacred Heart Hospital Guild and hold them over for our meeting next month." Edward looked up to see everyone, with the exception of Clyde, making notations. He felt his stomach flip and roll, anxious for the day when Georgia Congressman Posey's son decided to make his move to the tin-covered dome. That day couldn't come soon enough, he thought. "Moving on to the pharmacy department, Shelby, what do you have for us today?" Edward watched the son of his dear friend, Leonard Maddox, a railroad tycoon in Chattanooga, pull out his leather-bound notebook. Edward knew his treasured daughter, Opal, was smitten by Sacred Heart's medicine maker. He had observed them stealing glances at each other at their Christmas party last year and in the hallways of Sacred Heart. It warmed his heart—Shelby would make a great addition to the Alexander family. He knew to be patient, though he was anxious to see his daughter graduate from the nursing program and advance to a luxurious life of domesticity and motherhood. That was his ultimate desire for her and her older sister, Pearl. Proud of her accomplishments and desire to serve others, he hoped that Opal's nursing education would sate her ambitious desires. Edward's wife, Trudy, cautioned him during their pillow talk at night to refrain from interfering with the budding relationship and scaring off the hopeful suitor.

Shelby spoke in an articulate and measured fashion. "First, I would like to thank you for all of your support with the medicinal and herb garden. The profits we have saved from compounding our own plasters, poultices, and tonics have saved Sacred Heart thousands of dollars over these past months." He turned to Lena. "By having the nursing students helping me in the garden, it has enhanced their pharmaceutical instruction, too."

Lena replied, "I couldn't agree more. In life and, in my humble opinion, in order to develop the best nurses, you need hands-on practical teaching experiences in conjunction with structured textbook instruction."

Shelby continued, "In light of those cost savings, I'm finding that the costs of purchasing aspirin are skyrocketing. Our major supplier has cut production. My colleagues across the country are telling me that an ingredient in aspirin called phenol is becoming harder and harder to come by in the States. Evidently, it's also an important ingredient in making explosives and the shipments are being diverted to support the ally's war effort in Europe." Dejected, he added, "I feel like my efforts to save money are becoming futile. We're not even involved in this war and it's already affecting our country's economy, everything from cotton to aspirin."

"Really? That is very interesting news." Clyde pulled out a tiny notepad and pencil from his tan suit jacket and made a note to himself.

Edward responded to his future son-in-law, "I know what

you mean, Shelby. Please know that your efforts aren't going unnoticed." It dawned on Edward that his leadership team was beginning to feel overwhelmed as the severity of their patient's cases increased, their work-load mounted, duties expanded, and community expectations and demands of the hospital grew. He was also worried about the dark cloud of war spreading and beginning to loom overhead. He surmised that it was just a matter of time before America needed to intervene. Anxious to wrap up, Edward addressed the last item on the agenda: "Sacred Heart's 1915 nursing student cohort. Nurse Hartman, what updates do you have for us?"

"All ten students are scheduled to arrive next Monday. The installation of the bunk beds in the dorm will be finished later this week by Joshua Goode and his men." Lena stopped and toyed with a new idea. "Sir, may I say that managing nearly thirty young women under one roof will be an adventurous undertaking. I'm afraid you may find Nurse Scott and I checking into a nervous hospital before it's all said and done."

Edward loved Lena's sense of humor. He welcomed it. She had a magical way of unwinding the tension in any room. Chuckling, Edward recalled Pearl's most recent exhibition of her monthly mood swings and verbal bruising, which he and Trudy encountered over a trivial matter. Racking his brain trying to remember if it had to do with dress color or skirt length, he was thankful for their housekeeper, Ranzell, who managed to mitigate the diatribe. He understood what Lena was insinuating. "What do you propose?"

"I'm not sure yet. I want our third-year nursing students to feel special and that they have earned certain privileges for their accomplishments and hard work. To be frank, let me flesh out my ideas with Nurse Scott and present them to you when I'm ready."

"Fair enough. If you anticipate any additional costs to the program, please work out how you plan to offset them with Alan." Edward pointed his pen at Lena. "Bear in mind, we built out the nursing dorm to house everyone comfortably. You were a part of the initial discussions and planning phase of that process."

Lena waved him off. "I'm aware." She folded her hands, resting them on the edge of the table. "But, as I give consideration for our growth, I don't want the students feeling like they are stacked and racked in the dorm like sailors in the bowels of a ship." She unclasped her hands, pleading her case. "People need their space. I'm thinking of their emotional well-being."

Clyde directed his next remark to Edward. "We all know women are highly emotional creatures. Their moods and minds change like the wind."

Resisting every urge to punch Clyde in the face and call him a pompous ass, Lena sat on her hands, and then responded calmly, saying, "Mark Twain once said, 'What would men be without women? Scarce, sir...mighty scarce.'"

Three hours later, Dr. Williams stepped out of the operating suite and into the B-wing hallway, the first-floor corridor containing Sacred Heart's emergency department, medical-surgical unit, and pharmacy. While walking over to the nurse's desk, he reached into his black leather medical bag and retrieved the bottle containing the diet pills. "Nurse Owens, will you dispose of these? They could kill someone."

Deborah took the bottle from his hand. "Yes, Doctor Williams. I sure will." She tucked them away in her uniform pocket.

## MONDAY EVENING, THIRD WARD

"Good Lord! That roasted lamb with root vegetables was delightful. My compliments go out to your cook. The mint sauce was divine." Clyde pushed his chair back from the dining room table as he untucked his shirt and crossed his legs.

Hoyt Burdeshaw's six-bedroom home located near Solomon and Martin Streets was quite palatial for the chemical factory owner and philandering bachelor. The first floor had been recently redecorated by Stephen Jones, a well-known interior designer in Atlanta and another intimate friend of Clyde's. Stephen managed to add his special touches to refine and balance the look of Hoyt's new country aesthetic.

"I love Stephen's choice of colors, and he managed to intertwine classic and elegant elements in his styling. I appreciate you recommending him to me." Hoyt pushed his merlot aside and ran his fingers through the flame of the candle in the center of the table.

Clyde studied the triptych hanging behind Hoyt. Two hunting dogs, one black and white, the other golden and white, stood in low-lying brush, eyeing a pheasant nearby. He wondered if they had sniffed each other's rear ends before their image was captured in oil. "While country casual isn't for me, it does suit you, Hoyt."

"Why, thank you. I was hoping you'd like what Stephen

picked out for me. I think it suits me, too. Stephen managed to capture my animal instincts with the new leopard-covered chairs in the living room." Hoyt stood up and wandered over to the cordovan framed mirror that hung over the buffet table.

"What do you think of my proposal to become a partner in your chemical company?"

"It's a bit complicated," Hoyt replied with his back still turned.

"I'm aware of all the risks involved." Clyde appreciated Hoyt's tall, lanky frame and broad shoulders, in perfect balance over his slender hips. The blonde strands in his hair glistened in the candlelight.

"Are you? All of them? Including our business dealings with Germany?"

"I am."

"Alright then. I accept your proposal." Hoyt turned around. His blue eyes sparked, enhanced by the black ash mask that he had painted around his eyes with his fingers. "Are you ready for dessert?"

Clyde's loins burned with desire. "I'm ready to walk on the wild side."

### MONDAY NIGHT, FOURTH WARD

Exhausted, Garrett was the last fireman at fire station number six to slip out of his boots and lie down on his bed in the dorm. Tucking his feet under the covers, he pulled the heavily starched, white sheet up around his shoulders. He rolled over on his left side and tried to suppress the adrenaline surging through his body. He slowly ran his hands through his copper hair, finding it comforting after a busy shift.

*Brrr…uuuitt. Ppptt. Ppptt. Ppptt.* The noise came from the next cot over.

The less than gentlemanly aroma wafted over a few seconds later, Garrett rolled over, trying to evade the insult to his nostrils, and weighed which odor was worse: the smell of a coffee-garlic, bean-tainted fart or the smell of the burning flesh of an elderly gentleman who accidentally fell asleep while smoking a cigarette and had torched himself and his house tonight near Highland Boulevard.

Restless, random visions continued to swirl in his head. The recent death of one of their own at Engine Company number nine haunted him. Three months earlier, Atlanta lost a fireman on the job for the first time when the fireman succumbed to injuries sustained in an automobile accident. The hose wagon was struck by a vehicle at Georgia Avenue and Washington Street in the Second Ward. With the omnipresent rigors, threats, and hazards of the job, it had never dawned on Garrett that he could die in transport on the way to a fire until now.

*Zzzzzzz. Paaaaahhh. Zzzzzzz. Paaaaahhh.*

Hyper-focused on every sound in the room and now growing more agitated by the snoring of one of his other roommates, Garrett rolled on to his stomach and buried his head under his pillow. His thoughts shifted from Addie, to the newspaper headlines about the war, to his father on the farm in Hope, Georgia, and back to Addie. Longing to see her, he ached to hold her in his arms and surround himself with her lilac-scented, auburn hair, which reflected the sunlight like the rock containing iron pyrite he had given her—a loving gesture mimicking what penguins do when finding a mate—when she left Hope for Atlanta to care for his widow aunt nearly two years ago. Frustrated and aroused, he flipped over on his back.

Garrett whispered, "I love you, my dear Addie. Come back to me someday."

# 3

Moira Goldberg, Sacred Heart's concierge, was working overtime this morning trying to maintain Clyde's affections and coax the tiniest bit of gossip out of him. Her usual methods were of little avail. Clyde appeared distracted as they tossed and tumbled under her deep purple sheets, a new acquisition from Rich and Brothers Department Store in downtown Atlanta. His far-away gaze gave him away. She felt a pang in her heart, and it shifted to the pit of her stomach. It was obvious. He was tired of her. She counted in her head how long they had been romantically involved. Three years was a long time to be a mistress of the mattress.

Refusing to make eye contact with her in the missionary position, Clyde flipped Moira over on to her stomach and lifted her hips up to meet his. Pressing her head of brown, wayward curls into the pillow, he curled himself over her as he fondled himself. A few minutes passed. "Damn it!"

Moira brushed her hair from her eyes and watched Clyde rear back on his knees.

"What the fuck?" He stared down at the flaccid appendage lying in the palm of his right hand.

Flipping over, Moira observed his expression transition from anger to disappointment to dejection. "Don't worry, honey. It... happens."

"But, not to ME!" Clyde roared.

Moira threw a pillow at him. "Hey, I'm not your enemy. Stop yelling at me. What the hell has gotten into you this morning? You seem distant. You're here with me, but you're not here."

She scooted over to sit on the edge of the bed, turning her back on him. She knew which buttons to push to evoke a reaction.

Clyde released his grip on himself. "What the hell is that supposed to mean, 'I'm here, but I'm not here?'" He reached out and touched her shoulder, but Moira was quick to shrink away.

"By the way, where did these new sheets come from? Do you have a new lover?"

Moira stood up and slipped on her red velvet bathrobe. Had she misread him? Was he actually preoccupied with the notion that she was entertaining someone new? She meandered over to the dressing table and sat down. Glancing at her reflection in the mirror, it dawned on her that Clyde had been bitten by the green-eyed monster. She brooded, refusing to reveal that she was selling newsworthy nuggets about Sacred Heart Hospital to Charlie Finch, senior reporter at *The Atlanta Dispatch*. Sunlight streamed through the part in the heavy gold-tone drapery and fell across her face, splitting her reflection in half. Suddenly, a dark object sailed by her head, startling her.

*Crash!* The mirror exploded, shattering into thousands of pieces.

"AHHHH!" Moira screamed.

*Thud!* Clyde's two-tone, brown, lace-up boot landed on the floor beside her.

"I ASKED YOU A QUESTION!" Clyde stormed toward her.

"STOP! PLEASE STOP!" Moira spun around and held out her hands. Lowering her voice, she pleaded, "Don't take another step. You're about to walk on broken glass."

Clyde stepped back and picked up the bedside table lamp. "WHY AREN'T YOU GIVING ME AN ANSWER?" He reeled back and hurled it at her.

Moira ducked. The lamp narrowly missed hitting her in the head. It struck the far wall, leaving a large dent. She screamed, "NO, YOU FUCKING IDIOT! NO, I'M NOT SEEING ANYONE ELSE!" Moira stood up. She took a step. She felt a piece of glass pierce the bottom of her right foot. She grimaced only for a second and went to take another step.

Clyde held out his hand. "Moira, stop! You're going to hurt yourself."

"You need to know I would walk through broken glass for you."

Clyde pulled a blanket from the bed, folded it over on itself, and threw it on the floor. "Come to me." Fixated, he watched her gingerly walk back to him. Picking her up, he carried her back to the bed and raised her leg in the air. "This is going to hurt, but only for a second."

"Do your worst."

As Clyde tugged and pulled on the shard, Moira hollered and grabbed at the sheets. Clyde watched her thrash her head about. Aroused, he toggled and twisted it before finally yanking it free from her foot. Blood trickled from the site. Clyde licked at it. A while back, he had overheard Dr. Williams explain to one of the nursing students that saliva had coagulating properties. 'That's why we intrinsically stick our finger in our mouth when cut or prick it and why animals tend to lick their wounds,' he had told her.

Moira felt her skin get hot and prickly. Her crotch quivered. She squeezed her pelvic muscles to intensify the titillating sensation.

Clyde rubbed the bloody sole of her foot on his hairless, pale chest, painting it reddish-pink. Devoted to feeding his curiosities and adhering to his personal mantra, 'The bawdier, the better,' he regained his lustful appetite. He leaned over to the bedside table, licked up a pile of white powder, and then packed it into Moira's cut with his tongue. He had also overheard the surgeons discussing cocaine's powerful vasoconstrictive and anesthetic properties. He was learning a lot from the doctors at Sacred Heart Hospital.

### SATURDAY AFTERNOON, SIXTH WARD

Addie, Deborah, and Bertie had spent the last hour on their hands and knees, cleaning the bathroom floor of the Sacred Heart nursing dorm.

Addie grew dizzy as she scrubbed the black and white checkered tile floor with the wood-handled horse hair scrub brush.

"I think we need to take a break and crack a window. I'm getting quite the headache from the fumes of these powerful cleaners." Addie stood up and walked over to open the frosted glass window. As she turned around, she spotted Deborah doing the unthinkable. Addie rushed over to Deborah, shouting, "STOP! Don't you dare mix that bleach with ammonia!" Addie yanked the pail of ammonia out of Deborah's hand. "Oh my stars! Deborah, you want to create chlorine gas and let the fumes overtake and kill us? Lordy, girl, you have a lot to learn. Didn't your mother ever teach you how to properly clean a house?"

Deborah recoiled, like a cottonmouth about ready to strike. Her eyes narrowed and frosted as her bottom lip thinned. Addie could tell her scolding stung and struck a nerve. Bertie watched the exchange, scooted back on her bottom to the tile wall, and used it to shimmy up onto her feet. She snatched the broom propped against the door and held it across her body, preparing to defend Addie at all costs.

Addie backed away. "Deborah, I'm so sorry. I didn't mean to offend you in any way. Truly, I didn't."

Bertie thought Addie's tone was sincere. However, she kept the broom handle raised in front of her. She shook it for effect at Deborah.

And then, Addie saw something in Deborah's eyes she'd never seen before. *Tears.* They welled in Deborah's eyes as she rose to her feet.

Deborah swiped away a stray droplet off her cheek with the back of her hand. She wagged her finger at Addie and Bertie. "I know I may not be as smart as you or come from fancy families and homes like you did."

Bertie strutted around Deborah, saying, "Trust me. I've heard Addie's stories about her family. Believe me when I say she's not filled with as much fancy as you might think. I mean, her family didn't come from high cotton. Their cotton patch only grew to be about ankle high, if you get my drift."

"He-ey! Really, Bertie?" Addie said with raised eyebrows and a light chuckle. "Are you being helpful right now?

"Maybe this place would be better off without me," Deborah whined.

Bertie glanced over at Addie, then back at Deborah. "What on heaven's earth are you talking about?"

Confused, Addie pushed. "What, you want to leave this place?" Confusion gave way to concern. It was the same feeling she had experienced when she ran from the family barn back to their house and discovered her mother. "Deborah, are you thinking of doing something dire?"

Deborah fidgeted with her fingers before sticking them in her pocket. "I'm fine. Leave me alone for a while." She exited the bathroom and took a seat on her bed, the bottom bunk.

Bertie mouthed, "What the hell is wrong with her? Do you think she wants to kill herself? I could never imagine doing something like that."

Addie shrugged her shoulders and mouthed back, "I don't know." She set the pail down. "I'll be right back."

Addie made her way over to Deborah's bunk and stood behind her. "I'm really sorry. I know nursing school is tough and we tend to be tough on each other. Nurse Hartman and Nurse Scott expect a lot from us and we, in turn, expect a lot from each other."

Deborah sniffled. "I accept your apology, Addie. Don't bring up anything about my mother again. Promise?"

"Yes, I promise." Addie's head pounded and throbbed with every beat of her heart. She furled her brows and massaged her temples.

"I've got some aspirin. Would you like some?" Deborah asked.

"Oh, God! Yes, please."

"I keep a bottle of it amongst my things." Deborah extracted a corked dark green glass bottle from the bottom drawer of her nightstand and poured two capsules into the palm of Addie's hand.

Addie examined them while Deborah poured her a glass of water from a pitcher on her bedside table. "These don't look like aspirin. Aspirin is a white tablet."

"Oh, they are. I have a hard time swallowing tablets." Deborah reached up and stroked her throat. "I had Dr. Maddox crush these and put them into a capsule so that I can swallow them more easily."

"Oh, that makes sense. Down the hatch you go." Addie popped them into her mouth, took a sip of water, and swallowed.


### SATURDAY LATE AFTERNOON, THIRD WARD

From the fourth-floor window of Burdeshaw's red brick chemical manufacturing plant, located on Tennelle Street, Clyde watched the continuous eruption of dark gray smoke billowing from the three smokestacks from the Fulton Bag and Cotton Mill off in the distance in the Fourth Ward. The perpetual emissions rose high in the sky, undeterred by the rain and wind from a pop-up afternoon thunderstorm. He found the lightning mesmerizing as it streaked across the sky. A few seconds passed. *Boom!* The window panes rattled. "I could watch lightning for hours. I never paid any heed to my mother's instructions to stay away from the windows as a child."

Hoyt covered the receiver of the phone with his hand. "I gather from the other night you enjoy taking risks." He winked and grinned. Uncovering the mouthpiece, he said, "Yes, is this Mr. Sloan? My name is Hoyt Burdeshaw. I own Burdeshaw's Chemical Manufacturing Plant in the Third Ward. I wanted to talk with you about taking out some advertising space in *The Atlanta Dispatch*."

Clyde read Hoyt's body language. He could tell Hoyt was getting punted over to the sales and advertising department.

"With all due respect, I don't want them handling my account. I would rather deal directly with you. I was told by Edward Alexander...," he lied. "Yes, yes, Edward referred me to you for this matter. I would like to make a special contribution to you and ask that you run a special article that would directly appeal to your sympathetic German-American readers about the war efforts in Europe. It would highlight the accolades and accomplishments of Germany...."

Clyde watched Hoyt sit up tall in his chair. He stepped up behind him and started massaging his shoulders.

"While the sinking of the *Lusitania* was a tragic accident, did you know there is more to that story? If you are truly a non-biased paper, then wouldn't it be prudent to publish such articles, Mr. Sloan? I could definitely make it worth your while." There was a long pause in the conversation. Hoyt picked up his pencil and scribbled on a notepad. "What I had in mind was one thousand dollars. Uh, huh. No, I wouldn't call it that. I would call it an incentive to support your varied base of readers. It's simple. I'll provide you with the content and you run it. In addition, I'd also like to take out a full-page ad to promote my chemical company for a year."

Growing bored, Clyde stopped rubbing Hoyt's tense muscles and took a seat on the couch. He kicked off his shoes and propped them on the coffee table. He wiggled his toes, picking off a raveling from his left sock.

"What do you mean you have to answer to your board of directors? How many do you have? Don't you think they could do with a bonus this year, too?" Hoyt covered the receiver again, directing his whispered comment to Clyde. "God, this is getting expensive." He picked up his pencil and tapped the eraser on the desk. "Look, Mr. Sloan. I'll give you an extra one hundred dollars for each board member. What? Fine. Well, you drive a hard bargain. Yes, I'll agree to three hundred dollars. Who should I make the check out to?" Hoyt penciled another note. "Oh, well, I can make arrangements for a partial payment in cash and issue a check for the advertising costs, paid in full. I can have everything, including the content, ad layout, and money, ready to be picked up on Monday." Hoyt twirled the pencil between his fingers. "Pardon me? I'm sorry, but I didn't understand the courier's name. Can you spell it for me?" He wrote, spelling each letter out loud, "S-C-O-U-T. Oh! I got it. Cute name. You say he has blonde hair?"

"Don't get any ideas," Clyde interjected.

Hoyt dismissed Clyde's comment with a wave of the hand.

"Fine. It's a pleasure doing business with you, Mr. Sloan. I look forward to seeing Scout on Monday at noon." He hung up the phone.

"Who knew that buying off the press and planting storylines could be so difficult?" Clyde patted the empty space next to him.

Hoyt waltzed over to the door and locked it. Kicking off his shoes, he sat down on the far end of the sofa, placing his feet in Clyde's lap. "Can you finish what you started?" He folded his arms behind his head. "My German colleagues are working hard to help shape the public's opinion in America with such tactics."

Clyde squeezed Hoyt's feet. "It sounds like there is a bigger plan afoot."

Hoyt laughed. "Very funny. That's what I love about you. You have a sharp sense of humor." He closed his eyes. "Yes, there is a bigger plan. There are numerous agents like me scattered throughout the country to help Germany destabilize the U.S. economy and shift sentiments towards my homeland. And, as we discussed the other night, we need to help redirect America's production of phenol away from them so we can make our own munitions and manufacture a key pharmaceutical product, aspirin."

"I understand. Since this country isn't involved in the war, I clearly see how our neutrality can be of assistance to you."

"Precisely. It's a brilliant, yet complex and multi-faceted scheme. It involves many high-level officials, including our German ambassador, an interior minister, a German-American scientist, and a few bankers here and abroad."

"And, not to mention savvy businessmen like us who appreciate the dollar and who aren't afraid of taking a few risks." Clyde moved his hands up Hoyt's pant legs to remove his socks.

"Ahh. That feels so nice. Don't stop."

Sunlight poured in through the windows while it continued to rain.

Clyde raised Hoyt's leg up and began licking and sucking Hoyt's big toe. "My mother used to tell me that when it rains while the sun is shining, the devil is beating his wife."

"I've never heard that expression before. Why was he beating her?"

"She explained that the Devil was taking his anger out on his wife because God created a beautiful, sunny day." Clyde resumed flicking his tongue along Hoyt's foot.

"Oh, dear God!" Hoyt couldn't contain himself anymore. "Why, aren't you being a little Devil!" He pulled Clyde on top of him.

# 4

"Emiline! Emiline! Can you hear me?" Dr. Randall Springer, Sacred Heart's pediatrician, turned the convulsing five-year-old girl on her side and inserted a wooden tongue depressor into her mouth to prevent her from biting or swallowing her tongue. "Addie, watch her and let me know if she turns blue or stops breathing," he directed.

"Yes, Doctor Springer." Addie complied, brushing a few sun-kissed brown strands of hair off of the young girl's face. "I feel so helpless."

Flipping through the patient's medical chart at the end of the bed, Dr. Springer pulled out a radiograph.

"That is the most recent x-ray. The evening shift nurse told me it was taken early this morning. They also told me that her mother was completely inconsolable after learning about her daughter's terminal diagnosis. They said her father became irate, blamed the mother for being impure and consorting with Satan. He stormed out of the hospital screaming that he wanted nothing to do with either of the Devil's spawn."

"My God! How heart-breaking." Dr. Springer approached the nurse's desk and held the film over the lit desk lamp. He studied it before returning to Emiline's bedside. "Where's her mother now?"

"Dr. Williams said she experienced a psychotic break from the traumatic news. He had to transfer her to Milledgeville's Lunatic Asylum for hysteria."

"Jesus! I wouldn't wish that place on anyone." Randall quivered.

Emiline stopped convulsing.

"It appears that her seizures have stopped." Addie patted her patient's tiny hand.

Randall placed his stethoscope over Emiline's chest and listened to her heartbeat. He removed it from his ears. "Her seizures are going to increase in frequency as the tumor in her brain gets larger. Over time, the x-rays will tell us if it's a fast or slow-growing tumor. Right now, the mass is the size of a pecan."

"With no other family to care for Emiline and knowing there isn't an orphanage in town that accepts medically fragile children, it sounds like she's going to be with us until...." Her eyes moistened. *Pull it together, Addie. Remember Nurse Hartman's and Nurse Scott's classroom instructions to 'Be professional, reliable, and trustworthy. Maintain a Spartan spirit. Remain cheerful and optimistic. Possess foresight and good judgment. Develop a critical and scientific mindset. Control your emotions and be undismayed by the unexpected. Be vigilant, demonstrating sympathy, kindliness, thoroughness, punctuality, persistence, and a democratic attitude that leaves class and race prejudice behind. And, in the face of death and despair, provide hope and encouragement even when the patient's barriers have broken down and the conventions of life seem trivi-al.'* With a clear mission reestablished, Addie refocused on the task at hand. She peered up at the clock on the wall, converting it into military time. *Twenty-three thirty.* "This convulsion lasted nearly a minute."

Randall referred to the chart before he rehung it on the hook at the end of the bed. "I can't administer another dose of medication until midnight. Let's see how she does in the next thirty minutes. Now that she's in a postictal state and we know she's going to sleep for a while, let's check on the rest of the patients."

Addie gently released Emiline's hand, removed the tongue depressor, and pulled the sheets up around the little girl's shoulders. Quickly assessing the other patients as she walked by their beds, Addie stopped at bed #3. "He's tolerating the vinegar-soaked cloths and brewer's yeast gargles and tonics very well."

The boy in the bed was ten-and-a-half-year-old Phillip Gardner. 'Call me, Pip,' he had managed to say upon admission, despite his inflamed throat and abscessed left tonsil.

Dr. Springer removed the dry flannel cloth wrapped around Pip's neck and palpated the boy's neck region. "He is doing better. Any fevers lately?"

"Not since this morning. His nurse told me that his temperature spiked to 102 degrees." Addie picked up the cloth. "I'll go and prepare another for him."

Randall readjusted the pillows under the boy that kept his head slightly elevated. He recalled his training at the Children's Hospital of Philadelphia that patients with tonsil and throat conditions needed to be monitored closely. Their situation could take a quick turn for the worst and, if the swelling persisted, affect their ability to breath. He watched Addie prepare the neck wrap and return to Pip's bedside. He observed her skillful hands and offered assistance as he leaned in to catch the faintest whiff of her lilac-scented hair.

Addie flushed, feeling his eyes on her and his hands touching hers. *I dare not look him in the eyes. God, this is embarrassing. What the hell is wrong with me? How could I possibly have feelings for Garrett and Randall? Both men are completely different. Garrett is all the comforts of home; being around him is like being wrapped up in Maw's hand-made quilt. Randall, on the other hand, represents all the possibilities of a world yet traveled. When I'm around him, I feel more like slipping into Mrs. Gray's stylish ermine coat and heading out for a night in the city.* Suppressing the rising memories of Randall's kiss last year at the orphanage and his subtle glances at the Alexander's Christmas party, she turned her back to Dr. Springer to tuck in the sheets of the little boy sleeping soundly next to Pip. "How's Garrett doing?"

"He's doing well at the firehouse. We pass like ships in the night. Only the sound of our footsteps signals our existence in the house as we head up to bed or leave for work."

Addie touched the necklace hidden under her uniform and then she reached inside her pocket. Her fingers searched for the pebble containing Fools Gold. It provided her reassurance to know she was loved. *I love Garrett, but am I in love with him? How am I supposed to know the difference if I've never been in love with someone before?*

Randall's heart skipped a beat when she turned around and locked eyes with him in the dimly lit room. He ached for Addie—to feel her lips on his and her skin pressed against his. After all, he knew the key to her heart. It wasn't here. It was glued on a piece of cardboard and hanging from a blue ribbon tacked to the back of her bedroom door at her house in the Fourth Ward. A heart-shaped collage was filled with magazine pictures of cosmopolitan women and newspaper photos from faraway places surrounded by dried flowers. Inscribed on top was *Dreams are an aspiration of your heart, so dream big!* It caught him off guard that his feelings for her were growing in spite of his sworn allegiance to bachelorhood, medicine, and pediatrics.

*Creak!* The ward door opened. Opal tiptoed inside. "How's everything going in here? Y'all need a hand with anything? All of my babies are asleep in the 'Bawl Room.'" She laughed under her breath. "I just love that nickname for the nursery. It's perfect. I can't believe Bertie came up with that one. She is so funny." Opal mimicked Bertie's gestures, pretending to place her hands on wide hips, saying, 'All those babies do is eat, sleep, pee, poop, and bawl.'"

Randall and Addie returned to the sink to wash their hands and laughed silently right along with her.

"Hey, have y'all heard the latest gossip going around here at the hospital?" Opal sat on the edge of the nurse's desk.

Addie shrugged her shoulders. "Do tell." She sat down in the chair at the desk, preparing to write in her patients' charts.

Dr. Springer dried his hands and then cupped his hand to his ear. "Oh, how I love to be invited to a hen party. Y'all are always clucking and pecking about the best stories!"

"You know you love hearing about every juicy nugget we find in the barnyard," Opal teased. "Do you remember when I told you last year that I thought Mr. Goode was getting sweet on Miss Maybelle? She was often spotted sitting next to his mother, Ms. Mattie, at his church on Sundays before our mammy up and died. Well, I overheard Joshua asking my father for time off from his custodial duties here at the hospital."

"Why? I hope he's not sick." Randall grew concerned.

"Oh! Heavens, no! He and Miss Maybelle are getting married! Can you believe it? Isn't that the best news!"

"When's the big day?" Addie said, appearing busy by shuffling charts.

"I think he said they were heading to Birmingham where her family's from at the end of the month to carry out the nuptials. Then, they'll return to Atlanta as Mr. and Mrs. Joshua Goode. Isn't that just grand?" Opal squealed and clapped her hands.

Randall raised his finger to his lips. "Shhh! We don't want to wake the kids." He excused himself, walking over to Emiline's bed to examine her. "Addie, she appears to be doing much better now. Will you run to the pharmacy and get some magnesium sulphate? I want to have a few syringes of it on hand in the event you need to administer it subcutaneously to her in the night should she experience any more seizures."

"Yes, Dr. Springer." Addie pulled out the top desk drawer and retrieved the keys to the pharmacy department.

"Addie, I'll walk out with you." Opal yawned and stretched her hands above her head. "I've got to get back to the Bawl Room."

"Nurse Alexander, I'll be over there when Addie returns to make my last round on the babies before heading home. It's been a very long day and I'm exhausted," he said quietly.

Addie and Opal stepped into the hall.

"I can tell he's sweet on you, Addie," Opal ribbed her.

"Oh, hush!

"I don't know, I could see you with Garrett or I could see you ending up with Dr. Springer one day."

"Really, Opal? What about you and Shelby? You'd have to be blind not to see what is going on between you two. I've seen you taking walks together in the hospital garden and how he brushes the hair out of your eyes when we're working with him in the medicinal garden." Addie reenacted Shelby's actions on her own hair.

Opal began to laugh, but her attention shifted when she heard a noise from around the corner. She pressed her fingers over Addie's mouth. "Shhh! I think I hear something."

Addie and Opal strained to listen.

"Ooooo! Ooooo! Uhhhh! Uhhhhh!"

"Is that the sound of a woman moaning?" Opal whispered. "Where's that coming from?"

Addie turned her head in the direction of the sound. "It appears to be coming from outside." She started to walk toward the side door.

Opal grabbed Addie's forearm. "Wait! I'm not letting you go out there by yourself. Help me check on my babies first before we go and investigate."

The infants were checked and all were fast asleep.

Opal propped the nursery ward door open. "Just in case one of them wakes and cries out."

Addie and Opal, arm in arm, cautiously crept into the A-wing hall. The moaning and groaning noise continued to be coming from outside the door on their right. They inched closer. Pressing their noses to the door window, they strained to see two people cloaked in the shadows against the side of the travertine wall, engaged in the most intimate of acts.

Addie gasped and Opal hastily pressed her hand over Addie's mouth. The figures stopped moving. The girls scurried off. Opal returned to the nursery while Addie sprinted down the corridor, past the concierge desk to the door marked *Pharmacy*. She unlocked the door and slipped inside. She pressed herself against it, taking several deep breaths to calm her nerves. *Calm down, Addie. You didn't witness a murder, only two people caught in a conjugal act. Get a hold of yourself. Dr. Springer and Emiline are waiting for you.* Addie's hands shook as she flipped on the lights and retrieved the medicine from the locked cabinet. *But, who was it?*

Stepping back into the hall, Addie's saw a flash of white. She turned to see Nurse Owens glaring at her from outside the medical-surgical ward doors. Without a word, Deborah entered the unit.

An elderly man with a grapefruit-sized cancerous tumor on his neck and open sores on various parts of his body reached out from his bed and tugged on Deborah's uniform, startling her. He struggled for each breath. "Sorry...didn't mean...to scare ya. I'm hurtin'...awful bad. More... medicine...please?"

Deborah, repulsed by Mr. Pollock, thought he smelled of death. "Sure." She was growing weary of taking care of his draining wounds and cracking, oozing mass. Deborah mumbled to herself as she meandered about the ward, collecting samples of various medications in a glass syringe, before returning to his bedside. "This is only going to hurt for a second, Mr. Pollock."

She didn't bother swabbing the injection site with alcohol, as she was taught to prevent infection, and only wondered how his body would respond as she stabbed the needle into his right atrophied thigh and injected the toxic cocktail. Would he have seizures? Would he stop breathing? Would he go quickly or languish in agony? "This should take care of everything." Her tone was sweet and reassuring. "I'm your Angel of Mercy. I'm here to take all of your pain away."

Mr. Pollock's eyes immediately glazed over, his limbs jerked a few times before they fell still, and all body functions ceased any life-supporting activity.

### MONDAY, EARLY MORNING, SIXTH WARD

The hallways on the first floor of Sacred Heart Hospital were a buzz of lively activity this early morning. Lena, Edward, Alan, and Clyde were all exiting their offices and heading upstairs to the conference room. Passing the nurses who were giving their shift reports on the maternity, nursery, and pediatric patients to their day shift colleagues, Alan spun around, having forgotten to lock his door. Clyde also broke from the pack and continued to press on toward the medical-surgical wing, making a point to stop and to talk with one of the nurses.

Moira set her pocketbook down under the desk. She sniffed the air a few times, thinking it smelled more astringent today. Spinning around her circular desk, she locked her sights on Clyde. He was talking to Deborah. Her gut feeling was right. Her stallion was courting a new filly. Moira's heart crumbled as she watched Clyde reach out to gently touch Nurse Owens on the upper arm, draw her in close, and whisper in her ear. The scent of Deborah was now filling his flaring nostrils.

"Oh, God! That bastard! He *is* losing interest in me." Moira's knees buckled. She grabbed the edge of her desk.

*Ring! Ring!*

Moira watched Clyde walk away from Deborah and hastily stride by her desk without making eye contact. He rejoined Edward and Lena, who stood outside the elevator doors.

*Ring! Ring!*

"Damn it!" Moira's jade dress perfectly matched her current mood. She hastily picked up the phone and huffed, "Good morning. Thank you for calling Sacred Heart Hospital." In a staccato rhythm, she punched out the last five words. "How may I help you?" She plopped down in her chair.

"Good morning, Miss Sunshine. How's the weather today? Sunny and clear?"

Realizing her stud was leaving her corral and feeling like a nag, she was eager to saddle up another steed already in her pen. Moira adored her secret name and the code phrase Charlie devised so that they could talk undetected about scandalous topics that had the potential for publication. Feigning a lilt in her voice, she replied, "Good morning, Charlie. The weather is clear, complete with sunshine, unicorns, fairies, and rainbows. How's our best and brightest doing at *The Atlanta Dispatch*?" Moira swiveled her chair to face the front door.

"Any updates for me?"

"No, not at this time. But, I've got my eyes and ears open as always. You know that nothing gets past me."

Charlie laughed. "Well...."

"Hey!" Moira interrupted. "I want to run something by you. Don't you think the paper could use a good gossip columnist? Well, I want that job." Unwilling to take 'no' for an answer, she pitched, "'Hey, Hetta!' Doesn't it have a lovely ring to it? I've been toying around with column names since I prefer to remain anonymous."

"You mean you? And, you want to use a nom de plume?"

Moira swooned. "Listen to you with all of that fancy talk. Absolutely! I need to have a pen name. You know I run in many social circles. 'Hey, Moira!' doesn't have the right ring to it. I love the name Henrietta, but it doesn't roll off the tongue very well. Whereas, 'Hey, Hetta!' sounds so much better and personable. Don't you think so, Charlie?"

"I...uh...."

Moira twirled around in her chair before Charlie could utter another word. "I would make the perfect gossip columnist for *The Atlanta Dispatch*. How much do you think a columnist makes?"

"Uh, I'm not sure. We've never had one before, so we're in uncharted waters."

"Tell your editor, Sam Sloan, it was your idea. The *Chicago Record Herald* has a female gossip columnist by the name of Louella Parsons, and the South needs one, too! While she writes about movies, actors, and actresses, I'll focus on Atlanta's social scene: you know, the movers and the shakers in this town."

Charlie shifted in his seat. His wooden chair creaked. "You know, your suggestion isn't half bad. I'll give it some consideration and get back with you. In the meantime, call me if you stumble across any exciting news at the hospital. Readers are getting tired of articles about the war and are fired up about the Leo Frank murder trial and the appeal to Governor Slaton to commute his corporal punishment. I've got to fill the pages with something new and different."

"You're the best, Charlie." Moira hung up the phone and spun around to find Alan walking away from her desk toward the elevators. "Oh, shit!" Had he overheard her conversation? "Shit!" If so, how long had he been listening? Moira clenched her fists and stomped her foot. "Shit!" She couldn't resist the urge, lunging across the desk and calling out, "Mr. Waxman, did you need me for anything?"

The elevator doors opened. "Not a thing, Miss Goldberg. Thank you. I'm just heading up to my meeting." Alan stepped inside. The doors shut behind him. He scribbled a note in his journal as his thoughts shifted from Moira to the nineteen letters in the red box in his desk drawer at home. 'YOU TOOK MY BABY!' The words echoed in his head until he entered the conference room. "Good morning, everyone." Alan took a seat and asked Lena, "Would you pass the fruit?"

Lena reached over to pick up the bowl filled with juicy strawberries just as Clyde used his bare hands to pluck out a few. She shot him a disapproving look, knowing that he purposefully fingered the fruit to poke fun at Alan's germophobic tendencies.

Alan retrieved his white linen napkin and coughed in it, saying, "God, he's such a horse's ass!" He anxiously bounced his right leg up and down; the dishes began to rattle on the table.

Lena kicked Alan's shoe. Alan stopped; the clattering dishes stilled.

Edward finished chewing his buttered toast, washed it down with coffee, and then spoke. "Good morning, all. I hope y'all had a wonderful weekend."

Clyde jumped in. "Oh, I did. I had a marvelous…."

Edward raised his hand in the air. "It was a rhetorical question, Clyde."

"Oh." Clyde blushed. He stuck a finger between his white Arrow collar and flushed neck.

Edward resumed. "I want to discuss some carry-over topics from our last meeting and have Dr. Williams bring you up to speed on a new initiative. In compliance with our mission of providing compassionate healthcare at Sacred Heart and the soon-to-be four walls of Alexander Hall, which is slated to open two years from now, my wife, Trudy, is creating a guild for both hospitals to financially supplement non-budgetary expenses."

"The guild is of vital importance and will help offset many costs," added Alan.

"Trudy is the perfect person for that job." Lena was proud to learn that Edward's wife was finding her place among those at Sacred Heart.

The others agreed.

Edward nodded. "She'll do a fine job. In addition, in order to proactively maintain the competitive edge that we discussed in our meeting last month, we need to expand our mission beyond these four walls. I'm going to turn it over to Dr. Williams to explain how we plan to do that."

"Now that the new nursing students are here, I've been working with Nurse Hartman to devise a community outreach plan by providing care to a few of the social settlement houses in town. We've chosen to work with two. One is a Methodist settlement house at the Futon Bag and Cotton Mill in the Fourth Ward and the other is at the Whittier Cotton Mills in the valley by the Chattahoochee River."

Clyde wrinkled his face. "Why do we need to provide medical care to such places? Aren't they filled with immigrant workers, mountain folk, and poor people?"

Overwhelmed by a strong desire to smack Clyde on the back of the head, Lena restrained herself and instead clasped her hands together. "As Jane Addams, one of the founders of the Hull House in Chicago put it so eloquently, every immigrant is 'either a citizen or a potential citizen' of the United States." She stopped to look at everyone at the table. "After all, wasn't someone in our family an immigrant at one time before they became a legal citizen of this country?" She touched her nursing cap on her head. "I digress. My point is that with the changes in urbanization and industrialization, these multi-cultural centers are trying to give their workers a steady income while providing a sense of community. These social settlements offer housing, athletic programs, daycare, clubs, education, legal aid, and even medical care."

Edward rested on his elbows. "So, our job here at Sacred Heart is going to be to provide medical services to those in need. It will be a great learning opportunity for our nursing students and will also help us develop a relationship with these future patients. There will be those who will require surgery, labor and delivery care, and emergent medical management from work-related accidents. It's our job to establish that referral relationship now and build trust with these people for generations to come."

Clyde knew he was going to make a run for the State House in the next year or so, and added, "And, they are future voters, too. Perhaps, I should also go out with our medical team. You know, as a representative of the administration."

Lena bit her tongue. It wasn't her call to make, although she wanted to yell out, 'Oh! Hell, no! Over my dead body am I taking that hair-brained, narcissistic idiot out with us!'

Dr. Williams also filtered and suppressed his immediate thoughts of 'Fuck no, you opportunist! I will not have you tag along.' Instead, he replaced those words with, "Thank you, Clyde, for the offer. However, Nurse Hartman and I have it under control and we, too, represent the administrative team."

Clyde shrank back in his chair and crossed his arms.

"When will you begin making visits?" Shelby inquired. "I want to be sure you are adequately stocked with pharmaceutical supplies."

"Our service contract is being finalized by our legal team and that's going to take a few months. I anticipate we'll be ready to go by the fall. That will give Nurse Hartman, Nurse Scott, and I plenty of time to get some educational and clinical courses under the belts of the new nurses."

"Fine work, Dr. Williams and Nurse Hartman. We appreciate your willingness to serve others in this capacity." Edward glanced at the agenda. "The next item is Alexander Hall. How is construction going, Oliver?"

"The building project is right on track. They are excavating the last tunnel that will connect Alexander Hall to the colored nursing school. I'm glad they are taking advantage of the warmer months for that project in order to avoid the catastrophic event we experienced with the Greene tunnel."

Edward's eyes misted. It was hard to forget the images of his childhood friend and contractor Tom Greene's contorted body and the dirt-filled orifices on his disfigured face from the tunnel collapse. There wasn't enough single-malt scotch to drown them out.

"I'm sorry, Edward." Oliver regretted resurrecting the past. "I didn't mean to dredge up such terrible memories."

Edward cleared his throat, and said, "Well, what's done is done. It was a tragic accident. We've honored his name and family by naming the tunnel after him." Edward bowed his head, and then looked back up. "I'd like to name the new tunnel in honor of my housekeeper, Mattie Goode." He refrained from revealing that her son, Joshua, was the product of their affair years ago when Trudy was in a dark mood, grieving over a miscarriage while sequestered at her sister's house in Florida for months. "She was an honorable and respected woman in her community and a very active member at the AME Church where her son, our Mr. Goode, preaches on Sundays."

Oliver and the others chimed in. "I think that is a great suggestion."

Clyde laughed, "I didn't know that Mr. Goode was a preacher, too. I guess I need to watch my language around him in the future or I may just end up in hell."

Alan coughed into his napkin, whispering, "God willing."

Edward acknowledged the group's approval on the matter. "Let's keep that information confidential for now."

Alan feigned another coughing spell as he spotted the notation he had just scribbled in his notebook while in the elevator:

*Moira Goldberg, Concierge. Overheard discussing an idea for a gossip column.*

# 5

Sam Sloan rapped his knuckles on his senior reporter's door at *The Atlanta Dispatch*.

"Come in." Charlie took another long drag on his cigarette before snuffing it out in the brass ashtray. He swiped the smoke out of the air and motioned for Sam to have a seat. "What can I do for you, boss?"

"I've just come from my meeting with the board. I pitched your idea about adding a gossip columnist to the paper. The board agreed and felt that it would add a bit of color to our black and white reporting."

Charlie had heard through the grapevine that Sam pitched the 'Hey, Hetta!' column as his idea. He suppressed any smartass remarks, knowing Sam's reputation and job were on the line, not his. "Yeah, nothing like stirring up hushed whispers and controversy in this town," chided Charlie while offering Sam a cigarette.

Sam declined. "I'm trying to cut back a bit on the advice of my doctor and nagging wife. Speaking of stirring up controversy, that pro-German article we buried in the back of the paper last month unleashed a shit storm of letters. They came mainly from pissed off and angry patriotic readers. Although, there were a few supportive notes sprinkled in."

"Articles that evoke a response, whether good or bad, are always good for the paper. Isn't that what you keep telling me you want?"

Sam shifted in the chair to avoid the morning sun from blinding him. He rubbed his chin. "Yes, it is. I was thinking of publishing one of each in the 'Letters to the Editor' section later this week."

"What did the board have to say about it?" Charlie popped another cigarette in his mouth and lit it.

"It was a risk worth taking. They feel that our stories are provoking responses from readers, which, at the end of the day drives sales. When people ask each other, 'Have you read about such and such or so and so in *The Atlanta Dispatch*?' that makes our board members very happy."

"And, if they're happy, then you're happy." Charlie made O-rings in the air.

"Exactly. I prefer to keep those bastards fat, happy, and off my ass." Sam laughed. "After all, if they get grumpy, it'll be my head they'll cut off and put on the spike."

"So, what are the stipulations for the gossip column?"

"For starters, the board loves the name, 'Hey, Hetta!' Keep the column between 300-400 words in length, and start off with soft stories, like a socialite's party. Have Hetta focus on the guests, how they dressed, what kind of food was served, and other artsy-fartsy kind of shit like that."

Charlie grabbed an old copy of the paper and jotted a few notes in a blank space on the front page between the main headline and the weather report. "What's Hetta's pay going to be?"

"The board agreed to pay her twenty-three cents an hour. Since she's a woman, she's going to be paid ten cents less than the male writers."

Charlie calculated the figures in his head and scratched the final numbers on the paper. "Great. Thanks a bunch."

"I appreciate you bringing up the idea." Sam got up and sauntered over to the door. "I look forward to meeting Hetta soon." Before he slipped out of the office, Sam remarked, "I know you've been jockeying for a pay raise, so I hope I don't find you dressed in drag in my office!"

"Fuck you, Sam!" Charlie cackled.

Sam closed the door behind him.

### THURSDAY MORNING, SIXTH WARD

Lena stared at the two-story, yellow brick, neoclassical house across from her office window overlooking Spring Street. For the past year, she had grown accustomed to watching an elderly man puff on a pipe and walk out the front door to pick up the morning paper. Today, she observed a change in routine. A frail elderly woman stepped out of the front door and retrieved it instead. Lena had always admired the home's design. The second-floor embellishments included a marble carving of vines and flowers centered about the front door and the cream-colored wrought iron railings on the porches that were nestled on either side of the house. Beautiful landscaping complimented the look, consisting of evergreens, ferns, rows and rows of pink begonias, and boxwood hedges and shrubs that were meticulously manicured in an alternating pattern of spheres and cones. The three dormers on the third floor indicated the presence of an attic. Lena knew the green tile roof would never need to be replaced, only repaired in the unfortunate circumstance that a tree limb fell and broke some of the tiles. She shot out of her office and jogged past Moira at the main desk, chattering away on the phone.

Moira watched Nurse Hartman dart out of the front doors of the hospital. She turned her attention back to her caller. "Oh, Charlie! That is wonderful news." Moira pushed her brown curls up off her neck and back into her chignon as she spoke. She continued to futz with her outward appearance as she conversed, making adjustments to her garnet dress sleeves. "When do you want me to start? Of course, I can make arrangements to meet you at your place tonight." Moira glanced over her shoulders.

Stepping off the elevator, Alan flipped through his ledger as he walked around the backside of the concierge desk. He noticed Moira. She was hunched over talking on the phone, her conversation hushed. He stepped closer to eavesdrop.

"Yes, it's sunny out." She spoke quietly into the phone.

The hair on the back of his neck stiffened. He remembered her saying that phrase last year and strained to hear her next words.

"I overheard our medical director, Dr. Williams, mention something about seeing an increase in the number of deaths, especially on the medical-surgical ward." Moira sat up, spun around in her chair, and saw Alan staring at her. "I gotta go!" She slammed down the receiver.

"Come with me, now!" Alan barked. He pointed at her purse sitting underneath the desk on the floor. "May I suggest you grab that, too?" Sheepishly and in silence, Moira followed Alan out of the hospital.

Once outside, Alan cornered her against the side of the building and drilled his finger at her as he spoke. "I know it's you who has been leaking news to *The Atlanta Dispatch*. Whom were you talking to just now?"

Moira toyed with the notion to play dumb, and then the words fell from her mouth. "I don't know what you're talking about, Mr. Waxman."

"Yes, you do!" Alan ripped open his notebook. "On Friday, the twenty-second of May last year, I heard you say, and I quote, 'Is it sunny out? Of course not, it's very cloudy right now.' According to my notes, it was a beautiful sunny day for the hospital's grand opening ceremony." Flipping through pages, he stopped at another entry. "On Monday, the seventeenth of August, you were wearing a red scarf and acting quite squirrely while you were on the phone...."

"I wore that scarf because of the...."

"I don't want to hear your excuses. The leadership team wondered how stories broke about the lice epidemic and the orphans who stayed at the hospital last year," Alan hissed as he turned a few more pages. "On Monday, the seventh of July, I overheard you discussing an idea for a gossip column." He slammed the book shut and pushed up his gold, wire frame spectacles. Perspiration rolled down his forehead and nose. His glasses slipped back down. He ripped them off. "And, today I...."

Indignant, Moira fired back, "Fine! I get your point." She arched her back and shoved her nose in the air. "I was about ready to tender my resignation anyway."

Not wanting to draw any undue attention, he lowered his voice. "Let's not make a fuss about this. You and I both know you're a snitch. Pure and simple. Please understand me when I say that you are terminated and I don't ever want to see you step foot on this hospital's premises again. So help me, God, if I do, I'll have you arrested on the spot." Spittle sprang up in the corners of his mouth.

Moira pointed at her own mouth. "You got a little something…."

Flustered, Alan stomped his foot four times. "Get the hell out of here!" He pointed toward Spring Street. "Start walking, NOW!"

Without a word, Moira flipped out her skirt and sashayed down the sidewalk, brushing past Lena, who was making her way towards Alan. Alan turned to walk away from Nurse Hartman.

"Alan, wait!" Lena called out. "I want to talk with you about something."

He stopped and turned around.

She studied him for a split second. "What was that all about with you and Moira? Are you alright? You appear flushed and you've got something…." Lena pointed towards the corners of her mouth.

Irritated, Alan pulled out his handkerchief. "I know. I know!" He wiped the saliva away, patting his upper lip four times.

## THURSDAY AFTERNOON, FOURTH WARD

Garrett dipped the rag into the sudsy bucket, wrung it out, and applied more pressure to the caked and dried mud spattered on the side of the fire truck. Sweat rolled down his neck and back. His white t-shirt clung to his skin. Upon hearing the familiar sound of a truck engine pulling up in front of the driveway, he said without looking up, "To what do we owe the privilege of your visit to our fire department on this hot and humid day?"

Brice McDaniel roared; his Irish brogue thick, "For fuck's sake, Garrett. 'Ow the 'ell did you know it twas me?"

"How could I not know it was you after all of this time working alongside you and your brothers?" Garrett stood up, dropping the rag into the bucket. He approached the ambulance. Garrett shook hands with Brice and his younger, unassuming brother, Rob, who sat in the passenger seat, puffing away on a cigar.

Garrett shook his head. "I don't know how you can smoke that thing. It's hotter than Dante's ninth circle of hell out here."

"It calms me nerves. Hey, how's about ya puttin' some elbow grease to the sides of this here ambulance." Rob patted the side of the door, blowing white smoke out of the open window.

"I don't want to rub off Sacred Heart's fabulous logo, *Reliable. Reputable. Responsive.*"

Brice howled. His grand belly danced up and down. "You could rub me off any time ya wanted to, son!" He popped Garrett in the chest with the back of his hand. "Ya know, that's me personal logo, too. Did ya know that?"

Garrett fired back, "Actually, I overheard Madam McGuire

and her girls say that you were unreliable, unreputable, and unresponsive."

Brice's ruddy face blanched.

Rob doubled over in hysterics, saying, "Brother, ya dish it out, ya got to be able to learn to eat shit every once in a while, too."

"Ya, but I don't 'ave to acquire a taste for it."

Garrett stepped back, unsure if Brice was going to hit him again with a sense of purpose. "I'm just messing with you, Brice."

"Just for that remark, I'm definitely counting you in as one of our regulars to play in our little card game."

"I'm not one for gambling, Brice." Garrett turned out his empty pants pockets.

"I hear different from the fellas at this 'ere firehouse. They say ya got the luck of the Irish on ya side."

Rob urged, "Come on, Garrett. We'd love to see ya on Saturday night at eight sharp. That is if ya ain't working. We've already got me twin brothers, Wei Wu, who runs Sacred Heart's laundry department, and with the three of us, that makes it an ideal number of players."

Garrett mulled over the invitation. What harm could it do? "As a matter of fact, that's my night off." He thought it would be a great way to sneak over and see Addie at the hospital and could pass a message to her that evening through Randall. "Count me in, fellas! See you on Saturday."

"Great! Come over to Sacred Heart's garage. Park 'round back so as to not draw any undue attention. See ya on Saturday!" Brice waved and then turned on the siren before zooming off down the street.

ready to pop out of me skull reading about stimulants, cathartics, and depressants."

"Sure! Come join us." Opal shuffled the cards as Bertie and Mary Margaret sat cross-legged on the floor. Opal dealt the cards. "In my spare time, I've been reading Louisa May Alcott's *Little Women*. Did you know that before she was a famous author, she was a Civil War nurse who worked at Georgetown Union Hospital?"

"Where's that?" Bertie picked up her cards, rearranging them in her hand.

"It's in Washington, D.C." Opal breasted her cards. "Did you know that she earned the nickname, 'nurse with a bottle,' because she always wore a tiny bottle filled with lavender water around her neck to suppress the effluvia of the wounded and dying soldiers?"

Mary Margaret and Addie wrinkled their noses.

"That sounds horrible!" Bertie pinched her nares shut. "That reminds me of one of my cancer patients on the med-surg unit. The stench of death was so strong around him before he up and died earlier this month. Come to think of it, he died while Deborah was taking care of him." Bertie lowered her voice. "Hey, is it me, or is Deborah acting a bit more looney than usual?"

"Me thinks so, caught 'er talking to 'erself in the bathroom mirror last week," Mary Margaret whispered.

*Should I say something about seeing Deborah in the hospital hallway after Opal and I caught two people having sex?* Addie weighed her options. *Should I? Shouldn't I?*

"Deborah is a strange girl," Opal chimed in. "By the way, did

Addie tell you that we caught two lovers outside of the hospital a few weeks ago?"

The group gasped.

"No! Do tell!" Bertie cajoled.

"Well, Addie and I were working on the night shift. She was assigned to the peds unit and I was in the Bawl Room and ...."

*Knock. Knock.*

The girls jumped. Bertie's cards flew in the air.

Deborah stood in the hallway, her dark eyes vacant and affect flat. "Addie, you've got a phone call. It's Dr. Springer." She disappeared.

"Ooo la la!" Opal batted her eyelashes, fanning her face with her cards.

Addie set her cards face down in front of her and shot to her feet. The room began to sway. She sat down in the closest chair.

"Addie, are you okay?" Mary Margaret reached out to her.

"I'm fine. I must have gotten up too quickly." Addie stood and felt her tummy rumble. "Girls, go ahead and play a hand without me. I'm not sure how long I'll be." Addie hoped her call with Dr. Springer was quick. A prickling heat flowed over her and sweat emerged on her upper lip. Her tummy gurgled again. Luckily, the first-floor bathroom was right next to the phone in the hallway. She ran to the phone and picked up the receiver, pushing out. "Yes, Dr. Springer? This is Addie. How can I help you?"

"You sound a bit breathless. Did I catch you at a bad time?"

*It would be very unladylike of me to tell him I've got to use the bathroom and that I'm in the middle of a card game with my friends.*

With a deep desire to keep the conversation brief, Addie simply replied, "No."

"I wanted to pass along a message from Garrett. He plans on playing cards with the McDaniel brothers on Saturday night in the hospital's garage. He'd love to stop by and meet with you in the garden around seven-thirty that night. Is that possible?"

Addie's bowels twisted; the urge to use the restroom was now emergent. *God, I don't want to have an accident right here in the hallway.* "Please give him my sincerest apologies. I'm working the evening shift in the Bawl Room and can't leave the babies unattended."

"Oh, that's a shame. I'll …."

"Dr. Springer, thank you for passing the message along. I have to go. Good-bye." Addie hung up the phone and scrambled for the bathroom.

Deborah stepped out of the kitchen and blocked Addie's entrance into the restroom. "What was that all about?"

"What the hell is wrong with you, Deborah? Get out of my way." Addie pushed Deborah aside, finding the nearest stall in the nick of time.

# 6

Edward watched the Sacred Heart leadership team assemble around the table as he folded the morning edition of *The Atlanta Dispatch* and set it down on the table next to his bowl of oatmeal topped with blueberries and strawberries. The headlines included stories about Independence Day celebrations, complete with parades, fireworks, picnics, and brass bands, and a story about how the aspirin shortage was negatively affecting hospitals and adversely impacting patient care across the country. The sports section gave him the latest update on the Atlanta Crackers' recent game scores and the weather report predicted more of the same: sunny days with sweltering temperatures nearing 100 degrees that brought a chance of afternoon thundershowers and lots and lots of humidity.

While he enjoyed all of the seasons, he loved the sounds of summer most of all and relished the rare moments when he could sneak away to take solitary walks under the pillars of pines and hardwood shade trees along the hospital's back property line. Cicada, grasshoppers, treefrogs, and bullfrogs sang their songs in rhythmic, rattling, rolling waves back and forth throughout the day and night. While he had no idea of the bird species names, he could make out their distinctive calls, which ranged from "chewy-chewy, chewy-chewy," "nu-huh, nu-huh," to "birdie-birdie-birdie-birdie." The woods were his favorite office space and he did his best strategic thinking there.

"See anything of interest in there?" Clyde pointed at the paper.

Edward picked up his spoon and scooped out a heaping helping of oats and fruit. "Aside from the city's patriotic festivities yesterday, it looks like Atlanta is percolating over with all kinds of political unrest. I read a story where the public isn't happy with Governor Slaton for commuting Leo Frank's death sentence and giving him life in prison. To demonstrate their displeasure with his decision, some citizens up in Dacula last month hung Governor Slaton in effigy with a sign around the dummy's neck that read, 'The king of Jews.'" He plunged the spoon in his mouth.

Clyde took his seat next to Edward. "Now that his term is over, my father says that our new mayor will be different."

"I hope so." Dr. Williams inserted himself into the conversation. "I voted for Governor Harris and attended his swearing-in ceremony last month. My father and I have a long-standing relationship with him."

"How so?" Alan inquired.

"We worked behind the scenes to help get his proposed bill through the legislature that established Georgia Institute for Technology here in town."

Edward continued, addressing the rest of table. "I'm also

hearing rumblings in my Rotary and Masonic club meetings that we're about to have a new fire chief and that we'll probably be getting a new Chief of Police, too, since our current chief has failed to fulfill his campaign promise to rid Atlanta of the red light districts."

Lena nodded her head. "I've heard that rumor, too. The problems associated with the sex-trafficking of children and women still plague this city. Something must be done to safeguard the innocent who get roped into that despicable business."

Clyde reflected on his business dealings with the Preti sisters and Mr. Chang to sex-traffic young orphans last year, counting his blessings that he never got caught in that web. That business venture was short-lived, just like the foiled tonic adventure he embarked on with Lester Schwinn and Alvin Martin two years ago. *Surely*, he surmised, *partnering with Hoyt to funnel phenol to Germany will prove profitable in the end. With great risks came great rewards*, he thought.

Edward scanned the morning's agenda. "Let's talk about our concierge Moira Goldberg's replacement plan."

"Let's." Although Clyde was in charge of daily operations and support staff, Edward made it known from day one that the leadership team, at any point, was empowered to fire employees on the spot as long as it was justified. While Alan shared with the group that Moira tendered her resignation to him, personally, Clyde prayed that there wasn't any more to the story. He was actually relieved that he finally had an excuse to sever ties with her. Visits with Moira were waning over the past month since he had other suiters to pursue and only a finite number of days and hours to accommodate his sexual escapades. After all, with great risks came great rewards. Clyde chuckled to himself. While he appreciated their time together, he had grown bored of Moira. Now that she was no longer behind the front desk, Clyde felt free to explore more unconquered conquests at Sacred Heart and at Alexander Hall in the coming year. Aroused by the thought that he and Deborah had been nearly caught by two nurses last month, he wondered where their next rendezvous would take place. The tunnels? The garden? What about in the morgue? Clyde played out multiple sexual scenarios in his mind.

Edward continued, "I was sorry to learn from Alan that Moira had resigned from her job so unexpectedly. However, people, like politics and pathogens, are so unpredictable. Who knows what her reasoning was."

Alan shrugged his shoulders and adjusted his glasses. He patted his thigh four times. He blurted out, "I like our new plan."

Edward asked Nurse Hartman, "How's it working out to have the first-year nursing students rotate and cover the front desk?"

"Nurse Scott and I are finding that they are enjoying the break from the clinical environment and it actually gives them another level of education and understanding about customer service, how to handle and field questions, assist in enforcing visitor's hours, and monitor bed placements with admissions and discharges. Nurse Scott and I are even grading them on their performance."

Clyde's sexual fantasies ceased momentarily as he added, "I actually like seeing a nurse in uniform behind the desk. It adds a level of professionalism in our appearance to the public."

Heads nodded in agreement around the conference table.

"Do you think it's a long-term solution?" Alan posed to Lena. "It would be a grand financial saving to our operational budget."

Lena smiled, appreciating Alan's masterful segue. which allowed her to pitch her idea for the senior nursing students. She was becoming a wiz at managing the hospital's politics. "Yes, and in follow-up to our discussion about my idea to find special accommodations for our senior nursing students, I learned that the house across the street was going to be put up for sale."

"Really?" Shelby appeared caught off guard. "That house is a real beauty. I'd actually been eyeing it for myself from my pharmacy window."

Lena wanted to say, 'I'm not blind and know you have feelings towards Opal. I've seen how you look at her when she walks by and how you pay special attention to her in your hand-on instruction in the medicinal garden. I'm sure that Edward will find you both another beautiful house. So sorry, but I saw it first.' Instead, she chose to ignore his comment and plowed on. "I spoke with the owner and widow. Mrs. White's husband died a few months ago and she plans to move to Cincinnati, Ohio, to live with her spinster sister at the end of the year. To make a long story short...."

Clyde yawned and stretched his arms above his head. "How'd he die?"

Resisting the desire to punch Clyde in the stomach for interrupting, Lena continued, "He dropped dead in the kitchen from a heart attack. Anyhow, Mrs. White said she'd be willing to donate the house and property to the hospital as a tax write-off. I propose we allow the senior nursing students to live there. Perhaps, we could even expand the space to accommodate any unmarried, full-time nursing staff, too. I'm hoping to avert complete chaos with nearly thirty women living under one roof. In addition to the cost savings that Alan just mentioned, that should be a fine outcome for the hospital."

Oliver sipped from his coffee cup and pointed out, "Not to mention, Edward, that even though Alexander Hall opens next year, we should be looking at the acquisition of land around both properties and across Spring and Alexander Streets so we can continue to expand on your master plan to build a comprehensive medical complex. Remember, although the bricks around Alexander Hall and the Colored nursing school hide the travertine tiles underneath, we all know that Sacred Heart Hospital and Alexander Hall will become one medical complex. While it won't happen in our lifetime, it's a secret that will be realized one day."

Edward gave the idea careful consideration and then replied, "Yes, Nurse Hartman, you have my permission to proceed. Alan and Oliver have also raised compelling reasons why this is a true win-win solution for all involved. Alan, please work with our hospital attorneys to finalize the deal." He extended an open hand to Lena. "Congratulations, Nurse Hartman, on a well-executed proposal."

Lena wanted to shout from the rooftop, 'Yes, I did it!' Instead, she humbled herself to the occasion. "Thank you, Edward, for your support." She placed her right hand over her heart. "It means the world to me."

The group joined in the accolades for Lena.

"Speaking of 'congratulations,' I heard that Joshua and Maybelle got married last month. Is that true?" Dr. Williams asked.

"Yes, it's true. Joshua and Maybelle tied the knot in Birmingham and will continue to remain employed here at the hospital. Please pass along your best when you see them." Edward refrained from revealing his other secret, but he was proud of his son. Edward considered himself fortunate that Trudy forgave him for having an affair with Ms. Mattie. While Trudy felt that her absence and mental instability was to blame, Edward countered that his restlessness, anger, frustration, and grief led to the infidelity. He hated not being in control, unaccustomed to handling feelings of loss and powerlessness. Trudy, despite everything, demonstrated that forgiveness was powerful; she was his true love. Edward made sure she knew that. He also made sure that his attorney provided a generous anonymous donation to Joshua's church and arranged for the customary congratulatory bouquet of flowers to be delivered to the Goode's home on behalf of the hospital when they returned to Atlanta after the nuptials. With one wedding down, he needed divine intervention to marry off Pearl first, followed by Opal, and then, in due time, Trip. 'Marry your true love,' he always told them. His heart burst with pride knowing that Joshua did.

### MONDAY AFTERNOON, FIRST WARD

"Is she here yet?" Sam asked Charlie as he entered *The Atlanta Dispatch*'s conference room, setting his iced Coca-Cola bottle down on the long pecan table. He adjusted his yellow plaid bow tie and straightened his blue vest.

Sam's elderly secretary, Imagene Littleton, who was sharp as

Katie Hart Smith

a tack and always one step behind him, scurried to pick up the soda bottle and placed it in a cut-glass coaster.

Charlie peered through the window blinds at what he thought looked like cotton candy exploding out of the cab out front. "Holy shit!" Hastily, he pulled out his handkerchief and dabbed his brow. He turned his back to the window and grasped the bottom sill. "She's here. And, she's managed to outshine the sun today!" He laughed nervously.

Pure joy and excitement poured out of every pore of Moira's being. She was dressed in a dusty rose organza afternoon gown with a white, high-neck, heavily embroidered bodice, and matching three-quarter length sleeves, complete with three tiers of ruffles on her train skirt. A rose-colored hat with white ostrich feathers, white lace gloves, and a white ruffled parasol completed the look as she marched up the walkway and through the front doors.

Imagene's deep Southern drawl made it sound like she was chewing on her words. "I'll go and fetch her, Mr. Sloan." Wearing a beige two-piece suit, her cotton-white hair in a topknot, she raised her crooked index finger and pointed towards the office lobby before shuffling off.

A few minutes passed before Moira appeared in the doorway, dwarfing Mrs. Littleton, who was barely visible peeking out from behind the monstrous gown.

Sam, enamored by her extravagant appearance and platinum blonde hair, thought she simulated a porcelain angel figurine he had once seen in the Montgomery Ward catalog. He extended his right hand. "Miss Hetta. It's a pleasure to finally meet you." Taking her hand in his, he patted it repeatedly. "Charlie has told me such wonderful things about you. We welcome you to *The Atlanta Dispatch*. Please have a seat." Sam pulled out her chair before he took a seat at the head of the table. "Mrs. Littleton, please get Miss Hetta a bottle of Coca-Cola, will you?"

"I'll take one, too." Charlie took a seat across from Moira, trying to process the vision before him. Her rouged cheeks and lips were more befitting an evening affair, but what did he know about the appropriate application for women's makeup? Was her hair the work of peroxide and a flat iron or a wig? His curiosity continued. Was her southern region dyed, too? He knew the truth would be revealed later that evening. He continued to blot his forehead.

Mrs. Littleton returned with the refreshments and multiple sideways disapproving glances at Miss Hetta before she left the room again. Charlie took a big swig of his beverage.

Sam was enamored. "Miss Hetta, if you don't mind me saying so, I think you look like an angel. Charlie, don't you think she looks like an angel?"

Charlie grunted and nodded, his mouth burning with the fizzy drink. He was having a difficult time swallowing without choking.

Moira blinked a few times. "Why, thank you. Mr. Sloan." She retrieved a pink, hand-held ostrich fan from her handbag, popped it open, and began fanning herself. "Every true Southern lady needs her hand-fan. Don't you agree, Mr. Sloan?"

Sam melted. "Absolutely! This Georgia humidity can be tough on a frail flower like you."

Moira giggled from behind her fan and tossed a wink at Charlie, knowing whom she was ending up in bed with tonight.

Tiny pink feathers broke free and began to float in the air, which gave Moira the appearance of being in a shaken snow globe. When Mrs. Littleton returned with a tray of cookies, a pink down fragment landed on her bottom lip. She tried desperately to remove it. *Pah. Pah. Pah. Pah.* To no avail, Mrs. Littleton stuck out her tongue. *Thwip. Thwip. Thwip. Thwip.* It looked like she was spitting on the delectable sweet treats as she placed the serving dish on the table. She plucked off the fuzzy menace, flicked it in the air, and exited the room in a huff.

"I'm sorry about that. I'm not sure what's gotten into her." Sam wondered if Mrs. Littleton would reappear.

She didn't.

"I'm really looking forward to seeing what I can do for you both and the readers of Atlanta with my new gossip column. This town needs something bold, exciting, and new." Moira closed her fan and set it on the table. The feathers ceased falling and settled.

Charlie's nerves, like the wayward feathers, settled, too, pleased that Moira was working her charms on Sam. He knew in his heart that she was a hustler and a chameleon, merely using him as a stepping stone to make her way in this world. And, little did Miss Hetta know, she was his. In the unfortunate event that the gossip column offended an influential socialite in this town, the board would see to it that Sam would be the sacrificial lamb and Sam's vacant chair would finally be his.

"I couldn't agree more. I think that this town needs *someone* bold, exciting, and new. And, that's you, Miss Hetta." Sam raised his bottle. "Here's to 'Hey, Hetta!'"

They toasted. "Cheers!"

High Cotton and Magnolias

## MONDAY LATE AFTERNOON, SIXTH WARD

Mr. Wu hustled across Sacred Heart's side yard, passing the white picket fenced medicinal garden where Shelby was working alongside Opal and other nursing students, weeding and tending to the herbs and plants. He followed the dirt driveway behind the construction site for Alexander Hall to the garage and storage barn in the back of the property. Wei slid the barn door open and slipped inside. Walking over to the first horse stall, he unlocked the gate and high-stepped over the hay to the back wall. *Knock.* Pause. *Knock, knock, knock.* Pause. *Knock.*

A tiny panel slid open. "Who goes there?" a voice whispered from behind the door.

"Ringing in the sleeves," Mr. Wu replied in his best broken English.

"What the fuck? Me ears haven't 'eard ya right. That's not it. Try again," the voice demanded.

Mr. Wu tried again. "Bringing in the sheets."

"Ha, ha, ha, ha! Oh, my dear sweet Jesus. No! Try again."

Frustrated, Wei pulled out a piece of paper from his pants pocket. He studied it for a few seconds. "Bringing in the shits."

Brice, unable to contain his laughter any longer, opened the door, grabbed Wei by his arm, and pulled him into the hidden room containing a round wooden table, and six chairs. The soft amber glow from the lanterns placed around the room flickered, highlighting Brice's bulbous nose, ruddy face, and reddish hair. "Oh, dear Lord! Wu, we 'ave to work with ya on ya English a bit more, 'ey?" His blue eyes twinkled in the dim light.

"What? Like my English any better than you?"

75

Three times Wei's size, Brice bent down and exaggerated his enunciation. "The secret phrase is, 'Bringin' in the sheaves.'"

Mr. Wu watched Brice's mouth and mimicked him. "Bringin' in the sheee-ves."

"Attaboy, me li'l wee man." Brice patted Wei on the shoulder. "Ya needin' somtin' cold to drink?"

"Shi. Yes, please."

Brice walked over to a large round galvanized wash tub filled with ice. He pulled out a bottle of beer. "I brewed this batch me self," he said as he handed it to Mr. Wu.

*Knock.* Pause. *Knock, knock, knock.* Pause. *Knock.* "Bringing in the sheaves." Two voices called out.

"Enter!" Brice called back to them.

The door slid open. Brice's twin brothers, Tim and Jim, ducked into the room, closing the panel behind them.

"Just got back from making a run. 'Ad to pick up a poor bastard who got his 'and smashed by a trip 'ammer in a nearby grain mill." Tim removed his ambulance attendant's cap and smoothed down his auburn hair, wet with sweat.

Jim did the same, his strawberry-blonde short-cropped mop matted to his head. "Bet 'is 'and is a goner, for sure." He made a b-line to the beer, pulling out two bottles and handing one to Tim.

"Ya wanna put a wager on it, fellas?" Brice dared, eyeing the three of them.

"Oh, 'ell no. I'm not bettin' on that poor fella's 'and." Tim made the sign of the cross across his chest. "That's a great way to bring the púca in 'ere."

"I believe the Southerners refer to evil spirits as 'haints,'" Jim said between swigs.

"Ya, that's true, brotha'. That's why so many folks have their porch ceilings painted blue, to wave off the haints. An ol' lady tol' me that a few weeks ago when we were pickin' up 'er 'usband who fell out from the 'eat." Tim finished off his beer and wiped his mouth with the back of his uniform sleeve. "God, that goes down quick."

"I bet not as quick as one of Madam McGuire's girls!" Brice bellowed.

"That a good one, Mr. Brice!" Wei took a seat in one of the chairs.

The men joined him.

Brice gulped down the last of his afternoon nip. "Speaking of going down quick, Garrett could hardly hold 'is drink or 'is hand at our last card game. "I was gettin' tired of 'im ramblin' on 'bout one of the nurses. What was 'er name?"

"Addie," Mr. Wu said. "She a good girl. I can tell a good nurse from a bad one by looking into their eyes." Wei pointed to his own eyes. "I can tell if they got a good spirit or a bad one. Some are good. Some, not so good."

"Poor son-of-a-bitch was broken 'earted that she couldn't make time to see 'im that evenin'." Brice added, "'Ey was throwin' good money afta' bad that night. I don't think Garrett 'ad two pennies to 'is name when 'ey left 'ere."

Jim was eager to add to his winnings. "Let's be sure to invite 'im back."

Brice nodded. "We will, my li'l brotha'. We will."

Mr. Wu pointed at his eyes again. "Garrett has good eyes. Good jīng shén, a good spirit."

Tim punched Wei in the upper arm. "Do I have good, 'ow did ya say it? Jīng shén?"

"Shi. Yes, you do. I often hear you singing when you bring patients to hospital. I think singing is good for the soul. Why you sing?"

"When I was li'l, our Presbyterian minister told me, 'He who sings, prays twice.' I figure I'm doublin' up on me prayers for the sick and dying. I sing to make 'em happy on their journey, wherever they may end up and to keep púca away." Tim cleared his voice, directing his next words to Brice. "Since ya spoke of bettin' on the wounded, me brotha', I need to clear the ghosts outta 'ere. Join me if ya will in song. This 'ere's me favorite and that's why it's our code phrase, because that's what life's all about, sowin' and reapin'." Clearing his throat again, he sang out, "Sowin' in the marnin', sowin' seeds of kindness, sowin' in the noontide and the dewy eve; waitin' fer the 'arvest, and the time of reapin', we shall come rejoicin', bringin' in the sheaves."

Brice, a baritone, and Jim, a tenor, found their respective harmonies while Mr. Wu hummed along in a unique key of his own. "Bringin' in the sheaves, bringin' in the sheaves, we shall come rejoicin', bringin' in the sheaves; bringin' in the sheaves, bringin' in the sheaves, we shall come rejoicin', bringin' in the sheaves."

# 7

Overcast skies and sticky, high humidity didn't dull Addie's effervescent spirit this morning. Holding a notebook, *The Principles and Practice of Nursing*, and a glass of water, she skipped down the back stairwell, spilling a few drops along the way. Addie took a seat between Opal and Bertie in Classroom A, which was located across the hall from the library and parlor in the nursing dorm. While pulling out her pencil, she fumbled with Garrett's pebble in her pocket. The grandfather clock down the front hall, a gift to the school by Lena's parents, tolled seven bells. Addie smiled to herself, recalling Nurse Hartman telling the students on the first day of orientation that from the time you hear the first bell chime in the morning to the last one you hear before you fall asleep at night, keep asking yourself, 'What did I do today that helped another human being?'

"You appear to be a beam of sunshine today, Nurse Engel," Opal observed. "What's gotten into you? By the way, are you losing weight? Your uniform is looking baggier." Opal tugged at Addie's waistband.

Addie whispered in Opal's ear, "I think it's just the stress of school. My tummy's been a bit off lately. And, yes, I'm giddy because I received a lovely letter from Garrett yesterday," she gloated.

Opal whispered back, "Oh, so Garrett has gotten into you!" She reeled back, laughing.

Addie blushed; her neck flushed. "You're impossible!" She couldn't resist laughing right along with her.

"Shhhh!" Bertie scolded the two of them between sips as she drank from her coffee cup. "You're going to earn us demerits if you don't cut it out."

Nurse Hartman took roll as the student's filed in, noting one student's absence, Deborah. "Does anyone know where Nurse Owens is this morning?"

Heads shook and shoulders shrugged as the students looked around the room at each other.

Nurse Clair Scott appeared in the doorway. "Good morning, class."

"Good morning, Nurse Scott," they replied in unison.

"Nurse Scott, would you mind running upstairs to check on the whereabouts of Nurse Owens?"

Clair tucked a brown curl behind her ear. "Sure. I'll be right back."

Nurse Hartman wrote on the blackboard with white chalk. *Observation of the Sick.* She faced the students and addressed the class. "Nurse Scott and I have been teaching you that your observation of the patient is both subjective and objective in nature. You must employ all five of your senses in your cephalocaudal, or head to toe, assessment. It is imperative to determine which symptoms are improving and which ones are evidence of neglect." Lena picked up the textbook and read from it. "As Florence Nightingale pointed out and I quote, 'If a patient is cold, if a patient is feverish, if a patient is faint, if he is sick after taking food, it is generally the fault not of the disease but of the nursing.' Such symptoms, if they exist and if they are reported, are very misleading and obscure the diagnosis, for the doctor takes it for granted and has the right to expect that his patient is receiving the best nursing care. The whole purpose of the observation and reporting of symptoms is not to hinder, but to aid in the correct diagnosis to the end that the patient may be cured.'" Lena pointed to Mary Margaret. "Nurse O'Malley, can you give me an example of when your clinical observations were found to be of great importance to the treating physician?"

While Mary Margaret began to unwind her story, Opal nudged Addie, having written a note on her paper. *What did he have to say to you?*

Addie scribbled a reply, giving the appearance she was taking notes. She angled her paper so Opal could read it. *He was thinking of me. Hoping school was going well. Disappointed he couldn't see me a few weeks ago. Firehouse keeping him busy. Lost money in a card game. His dad and farm – O.K.*

"That was a wonderful example, Nurse O'Malley," Lena remarked. "Let's hear from another student."

Opal gingerly picked up her water glass, clueless about the topic at hand and praying she wasn't called on. Addie bowed her head, hoping to be invisible.

Nurse Hartman scanned the room and then pointed the chalk at Addie. "Addie, can you give us an example from your experiences?"

Addie lifted her head. *Shit. Shit. Shit. I wasn't paying attention. What was the question? Oh, dear, God! How am I going to respond? What if she walks over here and asks to see my notes. I'm doomed for sure.* A wave of heat rolled over Addie and hives broke out on her neck and chest.

Nurse Hartman began walking toward her.

"Well, I...I...I...." Addie stammered and then reached for her water glass.

*Boom! Boom! Boom! Boom! Boom! Boom! Boom!* And then, silence.

"What the devil was that?" Nurse Hartman froze.

"It sounded like it came from the back stairs." Addie didn't know if she should feel relieved or scared.

Nurse Hartman raced toward the stairwell. The room emptied behind her and they all found Nurse Scott lying unresponsive at the bottom of the stairs, her head and neck at an unnatural angle.

Lena rushed over. "Oh no! Nurse Scott! Can you hear me? Clair? Clair?" She felt for a pulse, knowing there wouldn't be one. Not wanting to scare the young ladies, she singled Addie out. "Addie, call the front desk and get a doctor over here, stat!"

Addie disappeared and made the call. When she returned, she found everyone in hysterics, huddled around Clair and Nurse Hartman.

"What's going on down there?" Deborah, still dressed in her nightgown, called out to the crowd below as she leaned over the second-floor banister.

Through the tears, Lena stood up and raced up the staircase, yelling at Deborah, "Where have you been? I sent Nurse Scott to find you."

Defiant, Deborah spoke rapidly. "I wasn't feeling well this morning. I've been in the bathroom with cramps. You know. That time of the month stuff. Cramps, bleeding, diarrhea, cramps, bleeding, diarrhea," she repeated. "Did you know I like the color red? I think I like blue and pink, too, but red is my favorite."

"What the hell are you talking about?" Lena took Deborah by the arms and shook her. "Did you do this? Wait until your uncle hears about this."

"UNCLE?" Deborah screamed. "I don't have an uncle! Have you lost your mind?"

Even through the shock, Addie recalled Nurse Scott's classroom instructions to her. 'When an emergency arises, try as best as you can to be objective, and observant. It's imperative to process everything and take mental notes of the time, place, condition of the environment, persons, and even conversations.' *Uncle? Who's Deborah's uncle? While she warned me to never bring up her mother again in conversation, I've never heard her talk about extended family. Why would Nurse Hartman accuse Deborah of pushing Nurse Scott down the stairs?*

"Stop! You're hurting me. You've gone completely mad. I didn't do anything! STOP!" Deborah pulled free from Lena's grasp and ran off.

Lena called out after her, "Deborah, I'm sorry! I'm sorry!"

Dr. Williams burst through the basement door that led to the Greene tunnel below. He quickly assessed Clair and hung his head. Looking around, he saw some of the sobbing students pointing to the landing above. He called up to Lena, "She's dead! She's broken her neck. She's dead!"

"Oh, God!" Lena buried her head in her hands and wept.

The light changed and shifted in the stairwell and something caught Addie's attention on the treads of the third, fourth, and fifth stairs. *Water. Oh my stars! Did I drop that water when I was coming down the stairs this morning? Did I cause Nurse Scott's death?*

### TUESDAY AFTERNOON, THIRD WARD

"Would you care for a glass of water or would you prefer something stronger?" Hoyt rummaged around the bar in his office.

"Something stronger, thanks." Clyde, captivated by a brown spider with a bulbous behind, watched it stick its minuscule fangs into the head of a wasp that was entangled in the heavy web in the corner window behind Hoyt's desk.

"She's fascinating to watch." Hoyt set the beverage down on the coffee table and took a seat on the sofa. "Come have a seat."

"It's amazing to see an insect capture prey four times its size and suck the living life out of it." Clyde grinned. "I know some people like her."

"I've named her Trudi. It means 'strong spear' in German."

Clyde meandered over and took a seat in a chair across from Hoyt. "Trudi's strategy and tactics don't differ from our corporate or political ones, do they?"

"No, they don't. It's not the size of the company or the political agenda that matters; what is paramount to our success is the initial planning and development of an overall strategy and the tactics to support a successful outcome."

"My father taught me to approach business, life, and politics with an end goal in mind."

"Precisely, and Trudi's end goal is to eat and provide food to her babies."

"Just like Germany. They want to eat and keep food on their tables, too, with the ultimate mission of disrupting American infrastructure."

"Yes, we, too, want to stick our venomous fangs into our prey and suck its very soul from existence." Hoyt reached into his coat pocket, pulled out a thick white envelope, and handed it to Clyde.

Clyde opened the envelope and flipped through the tightly packed bills inside.

"It's all there in the denominations that you asked for. Phenol sales are going well, and the acquisition of excess phenol is being funneled to an American subsidiary that is actually a German-owned chemical company. My motherland is very happy with our factory's production and our covert ability to buy off the press in an attempt to influence the public's perception about the war in Europe."

"That's great news." Clyde set the envelope down on the coffee table and picked up his drink. "Speaking of news, I heard from my father that the sympathetic stories about Germany you planted in *The Atlanta Dispatch* aren't going over very well. He said there are a lot of concerned influential people rumbling about it. While I know you didn't use your name in the article, I hope that those stories don't come back to haunt you."

"Why would they?" Hoyt crossed his arms and legs. "How could they? I've paid off that entire newspaper board and their editor. I've bought their silence and obedience."

"Oh, I don't think there's anything to worry about." Clyde emptied his glass, set it on the table, and retrieved the envelope.

"I sure hope not, Clyde. Just like most breeds of spiders, we have multiple eyes and are completely aware of our surroundings so we don't get caught. If we do, we have our ways of getting out of tangled webs."

*Ring. Ring. Ring. Ring.*

Hoyt picked up the black candlestick phone on the end table. "Hello? Yes. Yes. He's here. Okay. I'll tell him." He hung up the phone.

"Who was that?"

"That was your father. It seems that you are wanted back at the hospital for an emergency leadership meeting. Edward's been calling all over town trying to find you."

Clyde groaned as he pulled himself out of the chair. "Great! Just when I was starting to relax, that fucker pulls me back to work. He likes having me on a string."

"I hate that you are leaving me so soon." Hoyt pouted.

Clyde pulled out his timepiece. "Why don't you stop by my place this evening? Perhaps, we can spin a web of our own tonight."

Hoyt's countenance changed. "I'll be there by nine."

"Perfect. You can be the fly and I'll be the spider."

Lena wrung her hands and paced back and forth in Alan's office. Her hands flew above her head as she spoke. "I'm so sorry, Alan. I truly am. I screwed up. I'm so sorry. It just slipped out."

Alan grew dizzy and anxious as Lena's rambled. He had never seen her like this. His legs rattled. "For goodness sake, Lena, please take a seat. You're driving me nuts with all of the words falling out of your mouth and your hands flying about."

Lena reluctantly complied.

Alan pulled out his bottom desk drawer and set an unmarked corked bottle filled with a clear liquid on his desk blotter. Pouring a small amount in two glasses, he handed her one. "Cheers. It's moonshine. Don't ask where I got it." He took a hearty gulp. "Tell me exactly what happened."

She tossed her drink back and set the empty glass on his desk. She exhaled and blew through her lips. "It tastes like warm apple pie." She reached over and poured out another shot. She threw that one back, too. Lena pounded her chest, and then answered his question. "Like I told the leadership team this afternoon, I found Nurse Scott at the bottom of the stairs."

"Yes, I'm familiar. Move your story along to the part that may be of concern to us that you didn't share with the group."

"When I ran up the stairs and yelled at Deborah, she started rambling nonsense and I said, 'Wait until your uncle hears about this.'"

"And, Deborah said?"

"She said, 'Uncle? I don't have an uncle.' She called me crazy and ran off while I tried to apologize to her."

"Perhaps the chaos was too much for her to handle. Didn't you say she was sick with her menses and that's why she didn't show up for class? Don't you women get weird and emotional during that time of the month anyway?"

Lena shot him a wide-eyed look.

"And, then you accused her of doing something horrible. Perhaps she snapped like you did?" Alan shook his head. "I can't believe I'm saying this, but don't worry. As Dr. Williams told us in our meeting this afternoon, it appears that Nurse Scott just tripped and fell. There wasn't any evidence of foul play. The bottoms of her shoes weren't slick or wet. While they found some water on a few of the steps, they were still in droplet form, not smeared. It was an unfortunate accident."

"I swore to you that I'd keep your secret, Alan. I feel like I betrayed you."

"Oh, for the love of all things Holy, Lena, I can't imagine in all of the confusion that anyone would remember anything you said, let alone Deborah."

Lena played and replayed the event over and over in her head. "That's true. Dr. Williams did administer a heavy pain reliever to Deborah after the incident to calm her nerves and to help alleviate her monthly discomfort." Lena sighed. The creases in some of the wrinkles around her forehead and eyes started to ease. "I'll check on her tonight before I leave." Her head started buzzing. "Jesus, that stuff is strong. I've got to gather my strength to ride my bike back to my apartment."

"Nonsense. Go and check on Deborah and come back here. We'll toss your bike in the back of my car and I'll give you a ride home."

"If you throw in grabbing a bite to eat along the way, then you have a deal."

"Deal."

"I'll be back in twenty minutes." Lena exited. Wanting to avoid any questions from nosey and curious employees, she made her way to the nursing dorm through the Greene tunnel, passing the morgue and Mr. and Mrs. Wu, who were pushing racks of linens to the laundry room. Once on the second floor of the nursing school, she found Deborah asleep in her bunk bed. She shook her awake. "Deborah. Deborah. It's Nurse Hartman."

"Wha-wha- what time is it?" Deborah asked, rubbing her eyes. "Am I late for class?"

"No, it's seven o'clock at night. I wanted to check on you before I left for the night. Are you feeling any better?"

"Yes, the shot Dr. Williams gave me worked. My cramps have subsided." Deborah rubbed her abdominal area under the sheets."

"I wanted to apologize for my behavior earlier today."

"What are you talking about? The last thing I recall, I was in the bathroom stall and then I blacked out. I awoke in the bed to find Dr. Williams sitting next to me giving me a shot in my backside. You were there with him, but I don't recall you saying much of anything. He was the one doing all the talking about Nurse Scott dying in an accidental fall down the stairs."

Relieved, Lena patted and smoothed down Deborah's sheets. "Well, rest up and if you get hungry, ask one of the students to run down to the kitchen and bring you up something to eat."

"I will. But I'd like to rest a bit more."

"Okay. I'll take my leave. But I expect to see you in class in the morning. If for whatever reason you are still not feeling well, will you please let one of the nurses know?"

Deborah nodded, rolled over, and pulled the sheets up to her shoulders.

As Lena made her way back to Alan's office, she passed Addie in the hallway.

Addie, returning from the pharmacy, tightly clutched three bottles of medication in her hands. She felt her insides twist with guilt. "Good evening, Nurse Hartman." *Should I say something to her about spilling water on the stairs? Should I not mention anything at all? Dear Maw in heaven, I know you taught me not to lie, but I didn't mean to kill Nurse Scott. Am I a murderer?* 'You reap what you sow, Addie,' she heard her mother's voice say clearly in her head. "Nurse Hartman, I need to talk with you about what happened to Nurse Scott."

Lena stopped and took a deep breath. She turned back and ushered Addie into the Treatment room. She closed the door. "Look, Addie. Today was a tough day for everyone...."

"No, Nurse Hartman. I think I did it. I think I caused Nurse Scott's accident."

"What do you mean, Addie?"

Addie stuttered. "I...I...I think I dropped some water on the stairs that caused her to slip and fall."

"Oh, honey. Come here." Lena opened her arms up wide and Addie fell into them, sobbing. "Addie, you didn't cause Clair to die. This wasn't your fault."

Addie stammered, "Wh-wha-what? It...it...it wasn't?"

Lena squared Addie in front of her. "Heavens no, my dear. Dr. Williams, after careful evaluation of the incident, told us this afternoon, that there didn't appear to be any evidence of foul play, that the bottoms of her shoes weren't wet, and there weren't any slick spots on the stairs. They did find a few drops of water, but they were still beaded and intact. You didn't cause Clair to die. Dr. Williams thinks she tripped somewhere near the top of the stairs; the momentum from tumbling down the entire flight was what broke her neck."

Addie, still clutching the bottles, felt her knees go weak. She reached out to grab the edge of the hospital bed as Lena caught the bottles before they crashed to the floor.

"Addie, are you alright?" Lena set the medicine down on the counter.

"I'm fine." Addie pulled out a hanky, blotting her eyes, cheeks, and nose.

"Why don't you compose yourself before heading back to the peds unit? I'll tell Dr. Springer that I asked you to run an errand for me and I'll take this medicine to him."

"Oh, thank you, Nurse Hartman. I was so worried and fretted all day that I was the one to…."

Lena held up her hand in protest. "Addie, I can't bear to talk about this anymore. All I ask of you is that you please lift Clair up in your prayers tonight before you go to bed."

"I will." Addie sniffed multiple times.

Lena turned to leave and then turned back. "Good night, Addie."

"Good night, Nurse Hartman."

Lena shut the door behind her.

# 8

Rays of sunlight streamed into Edward's office, illuminating the contents piled on his executive desk as he discussed the agenda items for September's leadership meeting with Clyde and Dr. Williams. Clyde, growing bored, started picking lint off of his black suit while scanning the morning headlines of *The Atlanta Dispatch* lying on the edge of the desk in front of him. He studied the picture of the blonde-hair gossip columnist in the 'Hey, Hetta!' segment. Something about her looked very familiar, but he couldn't place her. He wondered if he had run across her at the Alexander home a few weeks ago, at a kick-off party for Trudy's hospital guild. Then he felt the hair on the back of his neck raise and tingle as he read, *How Germany Has Worked in U.S. To Shape Opinion, Block The Allies And Get Munitions For Herself, Told In Secret Agents' Letters,* an article reprinted with permission from the *New York World.* He lunged out of his chair, snatching the paper. Edward and Dr. Williams stopped conversing and glared at him.

Edward chided, "Clyde, I swear that you feel that we are here for your amusement. Having you as an employee is like having a fly tied to a string. You flit and fly all over the place; your mind is everywhere but here in this moment." He slammed his fist on his desk. "Would you please show Dr. Williams and I the professional courtesy that we deserve?" He forced a half-assed grin.

"My apologies. Please continue." Clyde folded the paper and set it in his lap.

Dr. Williams picked up where he and Edward left off. "Edward, in addition to having me investigate the National Birth Registry, I must insist that we add to next month's meeting a discussion about Sacred Heart's nursing care."

Edward balked.

"But," Dr. Williams ploughed on, "look, it's not that I'm questioning Nurse Hartman's skills, but in light of the tragic loss of our educator, Nurse Scott, we need to make sure that the skills and competency of the rest of the nurses, especially the new ones, are attended to." Dr. Williams was emphatic. He leaned back in the wooden chair in Edward's office and pulled out a piece of paper from his lab coat pocket. "According to my notes, the death rates, especially on the medical-surgical unit, are continuing to stay in the mid-twenties and I would prefer that number to be much less."

Clyde scrutinized and countered, "But, haven't you been telling us that the severity of the patient's cases has risen and the number of work-related injuries, compounded by the pellagra epidemic, is at the root of the matter."

Edward was impressed with Clyde's response. Perhaps there was a glimmer of hope in him after all. "Clyde is right. Since we have opened the doors of Sacred Heart and as the word of our excellent care has spread far and wide throughout Georgia, you are beginning to see an incremental increase in the acuity of your patients. With that said, doesn't that have the potential to correlate with the volume of deaths, too?"

"Maybe, but I do want to address the nursing issue next month." Dr. Williams stood up. "If you'll excuse me, Edward, I've got a surgical case waiting for me. Some poor woman needs a hysterectomy after giving herself too many Lysol douches over the years." He shook Edward's hand, patted Clyde on the shoulder, and headed for the door.

Clyde couldn't resist asking, "Dr. Williams, how do you know it's a nursing issue and not a physician issue?"

Dr. Williams didn't respond and left.

Edward pounded his fist again, startling Clyde. "Clyde, what the fuck is wrong with you? I see glimmers of competence and aptitude as you climb your mountain of success, and then the calculated timing of your inappropriate comments hit people like a rock slide. Everything you have accomplished to gain favor with them is all for not." Edward felt the acid in his stomach rise. "Have you not learned anything from me over these past two years? God, damn it! Learn when to speak and learn when not to. It's called tact! Dr. Williams and Nurse Hartman are working miracles out there every day."

He got up and walked over to his bookshelf on the far wall. Edward opened the oak, hand-carved humidor decorate with Masonic symbols—like the square and compass, trowel, plumb rule, and level—on the lid and around the sides of the box. He pulled out a cigar, shoved it in his mouth, and started chewing on the end. "Try not to hang yourself, Clyde, with your asinine remarks."

"What? Like that poor Leo Frank fella who got abducted from jail and lynched yesterday?"

Edward wanted to scream but instead weighed his next words carefully before responding. He pulled on his black suspenders. "People tend to take justice into their own hands when they feel that a situation hasn't been adequately handled. Be careful that the same doesn't happen to you because one day, neither your father nor I will be able to save you from your foul remarks and reckless behavior." Edward wrinkled up his nose and sniffed a few times.

Clyde did the same. "Speaking of foul, what the hell is that?"

Edward pulled the cigar from between his lips and burst out of his office, raising his nose in the air. "My God! What the hell is that awful smell?" Walking over to the door marked, *Treatment Room*, he twisted the handle and found the door locked. He started to knock, but resisted the temptation, "I don't really want to know what is going on in there." He retreated back to his office and slammed the door.

"Opal, should I go and see who was trying to get in here?" Addie inquired as she applied the sulphur ointment to the red rash on the middle-aged female patient's back.

"No, it happens quite a lot. Nosey people need to keep to themselves." Opal turned her attention to the patient. "Ma'am, as we explained earlier, this medicine is going to help treat your scabies." Opal scanned *The Doctor's Order-Book*, a book found on each ward that insured that the right patient was given the right medication at the right time. Various colored, two-inch tickets, ranging from yellow, pink, to orange, blue, red, green and white, indicated the time of medication administration. The paper tickets could be whole, the corners cut, or halved to represent the frequency. When a medication was not to be repeated, it was marked off with a red ink pen and the time it was given logged to prevent the drug from being delivered a second time. A two-inch pale orange square was secured by the patient's hand-written name, *Marsha Meadows*. "It appears that the doctor has ordered the ointment to be applied two times a day. We'll have to apply your medicine again tonight."

The weathered woman nodded and grimaced, revealing four missing upper front teeth.

Addie apologized for the stench, saying, "I know it stinks to high heaven. Sulfur smells like rotten eggs."

Mrs. Meadows shrugged. "It don't smell half as bad as my husband after workin' in the field all day."

The women laughed.

When the treatment was completed, a freckled-face student nurse, whose badge read *Nurse Harper*, was summoned by Opal to escort Mrs. Meadows back to the medical-surgical ward.

Opal returned to the room and waved her hands in the air. "We're going to have to air out this room before the next patient comes in here."

"It reeks for sure." Addie glanced at the *Procedures* roster. "It looks like Deborah has a patient scheduled in here in the next few minutes."

"Deborah." Opal shook her head. "Is it me, or do you get a creepy feeling when you are around her?" Opal lowered her voice. "I know Nurse Hartman put the fear of God into us if we ever talked about the Nurse Scott incident, but do you think Deborah was capable of such an act?"

Addie finished mitering the corner of the bedsheet and smoothed out the wrinkles. "Murder is a pretty serious accusation. However, Nurse Hartman's initial response was to lash out at Deborah. By the way, did you catch Nurse Hartman telling Deborah, 'Wait until I tell your uncle?'"

Opal pondered. "Gosh, so much happened. It's all a blur to me. I don't recall her saying that at all. Come to think of it, I've never heard Deborah talk about her family. I don't even know where she's from or who her people are." Opal collected the patient's chart and *The Doctor's Order-Book* off the counter. "Do you want me to ask my father?"

Addie lit a Berger lamp to help expel the odor. "I think you should." She blew out the match.

Opal reared back her head with confidence. "Okay, I will."

Addie and Opal exited the treatment room.

Deborah approached, snatching *The Doctors Order-Book* out of Opal's hands. "I'll take that." She entered the treatment room, closing the door behind her.

Ripping open the book, she flipped through the pages and stopped at an entry. *Daniel Huey. Diagnosis: Inflammation of the iris and adhesions - OD. Medication order: Atropine eye drops - one drop to right eye.* Deborah removed the pale orange ticket by Mr. Huey's name and swapped it with Mr. Adam's yellow ticket, a color that indicated his two aspirin tablets were to be given every four hours. In addition, Deborah changed the 'one' to a 'two' so that it read, *two drops.* She slammed the book shut and readied her room for her patient.

## WEDNESDAY AFTERNOON, FOURTH WARD

Clyde made a right turn and drove through the arched red brick entrance at Oakland Cemetery. He bobbled and bounced as the Model T Ford traversed the cobblestone road until he pulled up to a mausoleum marked with an angel on top. Hoyt's hunter green Cadillac Model 51 four-door Saloon was already parked on the side of the road. He had overheard Hoyt boast to one of his employees at the factory last month about how he had purchased the new V8 at a cost of nearly two thousand dollars when it rolled off the assembly line in September of last year. A very stately car, Clyde thought, tipping his Bowler to Hoyt's chauffeur as he exited his vehicle. Weaving through low lying azalea bushes and headstones, he found Hoyt standing next to a granite mausoleum, dressed in an ivory sack suit, matching vest, and straw boater's hat. "Don't you look dapper today?" Clyde's heart skipped a beat, appreciating Hoyt's fair skin, blue eyes, and blonde hair against the pale hues of the fabrics, his appearance pristine, unaffected by the stagnated breeze, oppressive heat, and humidity. Clyde pulled on his black suit lapels. "It appears that I'm the Yin to your Yang today."

Hoyt's eyes darted from side to side; skipping the small talk, he jumped straight to the point. "I'm guessing you read the newspaper headlines today?"

"Yes, that's why I chose this place to have a chat. I was afraid that your factory might be under surveillance by the Secret Service. Is it true that the conspiracy was exposed by the negligent act of a German agent who left his briefcase on a train?"

Hoyt stepped closer to Clyde. "Yes."

"What a dumbass!"

"That briefcase contained an outline of all of our activities, names, places, and accounts in the phenol plot." Rather than admit defeat, Hoyt added, "But, it really doesn't matter because we have diverted enough phenol to make nearly five million pounds of explosives and secure our world domination in the manufacturing of aspirin. The bottom line is we achieved our objectives."

"The article also points out that excess phenol was even funneled from American inventor Thomas Edison's factory in Pennsylvania. Is that a fact?"

"It's true. I explained that our roots run deep in this country."

Clyde, sensing Hoyt's restlessness, felt his own agitation growing. He didn't like feeling entombed, suddenly afraid that he was going to be caught up in the colossal web of a conspiracy. "May I suggest that you take an extended leave of absence from your chemical company?"

"I'm already one step ahead of you." Hoyt pointed towards the Cadillac. "My trunks are packed, I'm tying up loose ends, and I've secured my passage out of New York, where I'll take a passenger ship next month back home to Baden-Baden."

Clyde was taken aback by the suddenness of it all. He had known he would have to let Hoyt go eventually, but so soon? "What about the factory? Sales records? Accounting ledgers? Can anything be traced back to me?"

"No, it won't, not after tonight. I have an excellent fire insurance policy." Hoyt managed a slight smile.

Recalling the incendiary ending to the paint factory, a front for Lester Schwinn's tonic business a few years ago, he knew what Hoyt was insinuating. Hardening his heart, Clyde extended his right hand. "It was a pleasure doing business with you. If I ever get to southwest Germany, I'll look you up."

"Please do." Hoyt gently placed a sweet kiss on Clyde's cheeks, one and then the other.

The men walked back to their respective vehicles.

As the Cadillac's engine turned over, Hoyt rolled down his window and called out, "I've left a gift for you in your car. Auf wiedersehen, my love." He blew Clyde a kiss as the car drove off.

Clyde peered in his driver's side window and saw four thick, white envelopes bundled together with a piece of string sitting in the passenger seat.

### WEDNESDAY EVENING, SIXTH WARD

"Mr. Huey, it's time for your eye drops again." Bertie placed two drops of atropine into the right eye.

"Did the doctor up my dosage? The nurses use to give me just one drop twice a day and now I'm getting two drops four times a day." Mr. Huey grabbed Bertie's wrist. "Is there something wrong with my eye that you're not telling me?"

Bertie yanked her arm away. "Mr. Huey, I must insist that you behave yourself!"

Mr. Huey tossed and turned in the bed, rambling nonsense. He started laughing, and then began crying. He pointed behind Bertie. "Who is that man standing behind you?"

Bertie turned. No one was standing behind her. She scanned the room, spotting Deborah at the medication cabinet, and called out. "Psst! Psst! Deborah, I need your assistance."

Deborah hustled over. "What's wrong?"

"There's something wrong with Mr. Huey. He's acting very strange."

"What is he doing?"

"He appears agitated and confused, and is hallucinating."

"What meds is he on?"

Bertie held out the bottle of atropine. "Just this one."

"It sounds like he has atropine poisoning. How many times have you been giving this medicine?"

"According to the order book, two drops, four times a day."

Deborah took the bottle and studied it.

Mr. Huey's skin flushed. He smacked his lips and spoke rapidly. "I'm thirsty. I'm so thirsty. Get me some water. I'm having a hard time swallowing. Get me water! Get me water!"

Bertie reached for the glass of water on his bedside table and held up his head so he could take a few sips.

"Much better. Much better. Thank you. Thank you. Thank you." Mr. Huey rolled over and began babbling again.

Worry washed over Bertie's face. "Oh, Jesus! What do we do?" She looked up at Deborah. "I need to call the doctor." She took a step, but Deborah reached out and grabbed Bertie by the arm, stopping her in her tracks.

"You will do no such thing. It's late and the doctor will be upset if we bother him. You don't want him to yell at you, do you?"

Bertie shook her head.

"He will be very angry with you for making a mistake. You might get into serious trouble."

Bertie started to whimper. "But I didn't make a mistake. I gave the eye drops as they were ordered."

With complete command, Deborah spoke, "Of course you did. However, it appears that the doctor has made a medication error. He should have written for one drop, twice a day. We need to correct his mistake. We need to have Mr. Huey drink some old tea. The tannic acid will help neutralize the effects of the drug. In addition, we need to catheterize him so the drug isn't reabsorbed into his system, and finally, he needs a mustard bath to draw out the atropine from his organs through the skin."

Without a word, Bertie rushed off and complied with Deborah's orders. Mr. Huey's symptoms subsided the following hour. Bertie continued to keep a watchful eye on Mr. Huey for the remainder of the evening.

At the end of the shift, Deborah walked up to Bertie at the nurse's desk. "The night shift should be here any minute. You don't need to report this incident to the charge nurse during our shift report."

Bertie stopped charting. "What? Are you crazy? I have to tell her what happened."

"No, no you don't. The doctor will only blame you for his mistake. By the way, I went ahead and corrected *The Doctor's Order-Book*." She glanced back at Mr. Huey, who slept soundly in his bed. "I see that Mr. Huey is resting comfortably and that his side effects have abated."

Bertie, conflicted, said, "I just don't know. I don't think that's the right thing to do."

Deborah countered, "Bertie, he is better because of what I told you to do. I saved him. Did you know that Mary Margaret asked me to change shift assignments with her? Thank goodness

I was here and knew exactly what to do to save your patient's life. Otherwise, he could have died while under *your* care."

The medical-surgical ward door swung open. The night shift charge nurse and Mary Margaret entered the room.

"Bertie, you can thank me later."

Deborah and Bertie reported to the oncoming shift. But not a word was mentioned about Mr. Huey's episode. The vow of silence was defeating for Bertie.

As Bertie gathered her belongings, she couldn't resist the urge, and subtly asked Mary Margaret, "Just out of curiosity, did you ask Deborah to swap shifts tonight?"

"No, Deborah asked me. Why do you ask?"

Bertie tried to contain herself and not look shocked. "Oh, no reason." She exited the unit, ran to the back stairwell down to the basement, taking the Greene tunnel to the nursing dorm. She searched for Addie. Bertie found her in the library writing in her diary. "Addie, do you have a minute? We have to talk. Now!" Bertie closed the French doors behind her and leaned up against them.

Addie stopped writing. "What the hell has gotten into you? Are you alright?"

"I'm fine. But I think Deborah is up to no good."

Addie slowing raised her hand and pointed her pencil at Bertie. "I wouldn't say anything more, Bertie."

"Why?"

"She's standing outside the door right behind you."

Bertie paled, turned, and swung the doors wide open. "Well, I'm off to bed. Have a great night."

Deborah watched Bertie disappear around the corner before asking Addie, "What did she have to say?"

Addie shrugged her shoulders. "Not much. She just said that you all had a busy night and she wanted to let me know that she wasn't in the mood to play cards with me tonight," she lied. "Do you want to?"

"No. I'm exhausted, too. It's been a long day." Deborah hung her head and walked off.

Relieved Deborah chose to leave her alone, Addie opened her diary and read over her entry.

*Dear Blue,*

*Nursing school is so demanding, emotionally and physically. Lately, I've been finding myself getting more tired and weak at the end of the day. Sometimes I get up and am dizzy. I try to eat well. Actually, I find myself eating more, but feel less than optimal. It's probably the stressors and rigor of the profession. Sometimes I feel like I manifest all of the symptoms of my patients. If they have an itchy rash, I feel like I do, too. If they have a stomach ailment, I think that I do, too. I frequently feel my forehead to make sure I don't have a fever and stick out my tongue in the mirror, praying my tonsils aren't red and swollen.* Addie drew a smiley face in the margin of the paper with its tongue sticking out.

*I love caring for my little Emiline. She appears to be holding her own. Her headaches are still frequent, and the size of the brain tumor is increasing according to her x-rays. I noted on her chart that her birthday is on October thirty-first, a Celtic celebration called "All Hallows' Eve" or Hallowe'en. Lexie explained the Scottish custom of children guising in costumes through their neighborhoods for candy, fruit, and treats. Bertie, Lexie, Opal, and I think that it would be*

*most memorable for Emiline to have a birthday party for her to re-*
*member. Nurse Hartman and Randall are on board with the plan.*
*I have even asked Mr. and Mrs. Wu to make costumes befitting a*
*"fairy" theme. Emiline said that stories about fairies like "The En-*
*chanted Circle of Love," were her favorite. She adores fairies because*
*they sparkle, have iridescent wings, can fly about in pastel-colored*
*outfits, and have brown and pink glittering hair. Emiline will surely*
*be surprised; a special memory is the best gift we can give her. I'm not*
*sure how long she will remain on this earth, but I will do my very best*
*to make sure she is cared for and, more importantly, loved. I recently*
*read in one of my nursing textbooks about the importance of touch and*
*that while patients are at their sickest, touch and human interaction*
*are vital to their humanity and condition. Speaking of the human*
*condition, Randall told me today that he is getting worried about*
*Garrett's well-being. It seems that he is drinking a bit more when*
*he is at home and gallivanting off to play cards with the McDaniels*
*brothers every chance he can get. While Garrett's letters to me mention*
*some of these activities, my concern for him grows. Should I say some-*
*thing to him when I see him next time? Would that only betray Ran-*
*dall's trust in me? And, in turn, Garrett's trust in him? I don't know*
*what to do, Blue, except pray for him. That's what Maw always said*
*to do, 'Pray when you want to rejoice, pray when you are sad, pray*
*when you want to give thanks, and pray when times are bad.'* Addie
stopped and then resumed. *Blue, I'm worried about Garrett.* She
drew a frowning face next to his name.

## WEDNESDAY NIGHT, THIRD WARD

Worry and trepidation filled Garrett's inner being as the alarm went out to the local firehouses at nine thirty-two that evening after a fire pull box was activated in the Third Ward. The station and the location were telegraphed to Garrett's firehouse in the Fourth Ward, summoning them to provide additional support to put out the blaze at Burdeshaw's Chemical Manufacturing Plant. The telegraph read that residents in the surrounding area reported hearing explosions before seeing the building engulfed in a giant red and orange fireball.

Garrett fretted on the ride over to the scene. *Is this the day that I die? Will I survive to fight another battle with the red demon? Will my fellow brothers remain safe?* His hands started to shake. He felt his heart race, and then skip a beat or two as he grew restless. He couldn't wait to get out of the truck. Recently, feelings of dread and panic had consumed him. He found relief when he searched out and counted magnolia trees as they drove to a location. And, as soon as they were in the field, he was able to focus on his chief's commands and the job at hand.

Garrett stood by the firetruck watching the Atlanta city police dart to and fro, gathering evidence and picking up debris and partially scorched ledger books off the dirt road while his fellow firefighters battled the blaze with their fire hoses and axes. His chief shouted orders to his men as they ran in and out of the building. Between the cracking and breaking beams, mini-explosions, and collapsing walls, Garrett stopped, looked down, and focused on the puddle of water he was standing in. He saw a brown spider with a large abdomen swimming by his right foot.

Due to its size, he suspected she was a female. He stooped down and scooped it up with his gloved hand. He reminisced about his dad teaching him about the usefulness of spiders on the farm and how they helped to control other pesky insects like mosquitoes, wasps, and flies. He heard his father's voice in his head as he stepped away from the fire truck and walked across the street. 'Did you know these little critters have up to eight eyes, and eight legs, six joints on each, giving them a total of forty-eight knees. Can you believe that?' Garrett stopped in front of a small Camilla bush and tossed her out underneath it. He pulled out a flask from his coat pocket, uncapped it, and took a nip. He mumbled to himself, "We're all just trying to survive, aren't we?" He took one more swallow before tucking it away and rejoining his brothers to battle the flames.

# 9

Edward watched John chew on a strip of bacon. He waited for him to swallow it before asking, "Dr. Williams, would you debrief us on the National Birth Registry?"

"Absolutely." Dr. Williams had started to pick up his cinnamon roll, set it down, licked his fingertips, and shuffled through the stack of papers lying in his lap. He pulled out an article. "Here it is. This article was put out by the U.S. Labor Department." Using his finger, he scanned it and found what he was looking for. "It appears that they are seeing rural birth rates declining due to urbanization."

"Huh?" Clyde interrupted. "I don't understand. How are our own farmers being affected by urbanization? I thought social settlements were cropping up due to urbanization and immigration."

"They are." Lena pointed out. "But, because there are more jobs in the city with the potential to earn a higher or more stable income, and with the war in Europe, compounded by the closed cotton exchanges, farmers are abandoning their fields."

Dr. Williams interjected, "With that shift, pregnant mothers are coming into the city and choosing to have their babies in a hospital and not at home. As a result, the national government is instituting a national birth registry. According to their report, there are currently ten states and the District of Columbia who have voted to participate. Georgia has yet to adopt it into law at this time. With that said, Edward and I were talking about this last month and wondered if we, as a hospital, should begin collecting these statistics. What are the thoughts of the group?"

Clyde persisted, "So, with everyone moving into the city, who is going to grow our cotton and food?"

Alan laughed. "This isn't a theory of absolutes, an all or nothing idea where everyone is abandoning their farm, Clyde. It's merely an observation in a shift in societal thinking and behaviors." He posed his next question to Edward. "When do you think the state will vote on this?"

Edward shook his head. "I have no idea. I'm keeping my ear to the grindstone at the capital and will keep you posted. Dr. Williams and I are of the opinion that since we already track mortality rates for the National Death registry, that we should be proactive and set the standard for other healthcare institutions in Georgia to follow."

"To that end," Dr. Williams retrieved another piece of paper, "I would like to read a quote to you from Frederick Hoffman, a statistician, who generated a report for the Prudential Insurance Company of America. He writes, 'Accurate and comparable vital statistics are the first prerequisite in every local effort to arouse public interest in the control and reduction of preventable and postponable diseases.' He goes on to say, 'In the furtherance of the nation-wide movement for the deliberate betterment of health conditions and the more effective public service of health-promoting agencies, there is the widest possible dissemination of trustworthy information regarding methods and means by which the prolongation of life may be more effectively a matter of individual and public control.'"

Shelby recognized the author's work. "Didn't I read about Hoffman in the paper earlier this year? Didn't he put out a report for the U.S. Bureau of Labor and Statistics in March that tracked the number of deaths and injuries as a result of industrial accidents?" Shelby reflected on the article. "I believe he said that out of the thirty-eight million in the total labor force that 25,000 died and 700,000 suffered serious injuries because of industrial accidents. In response, the American Association for Labor Legislation drafted a bill for government-provided healthcare and workers compensation."

"Right you are, Shelby." Edward recalled reading that same article. "The AALL is garnering support for a draft bill called the Health Insurance Act from a few states and the American Medical Association in an effort to improve healthcare standards, decrease the volume of workers' absenteeism, and increase job productivity. I believe they summed it up by saying that a company that cared about and took care of its employees would generate greater profits in the end."

Lena raised her hand. "I've got an idea. I propose that my nursing students incorporate this as a part of their concierge coverage duties. They are already working with the Sacred Heart patient log book at the desk. Let me know what categories we want to track, like births and work-related injuries, and I will ask them to begin tallying up the numbers and have Dr. William's start reporting them next month. Then those figures will become an official part of our meeting minutes."

Dr. Williams was pleased with that proposal. "And to build off the suggestion of Hoffman, from the data we compile, we can track and trend the volumes. Moving forward, it will provide me with very useful information to submit for future publications and reports."

"Not to mention, it will be helpful in our legislative causes, discussions, and endeavors at the state capital," added Alan.

Edward started to speak. "Wha...." But he was interrupted by Clyde.

"What a brilliant solution, Nurse Hartman."

Alan whispered to Lena, "How does Clyde go from being an ignorant jack ass to an omnipotent leader in two seconds?"

She picked up her coffee cup with both hands while waving her left pinky finger in the air.

Alan whispered back, "Yes, he is a little prick!"

Lena thought it wise to redirect the conversation elsewhere, lest she burst out in hysterical laughter. "Edward, I must thank you so much for covering the costs of Nurse Scott's funeral in Valdosta. Her family was so appreciative of your generous gesture."

"It was the least we could do in the unfortunate set of circumstances."

"It was such a tragic accident," Shelby added.

"It was, Shelby. We have endured our fair share," Edward said, referring to the tragedy in the operating room, the lice epidemic last year, and tunnel collapsing on Mr. Greene two years ago. "I want you to know that I will be working with Alan and

Nurse Hartman to set up a nursing scholarship in honor of Nurse Scott. It will go into effect next year. That will allow the guild plenty of time to do some fund-raising."

Heads around the table nodded. Lena, along with a few others, wiped away a stray tear and sniffled.

Dr. Williams said under his breath, "Since we're on a somber subject, let's table my discussion about the quality of nursing care with Lena. May I propose a private meeting in Nurse Hartman's office later today?"

Edward agreed with John. There was no sense in beating down his team any further. The sands of time, he thought, were his best friend. Let them pass through the hourglass one crystal at a time until emotions and feelings were tempered by the collective weight of the individual grains.

### MONDAY AFTERNOON, SIXTH WARD

Lena sat behind her executive desk in her office. She flipped the page of the morning edition of the *Atlanta Dispatch* while she gazed out of her office window at Mrs. White across the street. Lena chuckled to herself as she watched the elderly woman chase stray leaves after the wind swirled through the debris piles. Widow White ran around the front yard swatting after them, her rake held high in the air. Mesmerized by the kaleidoscope of colors falling from the trees, Lena sprang forward in time to spring, where she envisioned the house bursting forth with life. She imagined brightly colored red and pink begonias and white, pink, and red azaleas filling the flower beds and the grounds bustling with all kinds of activity—nursing students chatting away while in rocking chairs on the front porch, sitting on blankets and studying in clusters on the green front lawn, or walking down the front porch steps clad in their white uniforms, nursing caps, and blue capes as they headed to their respective classes or shifts. She was growing excited about their new venture and the nursing program's expansion plans. Lena turned her attention back to Atlanta's latest news, erupting in more spontaneous bouts of laughter as she read the "Hey, Hetta!" column.

## "HEY, HETTA!"

*Uncovering pearls and gems from Atlanta's social scene*

Mrs. Betty Burch was pregnant until she couldn't be pregnant anymore. She gave birth to a baby girl, named Sarah Ann. The proud parents, Mr. and Mrs. Robert Burch, will be hosting a celebration of the birth at their home on Sunday afternoon. Friends welcome.

Rumor has it that a local minister's wife cried herself to death because her house was built on an alley and not a formal street. Family members said that she died of a broken heart.

Mrs. Barbara Beach got her blue satin evening gown caught in the door of their Studebaker on Saturday night at the Canfield dinner party. Their driver pulled away and she was drug down the street for a ways before he realized her dilemma. Mr. Roscoe Beach was overheard saying that had she wore the red evening gown that he had bought for her earlier that day from Rich and Brothers, that this wouldn't have happened. She walked away with a few scratches, bumps and bruises. It was later reported that Mr. Beach suffered similar injuries that night due to 'an unfortunate incident at home.'

Mr. and Mrs. Henry Maxwell are happy to report that their eldest daughter, Sadie, is engaged to Mr. William Bryant from Cordele, Georgia. While her mother hoped for a church wedding, they will be married next Wednesday at the courthouse. A reception will follow for family members at the Maxwell home.

### *City of Atlanta Social Activities*

#### TUESDAY MORNING

The Poetry and Book Club Society will meet at the Georgian Terrace on Tuesday morning. They will be discussing the novella The Metamorphosis by Franz Kafka. It's a story about a man who wakes up one morning and finds that he has turned into a bug and the struggles he endures due to his transformation. The Scarecrow of Oz by L. Frank Baum will be discussed next month.

WEDNESDAY MORNING

The Bible Scholars will meet at Atlanta First United
Methodist Church on Wednesday morning.

WEDNESDAY AFTERNOON

The Sacred Heart Hospital Guild will meet at the home
of Mrs. Edward Alexander II on Wednesday afternoon.
All members are required to attend.

A Fourth Ward community picnic will be held at Grant
Park on Wednesday afternoon. Neighborhood residents
welcome.

THURSDAY EVENING

The "Peach of a Story" Tellers will meet at the home of
Mr. Gerald Goodrich on Thursday evening. A contest
will be held for the best story. All members are urged to
attend. Last month's winning story was told by Mr. Jerry
Brown, titled, "There are things born in kids that you
can't beat out of them."

FRIDAY MORNING

The Sewing Club will meet at the home of Mamie Out-
lander on Friday morning. New members are encouraged

to attend. Please note that sewing skills are not a requirement to belong to this group.

*Knock. Knock.* Two shadows moved behind the frosted glass
of Lena's office door.

"Come in," Lena called out. She folded the paper up as Edward and Dr. Williams walked into her office.

Dr. Williams made his way over to the small oval conference
table and pulled out a chair for her. "We were afraid to come
in. It sounded like you were courting a suiter in here with all of
your giddy laughter." He and Edward remained standing until
she took her seat.

"Hearing you laugh like that suits you, Lena." Edward tossed
her a wink.

"You caught me doing some heavy reading. I was catching up
on the latest town gossip in the new 'Hey, Hetta!' column. I don't
know who this gal is, but she sure has got a lot of moxie to write
that stuff."

Laughing, Edward remarked, "I've read a few of her columns
and I'm willing to bet she's a real ball buster."

Dr. Williams winced. "I'm not up to feeding my mind with
that kind of rubbish." He glanced at his pocket watch. "Look,
Lena, in light of my tight schedule, I'd like to get straight to the
point. I'm growing concerned about the quality of nursing care."
She twisted her face as he pulled out a piece of paper from his
lab coat pocket and unfolded it. "It appears that the numbers of
deaths are still high, especially on the medical-surgical unit." He
pushed the paper towards her.

Picking it up, Lena reviewed his handwriting and figures. She handed it back to him. "I would agree with you up to a point, but we must take into account that our patient acuity is much higher than when we first opened our doors. With the pellagra epidemic, TB, complications from childbirth, childhood diseases, and work-related accidents, we're up to our eyeballs in germs, infections, and illnesses. After all, isn't that why we're here? For sick people?" Her tone was sarcastic.

"Yes, but I'm seeing an upward trend specifically with the med-surg patients." Dr. Williams' nostrils flared as he refolded the paper and shoved it back into his pocket.

Lena bristled. "Now hold on a minute, are you insinuating that our nursing care isn't up to *your* standards? Let's recap, shall we? The standards were developed by you and me."

Edward intervened hoping to quell the rising tempers. "I don't think that's what he means. I think what he is proposing is that why don't we begin tracking and trending the patient outcomes on that unit. Take a look at the historical data for the mortalities, caregivers, diagnoses, medications, and see if there is anything that looks like we have a broken process. As you know, healthcare isn't cookie-cutter medicine. It is the holistic management of a patient's disease processes. Not all medicines and treatments work exactly the same from one patient to another. Sometimes there isn't a quick fix to what ails someone. Sometimes, an individual may have an adverse reaction to their treatment. Why? Only God knows why that happens." He let his words sink in before adding, "Are you both okay with that plan and taking those next steps?"

John and Lena nodded their heads, answering in their own time. "Yes."

"Lena, I'll give you a month to do a retrospective evaluation of the patients' charts. Trudy and I are taking the train up to the Greenbrier for some rest and relaxation in two weeks. I made a promise to her to carve out time for just her and me. We return on the second Monday of November. We can reconvene after that to review your findings before my next board meeting, which is scheduled for the day after Thanksgiving."

John tempered his words. "I know you are organizing and finalizing the hospital's outing to the Whittier Cotton Mills social settlement next month in addition to your other duties. Will a month give you enough time? Unfortunately, my schedule is extremely tight; otherwise, I'd offer a helping hand."

Pissed and hating feeling like she was under fire and being hung out to dry, she responded with a simple, "Yes," choosing not to add anything more to the discussion. It was bad enough that they had lost a nurse to electrocution in the surgical suite last year, compounded with the devastating accident of Nurse Scott this summer; the notion that she wasn't doing her job well enough training her nursing staff rocked her to the core. Her head reeled. There were checks and balances at Sacred Heart, policies to ensure safe practices, and quality controls in place. There had to be an outlier, she thought. Someone or something was acting not according to normal operating procedures. But who or what was it? She only had until November to figure it out. Otherwise, she feared the board may take their revenge out on her, use her as a scapegoat, and fire her. Lena swore to get to the bottom of it.

MONDAY EVENING, CUNARD PIER 54, MANHATTAN, NEW YORK

*Brrrrrrrrrm.* The long horn blast from the *Isabella* signaled her departure from Manhattan, one of the five boroughs in New York City. With all passengers and crew aboard—*Brrrm. Brrrm. Brrrm*—the three short horn blasts indicated that the captain was backing the passenger ship out of the slip. Hoyt watched the white steam from the smokestacks disappear and meld into the shifting ceiling of white fog that cloaked the city from view. Not even the Woolworth building, the city's tallest skyscraper, was visible on this chilly night. Hoyt couldn't shake the ominous feeling in the pit of his stomach. Maybe the fog was nature's way of closing the curtain on the final act of his time in the Americas, or was it the fact that the *Lusitania* had also departed from the same pier four months earlier before being torpedoed by a submarine from his home country? Regardless, he was hoping that a 1910 Italian bottle of Bottega Millesimato Spumante Brut would settle his nerves. Relieved by the quick financial settlement from the insurance company for the devastating fire that destroyed his chemical company last month, he took a final mental inventory while standing outside on the balcony of his starboard suite and was reassured that all of his loose ends were shored up in this country. Would he ever be really free from his time spent here? Would he find enlightenment from the assignment, memories, and experiences that shaped him on this mission? What new intriguing adventures lay on the horizon for him? Hoyt's thoughts continued to whirl as the ship's engines churned up the briny scent of the Hudson River and a faint mist fell on his face. Dressed in his white tie formal wear, he glanced back over his shoulder to make sure he had propped his balcony door open so he could keep an ear out for his cabin butler. As the ship made its way down the waterway, Hoyt could see halos of red, yellow, white, and blue lights along the shoreline where the haze was beginning to dissipate.

*Knock. Knock.* Hoyt's suite door opened. *Rafael,* according to the brass nametag on his white mandarin collar coat, rolled in a serving cart covered with a white linen tablecloth. Atop sat a white porcelain vase filled with short-cut yellow roses and a sterling silver champagne bucket. Hoyt took a quick liking to his butler, a well-groomed lad whom he estimated was in his early twenties. Rafael's sharp brown eyes, dimpled chin, and olive skin checked all of the boxes on his ideal wish list for a travel companion. Hoyt watched Rafael pull the bottle of chilled bubbly beverage from the ice bath and skillfully uncork it. With graceful elegance, Rafael poured and handed the refreshment to Hoyt. Rafael smiled, revealing perfectly straight white teeth. How unusual. Hoyt pondered over it for a half of a second. *Having good teeth typically means you come from money. Well, he's a far cry from the gapped-tooth lover I enjoyed on the voyage.* Hoyt fell immediately in lust.

"I'm so sorry, sir. It's not a great night to view the city. But perhaps you'll be able to catch a glimpse of my lady."

Curious, Hoyt questioned. "Your lady? What lady are you referring to?"

Rafael walked through the open door onto the balcony and pointed into the darkness. "Come here. I can see her from here now." He turned to see Hoyt still standing in the low-lit suite. He held out his hand. "Come."

Curiosity took over and Hoyt joined him. With his full glass in one hand, he placed his right hand on the high-gloss, heavily lacquered teak railing and leaned over it. "I'm not sure I see what you are talking about."

Rafael quickly bent over, picked up both of Hoyt's feet, and flipped him over the side of the ship. Hoyt face held a look of horror as he plummeted twelve stories to the ocean. His screams were inaudible, the horns of the ship drowning out any possibility of him being heard by another employee or guest. Peaks of hissing, foamy white waves reached up and swallowed him. He never resurfaced.

Rafael moved swiftly, removing Hoyt's personal belongings from his cabin. An awaiting porter who stood guard outside helped Rafael load the trunks onto his cart, and the two disappeared behind an interior door marked in red bold letters, *Staff Only*. Fifteen minutes later, the porter and Rafael were accompanied by another man, who was much shorter and older than the two and had a pencil-thin brown mustache; all fled to the lower level of the ship, where he opened a starboard side door. A small boat emerged and pulled up alongside the *Isabella*, making sure to match her speed.

Rafael called out to the man as he and the porter jumped into the back of the boat. "Remember to erase his name from the passenger manifest."

The man at the door signaled Rafael with a thumbs-up gesture as he watched the watercraft veer off and vanish behind a gray curtain of mist before he closed and locked it. The players were finished, their final act complete.

As the *Isabella* made her way to the Atlantic, the fog had

lifted around Rafael's "lady," a copper statue gifted to the United States by the citizens of France called "Liberty Enlightening the World," also referred to as the Statue of Liberty. Her right hand lifted a beckoning torchlight, illuminating the way to freedom, opportunity, and hope.

# 10

Addie, Bertie, and Opal were the last of the Sacred Heart medical
staff to step off the streetcar and join Nurse Hartman, Dr. Springer, Deborah, and Mary Margaret. The remaining students in Addie's class, Susan Kessler, Alice Fein, Isabelle "Belle" Esposito,
and Alexis "Lexie" Carmichael, remained behind at the hospital,
and were scheduled to cover the mill medical clinic next month.

All huddled around Mr. Hayes, a spry man who stood five-
feet-three inches tall with a brown Fedora wrapped with a ce-
dar-colored band perched atop his head. Salt and pepper colored
hair, a mustache, and a closely cropped beard indicated that he
was in his mid-forties. Voice high-pitched and talking quickly,
he began his introduction. "Welcome to Whittier Cotton Mill
and Village. We are happy to have you assist our physician today.
You will be seeing and treating all ages and sexes and we have
everything set up at the medical clinic." He turned his back to
begin walking; the group followed. He stopped abruptly and the
tightly packed group nearly ran up on each other. Mr. Hayes took

a few steps back. "Sorry, I'm new and I'm still getting adjusted to this new role as Whittier Cotton Mill's host. Where was I?" He pulled out a few white notecards from his coat pocket, shuffled through them, and read directly from one. "The cotton mill was established in 1896 and shortly thereafter residential homes were built for the mill workers to lease for about a dollar a week. The overarching idea behind the establishment of settlement houses in mill villages was to help improve the laborer's quality and standard of living. There are a few other places like this all over Georgia, like the Methodist settlement house at the Fulton Bag and Cotton Mill in the Fourth Ward. Georgia and the Carolinas are becoming the new hot spots for mill towns." He slid the card behind the others.

Bertie waited for him to take a breath. "Why is that?"

"Good question, miss. We have better weather down here, tax breaks, and we employ men, women, and children. Mills in the north rely on male immigrant workers who demand higher wages, eat more meat, require more clothing, and need heat for their houses. Operating expenses are so much higher there. Well-insulated factories are imperative since the freezing cold winters can mess with the machines." Mr. Hayes shuffled one card over the other. "Moving on, follow me and stay close behind. I'm just going to talk while we walk over to the clinic. The settlement house for our workers is that large three-story building over there." He raised his hand, pointing to the southeast corner of Parrott and Whittier Avenue. "Like other settlement houses in Georgia and throughout the country, we provide the employees and their families with clubs, schooling for the kids, daycare, and organized athletics—for example, we have a baseball team. We even sponsor fairs and bazaars so our textile workers can sell their hand-made wares and earn some extra spending money. Medical and legal services are also free."

Addie mulled over what Mr. Hayes said before asking, "If the textile workers work such long hours, how can they take advantage of your amenities?"

Mr. Hayes stopped and flipped his cards over and over, growing frustrated. He hadn't anticipated that question. He blurted out, "They have to find the time or find someone to cover their shift."

Mary Margaret jumped in. "But, then wouldn't they lose out on their wages, and if the whole family is workin' how does that work for 'em exactly?"

Mr. Hayes continued to shuffle his notes. Nurse Hartman and Dr. Springer sensed Mr. Hayes's growing exasperation.

Lena pointed to a gazebo off in the distance. "What is that used for, Mr. Hayes?"

"The gazebo is used as a bandstand and is home to our brass band. They are remarkably very good and play some real toe-tapping tunes."

"I bet." Deborah groaned.

"The Whitter Mills are served by the electric shorts, which you took up here today. The Southern Railroad also runs through this valley, along with the Chattahoochee River over there." He waved his notecards and pointed toward the west. Suddenly, a gust of wind blew the notes out of his hand, scattering them all over the road. Everyone dispersed, trying to stomp on and pick up the loose paper. Gathering them one by one, Mr. Hayes brushed off the dirt and dust and stuck them back in his coat pocket while mumbling self-deprecating comments to himself.

Unable to find time on the ride over to the mill, Addie seized the moment to ask Randall about Garrett. "How's Garrett doing these days?"

Randall knew Garrett was struggling with his newly acquired addictions. His late-night comings and goings and the stench of alcohol on his breath in the early morning hours betrayed Garrett's secrets. However, this wasn't the place to have a full-blown discussion about the poor gent's vices. Knowing that he, too, had his own tightly-guarded secrets, an affinity for booze and bordellos, he snapped, "He's fine."

Unwilling to take the bait, she probed, "Really?"

"Not now, Addie," he hissed.

His reaction caught her off guard. *I've not seen this darker side of him before.* Addie backed away and blended into the group, rejoining Opal in the rear.

Lena chose to lend Mr. Hayes a hand with the guided tour, asking, "Does anyone know where settlement houses originated?" They resumed ambulating through the streets. "Do you remember our class lecture about Jane Addams and the Hull House in Chicago?"

"Wasn't it in London?" Bertie shouted out from the middle of the pack. She glanced back at Addie and Opal, giving them a broad-faced grin.

"Good job, Nurse Jones. At least someone was paying attention to my lecture."

Deborah slipped in next to Bertie and mocked in her ear, "Good job, Nurse Jones." She firmly grabbed Bertie by the upper arm and squeezed. "You haven't told anyone about what happened to your patient, have you?"

Feelings of guilt arose along with a shooting pain in her left arm. Bertie elbowed Deborah. "Get away from me." She jogged up to the front, looking back to make sure Deborah didn't follow her.

Addie, observing the interaction between Deborah and Bertie, stumbled.

Opal caught Addie's arm before she fell completely to the ground. "Are you alright, Addie?"

"Yes, I'm fine." Embarrassed, she brushed herself off. "Oh my stars! I'm such a klutz these days."

The party disappeared around the corner of a white-washed building. Addie and Opal ran to rejoin them.

Addie took notice of the mill houses. They were built in a semi-circle and faced the mill. Off in the distance, a large brick home was perched on a hill. "What a way to live. Nothing and no one would go unnoticed here, huh?" she remarked to Opal.

Mr. Hayes regained his composure and took the reins of the guided tour back. "The tall brick mill tower over there has offices and a water tank to help put out any fires." Mr. Hayes turned around and redirected everyone's attention. "That building over there across the street from the company store is what we call the 'Ark,' and it contains the barber shop, pharmacy, a shoe shop, and the men's showers."

Dr. Springer watched a group of ten children walk by carrying bundles of beige yarn and grey wool. He figured they ranged in ages from thirteen to as young as seven or eight years old.

Mr. Hayes saw the expression on Randall's face and anticipated his question, answering, "Georgia, like many other Southern states, doesn't have any laws to compel small kids to go to school. The mill can employ kids as young as seven years old to work here."

"I grew up in New York and worked in Philadelphia. So, I'm still trying to adjust to seeing such young workers. In my humble opinion, kids need a proper education so they can grow up and break the chains of poverty. At least an education or training in a skilled trade can give them that chance," said Dr. Springer.

Overhearing, his remarks, Opal murmured to Addie, "Did you hear his thoughts about children? By the way, what does Garrett think about having kids?"

Addie nudged Opal back. "Oh my stars! Would you stop?" The two continued to chide each other.

Nurse Hartman observed them out of the corner of her eye, walked over and stood behind them. "Ladies, if you please. Let's try and contain ourselves, shall we?"

"Yes, ma'am," Addie and Opal replied in unison.

"By the way, would you both mind helping me with a special project? It will require us to work late into the night to review patient charts."

Intrigued and curious, both agreed.

"Great. Please sit by me in the streetcar on the way home and I'll provide you with the details." Lena knew the sands of time were slowly running out for her to review the deceased patients' charts from the med-surg unit. She had even reached out to Alan, who helped devise a spreadsheet for her. She knew that either Addie or Opal could be possible replacements for Nurse Scott after graduation. However, it wasn't uncommon for nurses to run off and get married right after they finished school. While Opal and Shelby might be making future plans together, even the most loving relationships evolve and change as people change. She knew from experience that you either grow together or you grow apart. Time would tell.

The Sacred Heart medical team was ushered into a white shiplap building. Inside, there were folding screens, denoting three separate areas in the long rectangular room. "The women will be seen over here." Mr. Hayes pointed toward the far right. "The kids will be seen here in the middle and the men over there." He pointed to the left. "If you need the restrooms, they are in the outbuilding behind us. And, as I mentioned to you before, prescriptions can be filled in the pharmacy, which is in the ark." Mr. Hayes started to exit the building and saw a small group of men and women walking toward him. Some were holding the hands of their children. He called back inside to Nurse Hartman. "I see people making their way over here now."

"Nurse Hartman, if it's alright with you, I'll take Addie." Randall was already motioning for Addie to come and join him. "We'll take care of the peds patients."

"Have fun!" Opal teased.

Feeling reprimanded by Randall's earlier response, Addie's stomach fluttered, and she could feel her cheeks blush. She dropped her eyes. *Dear Lord, please get me through this day. Help me to focus on my work at hand and not on Garrett's troubled soul or Dr. Springer's gentle healing hands. Amen.* Once at Randall's side, she whispered to him, "My sincerest apologies for my probing question about Garrett earlier."

Randall nodded and smiled as the two of them stepped behind the white cotton cloth partition.

Lena corralled Opal and Bertie. "Why don't you two help me with the female patients? Mary Margaret, you can help the mill physician with the male patients. Deborah, let's have you sit by the front door and triage the patients, assigning them to their proper place upon arrival." Lena introduced her team to the mill doctor, organized her space, and readied them for the onslaught of men, women, and children. She tried to see the good in the former rural and mountain-dweller's choice to leave the familiar behind. Was this a virtuous pursuit of a better life? Did their long, arduous hours here bring valuable meaning to their lives? She reflected on her recent readings of *Democracy and Social Ethics*, published in 1902 by Jane Addams. "The Hebrew prophet made three requirements from those who would join the great forward-moving procession led by Jehovah. "To love mercy" and at the same time "to do justly" is the difficult task; to fulfil the first requirement alone is to fall into the error of indiscriminate giving with all its disastrous results; to fulfil the second solely is to obtain the stern policy of withholding, and it results in such a dreary lack of sympathy and understanding that the establishment of justice is impossible. It may be that the combination of the two can never be attained save as we fulfil still the third requirement—"to walk humbly with God," which may mean to walk for many dreary miles beside the lowliest of His creatures, not even in that peace of mind which the company of the humble is popularly supposed to afford, but rather with the pangs and throes to which the poor human understanding is subjected whenever it attempts to comprehend the meaning of life."

As the mill workers entered one by one, Lena noticed that some had a jovial spirit with a gleam in their eyes while others had vacant expressions, their eyes void of life. She could tell those were the ones still wrestling with their new meaning of life. Lena remembered that Addams went on to write, "Yet in moments of industrial stress and strain the community is confronted by a moral perplexity which may arise from the mere fact that the good of yesterday as opposed to the good of today, and that which may appear as a choice between virtue and vice is really but a choice between virtue and virtue. In the disorder and confusion sometimes incident to growth and progress, the community may be unable to see anything but the unlovely struggle itself." Lena knew that in addition to classroom and textbook teachings and exposing the nursing students to the varied healthcare needs of the community that life itself was also a respected teacher. On this day, her medical team observed the realities of life and the 'unlovely struggle,' first hand.

### SATURDAY EVENING, SIXTH WARD

Garrett dealt the next hand, placing the last playing card in front of Mr. Wu. Wei picked it up and immediately folded, laying his cards on the table. "I'm out. Must go pee. Be right back."

"Wei must go wee!" Brice taunted.

Garrett, Rob, Tim, and Jim joined in the teasing. "Wei going wee wee."

Wei stumbled out of the hidden room in the Sacred Heart garage, clomped through the straw in the stall, and emerged outside, where he leaned against the corner of the building to relieve himself. Gazing up at the star-filled sky, he heard moaning noises coming from one of the ambulances parked out front. Buttoning up his trousers, he crept closer to the vehicle and hid behind stacked crates. Peering out, he caught a glimpse of Clyde and Deborah entangled, ravaging each other in the most primal way. He could see their breath in the cold night air, rapid and panting like two of the four Chinese fiends – the devious winged-tiger that barks like a dog, Qiong Qi, and the flesh-eating, gluttonous beast, Tao Tie. Should he make himself known, run back inside and tell the others, or simply let them be? Not wanting to make any trouble for his wife and him, nor the others, and since Clyde was their boss with a powerful father, he chose the latter.

A few hours later, Garrett was giddy with excitement, having won the evening's pot. Inebriated, he walked through the backyard of Alexander Hall over to the Sacred Heart Nursing dorm. From behind a large maple tree, he searched the shapes and shadows in the upstairs and downstairs windows, unable to find Addie's familiar frame.

"Psst. Psst." Brice had followed Garrett. "Get ya arse over 'ere. It's time for me to take ya back to the firehouse."

"I'm going to marry her one day." Garrett stuck his hands in his pockets and sauntered over to join Brice. A goofy grin emerged.

Brice threw his large arm over Garrett's shoulders. "Who are you gonna marry, lad?"

"Addie. I'm going to marry Addie one day." He stopped and drilled his finger into Brice's coat. "Mark my words."

"The lass will only marry ya if you straighten up and fly right. She won't want to marry a broke tosser. Ya gonna 'ave to find it in ya to grow up one day and be the man she needs ya to be for 'er."

Garrett's head bobbed.

"Ya young, lad. I know ya sowin' ya seeds wildly about and that's perfectly within ya right to do so. But, one day, ya gonna 'ave to put an end to it. Men, who lack self-direction and motivation will always fail and find 'emselves wallerin' in the ditches of life. I won't let you become that kind 'o man."

"Promise?" Garrett squinted, his eyes swollen and blood-shot.

"Promise."

# 11

"Oh my stars! Mrs. Wu, these fairy wings are gorgeous! Emiline is going to absolutely love her costume. You made it look just like Princess Dasha's wedding gown in her favorite story."

Joshua set two large boxes down on the conference table. "This is such a wonderful idea, Addie."

"Thank you. I wanted to make Emiline's final days here special." It was difficult to suppress the stream of tears falling down Addie's cheeks as she sorted through the various pastel-colored silk, iridescent, and glittering wings in one box, and then found a wide array of ribbon-wrapped wands in the other. "Why are there so many wings and wands?"

"When Mr. Alexander heard about the fairy garden birthday party for Emiline, he made it mandatory for the entire leadership team and available medical staff to attend. He even asked able-bodied patients to come, too." Joshua pulled out a hanky and handed it to Addie.

"Oh, my heavens! He did that for her? Did he happen to make today the absolute perfect day to be outdoors this evening, too?" Addie dabbed at her eyes and then pointed toward one of the large, arched windows.

"He's a very good man and I believe God heard all of our prayers to have the warm weather for us this evening." Joshua peered inside the box, pulling out two pairs of blue wings. "One for me and one for the Missus." Joshua put one arm through a shoulder strap and then the other. He shook his shoulders back and forth; the wings fluttered. "How do I look?"

Addie jumped up to take a closer look. "You look amazing. Wait until Ms. Maybelle sees you."

Joshua retrieved two wands, flapped his arms, and spun around. "She's down in the kitchen baking up a few goodies for the party. Wait until you see what she's created."

"Addie, Mr. Alexander, Mr. Wu, Joshua, and I have more surprises in store for Miss Emiline."

"More? How could you have any more?"

Ying handed Addie a smaller box. "Open it!"

Addie carefully opened it. "Oh, my goodness!" She pulled out a sparkling pink wig made from curly, long strands of human hair and a delicate white and iridescent floral crystal tiara. She dashed over to embrace Joshua and Ying.

"Don your fairy wings, grab a wand, and get Miss Emiline dressed. We'll take care of the rest." Mrs. Wu stacked the costume boxes in Addie's awaiting arms.

Darting towards the door, Addie turned back, "I'll meet y'all in the garden in twenty minutes."

True to her word, Addie, with the assistance of Dr. Springer, had Emiline dressed in a glittering white dress, complete with pink wig and tiara, and placed her in a white wooden wheelchair with tiny pastel flowers all over it, hand-painted by Brice and his brothers. The McDaniel brothers even added ribbons and gold-gilded finials on top so it looked like a throne fit for a fairy princess. Addie lifted a hand-held mirror so Emiline could see her reflection. Emiline's green eyes widened and tears rolled down her cheeks. Growing frailer with every passing day and having lost the ability to speak a few weeks earlier, Emiline waved her hands, motioning for Addie to come and give her a hug and a kiss on the cheek.

Once the three of them composed themselves, they proceeded to the back doors that led to the garden. They swung open. Winged-employees, doctors, patients, nurses, and nursing students lined the right ramp, all blowing bubbles into the air, sprinkling glitter, or waving their wands as Emiline rode by them. The sweet sounds of a string quartet accompanied by a harpist playing "Arabesque No. 1" by Claude Debussy filled the floral garden. Torches lined the stone paths and even the fountain water had been dyed pink for the occasion. Tiny white lights on strings were strung in nearby trees and shrubs. A man wearing a black tux and top hat emerged from the side of the building. He escorted two white ponies with silver unicorn horns and ribbons flowing from their manes and tails. The pair pulled a white flower cart that had jingling bells attached to the sides. Emiline grew wide-eyed, clapped, and pointed.

"Do you want to go for a ride?" Randall stopped the wheelchair in front of the horses so Emiline could reach out and pet them. He picked her up, gently placed her on the pink-pillow inside the cart, and followed behind as the team pulled Emiline up and down the dirt road in the back of the property.

Food and drinks were housed under a white tent that was decorated with baby's breath, green ivy, fresh-cut white and pink roses, and white, gold, silver, pink, and green ribbons. Ms. Maybelle ladled out cups of sparkling cranberry punch from a large sterling silver bowl, borrowed from Mrs. Edwards, while Joshua offered finger sandwiches and pink and white petit fours to the guests.

Once back in her wheelchair, Emiline glowed and smiled, tapping patients, nurses and doctors on their shoulders with her wand as they walked by, all vowing to become loyal subjects to the birthday fairy princess. Even Alan, after much coaxing from Lena, coupled with a few shots of moonshine, put on fairy wings and joined in the fun.

Addie retreated to the top landing of the outdoor staircase to catch an overall glimpse of the party and soak in the magic. She thanked the divine for intervening tonight as the setting sun turned the sky pink and pale blue, as if to coordinate with the festivities. With a full heart of gratitude, she prayed, *Dear Lord, thank you for putting Emiline into my life. While I don't have a child of my own, I am humbled that you gave me the opportunity to love her while she was here with us. Dear Maw, I ask that you be there to greet Emiline when she becomes an angel. She doesn't have a family to call her own and I think we should adopt her into ours so that she isn't alone in heaven. I think she would love to play with Sissy and Ben. I love and miss you dearly, Maw. Amen.*

Edward emerged from the crowd, sporting large silver wings, while sparkling white grape juice was distributed to the guests. Lifting his glass into the air, he toasted, "Join me in wishing Miss Emiline the happiest of birthdays."

The guests erupted in cheers and well-wishes. The musicians struck up "Happy Birthday" and the staff sang along, waving sparklers in the air. Randall brought Emiline over to cut the four-tiered white cake with cascading pink and white icing roses and helped her blow out the six candles.

Following dessert, Emiline was positioned at the top of the stairs in front of the closed double doors. Edward sat in a large chair placed next to her. Patients leaned out of the windows on the TB ward while Deborah and other nurses held up the sick children in the pediatric ward windows so they could be a part of the party, too.

"That's our cue, brothers. You too, Wu," Brice said to Rob, Tim, Jim, and Wei as he inconspicuously topped off their punch-filled cups with booze from his flask. "We best get to our stations behind the garage." The five men, still wearing their wings, flittered away.

Addie joined Opal and Shelby on one of the garden benches. "Your dad is the best, Opal."

"He is, isn't he?" Opal put her arm around Addie.

Edward leaned over to Emiline and whispered in her ear. She clapped and nodded. "Emiline has commanded me to read her favorite story, "The Enchanted Circle of Love." He cleared his throat while he opened the book.

"This is the enchanted story of the fairy wedding of Princess Dasha to Prince Nasus, which takes place in a magical setting.

Princess Dasha is a snowflake fairy princess, who is so invisibly small. She lives in Traheirmanel, where the mountains are so tall.

She lives with her clan atop snow-capped mountains so high.

The Traheirmanel Mountains are hidden by the white clouds floating by.

Prince Nasus is a woodland dweller in Thimstrah, located at the edge of a deep lake of blue. It is found in the mist and is difficult to travel to.

The woodland fairies are just wee folk and are quite mythical. The snowflake fairies are just as tiny and are quite magical.

Fairies are people of peace and have big, beautiful wings. They love to fly and even travel on the backs of birds and other things.

The Thimstrah fairies have brown skin, green eyes, and shimmering hair. The Traheirmanel fairies have pink hair, purple eyes, and skin so pale and fair.

On the day of the wedding, the woodland fairies flew on the backs of dragonflies, flying high above Thimstrah between the sunbeam rays and the blue skies.

Prince Nasus and Princess Dasha were married under the crystal blue ice dome, by the oldest snowflake fairy. His name was Kerome.

After they exchanged vows, the clans joined together for the ceremonial dance, in the silver and pink ballroom that was decorated with such elegance.

The ballroom had flowers and a band of harps and strings. It sparkled under the lights of lanterns that hung from golden rings.

The fairies gathered round to form the enchanted circle of love, around the Prince and Princess as bells rang out from above.

The dance began with a simple bow to each other from the men, as the ladies curtsied to the fairies on the right and on the left of them.

They stood shoulder to shoulder, spreading their wings out like birds, and began to hum to the ceremonial song, one that has no words.

The fairies walked two steps forward and took two steps back, as the band played, the bells tolled, and the fairies raised their hands and clapped.

They clapped their hand above their heads, one, two, three, four, while fairies spun and twirled on the ballroom dance floor.

And, with a click of their heels, they shouted out, "Wee!" They patted the sides of their legs for a count of one, two, three.

They flicked their hands at the wrist and moved their arms up and down. Princess Dasha laughed with glee as she danced in her shimmering white wedding gown.

The fairies began to flap their wings and lifted off the ground. They took flight and sprinkled their fairy dust all around.

The fairy dust gently fell like snowflakes on the crowd. It glittered in colors of gold, silver, white, and pink as it gently floated down.

Princes Dasha and Prince Nasus danced the night away, with their family and friends on their magical wedding day.

The Enchanted Circle of Love dance symbolizes the real act of love, for love has no beginning and no end. It's a blessing from heaven above.

Love abounds throughout the world, from Thimstrah to Traheirmanel, lands where even the tiniest snowflake and woodland fairies like to live, love, and dwell.

The end."

Edward closed the book while Emiline, overjoyed, clapped

and clapped. He stood to address the crowd. "Thank y'all for being a part of this enchanted evening. I have one more surprise."

The instrumentalists started playing "The Dance of the Sugar Plum Fairy" by Tchaikovsky while the McDaniel siblings and Mr. Wu lit the fuses to the fireworks display. *Boom! Boom! Boom! Boom!* Colors of blue, yellow, red, and white exploded high above them. The fiery fragments floated down, eventually fading and disappearing into the night sky while patients and staff oohed and aahed. The pyrotechnics show concluded with a vibrant and explosive ending. Following the finale, Addie and Dr. Springer rejoined Emiline and took her back to the ward. Although exhausted from the affair, Emiline mustered up just enough willpower to refuse to remove her costume when Addie readied her for bed.

Randall intervened. "It's completely alright for our fairy princess to go to bed dressed just as she is." He tucked her under the covers while Addie checked on the status of the other pediatric patients and Deborah returned to the nursery.

Emiline motioned for Dr. Springer to hand her paper and crayons.

"What? You want to color a picture?"

She nodded.

He opened up the drawer of her bedside table, pulling out a box of crayons and a clipboard that had a couple sheets of blank Sacred Heart stationary secured under the metal clip. "Here you go. I'll let you draw for ten minutes, but after that, I need you to get some sleep."

Emiline tugged on his lab coat and pointed at Addie. She pointed at the blank paper and then pointed at Addie again ,who was now three beds away, rewrapping vinegar-soaked bandages around eight-year-old Craig Sewell's arms and legs, his hands bound to prevent him from scratching at his bad case of poison ivy.

"Yes, I will give Nurse Engel your picture when you are done with it." Randall joined rounding with Addie and Lexie on the remaining patients before making a final stop back at Emiline's bedside twenty minutes later. The pallor of her skin, pale blue lips, and fingertips immediately grabbed his attention. He knew without having to place his stethoscope on her chest that she was now a fairy princess flying high amongst the angels in heaven. Fighting back tears and praying not to draw any attention to himself, he picked up Emiline's clipboard and collected her crayons. She had drawn a picture, stick figures of what appeared to be Addie and Emiline in her wheelchair. They were holding hands while fireworks exploded above their heads in the sky. Written at the bottom, she had scribbled, *Thank you, Mommy. I love you. XO E.*

### SUNDAY EVENING, SIXTH WARD

Alan escaped the party through the back doors of the hospital and eagerly took off his fairy wings, setting them on the concierge desk. While he retreated to his office, he overheard someone singing, the tune hauntingly familiar. Curiosity took over. He turned right down the corridor after the treatment room and turned right again, landing in the hallway of the pediatric and newborn nursery wards. He pressed his ear to the door of the nursery, twisted the glass-handled knob, and peered in. He saw Deborah rocking a newborn infant in her arms and was relieved that her back was to the door. He watched her rock, back and forth, and sing. Then hairs on his arm rose and tingled as he remembered where he had heard that same lullaby twenty years earlier. He hastily closed the door and sought refuge in his office. Without turning on a single light, he retrieved the bottle of moonshine from the bottom desk drawer. Flashing before his eyes were the images of the bloody words on the twenty letters, one for every year, kept under lock and key at his home office: *YOU TOOK MY BABY!* Taking a seat behind his desk, his hands shook as he poured out one shot, downed it, and followed it with two more. He tapped his leg four times, unable to stop the surging memories from flooding back.

### SUNDAY AFTERNOON, FEBRUARY 10, 1895, EASTERN STATE PENITENTIARY, PHILADELPHIA, PENNSYLVANIA

"Hush a bye baby, on the tree top, when the wind blows, the cradle will rock, when the bough breaks, the cradle will fall, down tumbles baby, cradle and all."

"She sings that lullaby every morning at the same time, like clockwork, to her daughter. You could set your pocket watch by her. I don't know how she does it, since there aren't any clocks on the rock wall or timepieces in her cell," the Eastern State Penitentiary prison doctor remarked as he moved aside to let Alan peer inside at his younger sister, who stood cradling and rocking her infant daughter in the stark white room.

A narrow rectangular skylight in the arched ceiling above her was the only source of light. The morning sun cast yellow rays on his sister's face. Alan chuckled to himself as he gazed upon her angelic profile, the family resemblance plain as day. She was far from an angel or any version of her fragile, floral nickname: Lily. He knew she lacked a penitent heart and the devil dwelled in Lilith's soulless body.

Despite his parent's attempts to quell her unruly nature and mouth with harsh words, strict house rules, and countless slaps across the face, Lilith eventually ran away from their Atlanta home when she was nearly seventeen. The police were never able to track down her whereabouts. Her trail grew cold until one day, nearly six years later, Alan's father received a phone call from the police department in downtown Philadelphia.

The newspaper headlines dubbed her "the lascivious night monster," for preying upon unsuspecting men, drugging them with a tainted elixir, and robbing them of their possessions. However, after the disappearance of a prominent banker, the police uncovered clues that led to the discovery of his naked body in an abandoned house, stretched out in the middle of the living room floor. The crime scene was described as 'gruesome' and that 'only a monster' could have done this to the poor man. The police report read, *The thirty-three-year-old victim was found with a five-inch gash across his abdomen with his entrails stuffed in his mouth.* Based the black and white photos of his ghastly expression, it appeared that he had been alive during the torture, before he either choked to death or bled out. They weren't exactly sure which occurred first. With the slam of a judge's gavel, Lilith Waxman, age twenty-three, was sentenced to life at Eastern State Penitentiary for the murder of Harold Frances Blake, loving husband and father of five children.

The prison physician leaned against the sliding barn door. "She hid her pregnancy from us for the first three months. Lilith soiled her menstrual rags with rodent blood in an effort to conceal her secret."

Alan winced, patting the side of his right thigh four times. He hated frank discussions about such delicate matters. Self-conscious of his rituals, Alan pushed up his spectacles. "Explain to me how she got pregnant in here?"

"Do you want the truth?" The doctor shifted, hesitated, and shoved his hands in his white lab coat pockets.

"Don't bother. I don't think the truth is helpful to us now, do you?"

The doctor shook his head. Eager to switch the subject, he added, "Well, there is a bit of good news."

"Do tell." Alan walked over to the next cell. The sliding door, marked *Hydrotherapy* in black paint above the tiny window, was closed.

"She's stopped killing tiny critters and such exactly a month ago, when she gave birth."

Alan peered over his glasses. He began tapping his left thigh four times. Afraid the physician would notice, Alan crossed his arms, and unfolded and folded them four times before they came to rest across his chest. Worried about wrinkling his wool suit jacket, he uncrossed them and let his arms rest by his sides. "I didn't know."

The doctor tapped on the Hydrotherapy door. "This treatment works wonders. I prescribed hydrotherapy for her five times a week during her pregnancy. I'll think I'll continue treating her in this manner and add a little electroshock into her regimen."

Alan nodded his head, not knowing what words would be helpful to add. "May I visit her?"

The doctor waxed and waned, before responding, "Yes, I gave her a sedative before you arrived. Let's check in on her together."

The gentlemen crossed over the raised threshold into the cell. Lilith ignored them and hummed a sweet tune to her baby as she rocked the infant from side to side.

The doctor spoke, his tone calm. "Lilith, there is someone here to see you. It's your brother, Alan. He's come all the way from Atlanta after he heard he became an uncle. He wants to meet your daughter. Why don't you tell him her name?"

Lily continued to rock the tiny bundle, swathed in a hoary wool blanket. She muttered, "Deborah. Her name is Deborah."

A commotion erupted in the hallway. Two prison guards ran past Lilith's doorway, batons raised.

"Come back here, you naked bastard!" one of the guards yelled out.

"Catch me if you can!" the male voice dared.

"Excuse me, please." The doctor rushed out of the room and was immediately bowled over by the cackling inmate.

Oblivious to the chaos outside, Lily slowly turned toward Alan. Her eyes were darker than he remembered, lacking any spark or joy. She shoved the sleeping infant into Alan's arms. "Take her. Take her far from here. You know it's customary to keep babies and mothers together in prison. There's no life for her here. I don't want her to grow up like me."

146

*A murderer?* Alan refrained from saying it. For a split second, he thought he saw a flicker of empathy in her, but it vanished when she stepped out of the light.

"Go! Go, now!" Lily turned away from him as she pulled her black, hooded cape up around her shoulders and sat down on her cot.

Alan removed his jacket and draped it over his arm, concealing the baby, who continued to sleep, oblivious to the shouting in the corridor. He hastily walked out of Lily's cell as a guard closed and locked the door behind him. Passing the open door of the Hydrotherapy room, he saw corrections officers, medical staff, and the physician wrestling with the naked inmate inside. Another prison guard unlocked the white iron gate—bearing a circular red cross emblem—that secured the wing. Alan stepped into the center of the hub and where the escalating convicts' screams, yells, and hollering echoed under the stone dome spoke designed penitentiary. An awaiting jailer escorted him to a nearby exit. Once outside, beyond the thirty-foot-high and ten-foot wide rock fortress walls, Alan hailed a cab.

"Where to?" the driver inquired with a tip of his black cap.

"The train station." Alan lifted his jacket. He watched his niece stir, lift her fist to her pink lips, and suck on it. Trembling, he came to the realization he had never held a baby before.

Seventy-two hours later, Alan, grateful for the aid of a nursing mother on the train to help feed, clothe, and care for Deborah for a nominal fee and relieved to be back on the red clay soil of Georgia, clenched the pencil in his hand as he filled out the admission forms at the local orphanage, the Fulton County Children's Home. Hesitating, he rapped the pencil on the desk four times before he wrote *Deborah Owens*, giving her his mother's maiden name. His shiksa mother, she was called by his paternal grandmother. He remembered Bubbe clearing her throat and spitting on the floor every time his mother walked by her. Those were dark times, then.

Next to Deborah's name, Alan made two dots an inch apart and connected them with a line on the sheet of paper. He made two more dots and drew an intersecting line, forming a cross, whispering, "Father in Heaven, watch over Lily and Deborah." Alan gently touched each dot with the sharp point of the pencil, tapping his black leather shoe in sync on the floor four times, and saying, "In the name of the Father, and the Son, and the Holy Spirit. Amen."

# 12

Scout removed his tweed cap, dampened by the afternoon rain shower. Brushing his sandy blonde hair out of his face, he stood in front of the frosted glass window marked *Charlie Finch, Senior Reporter* in painted black letters. He tapped his knuckle on the large oak door. There was no response, but a rustling came from within. Pressing his ear to the door, he overheard hushed voices. He knocked again, knowing better than to barge in with urgent news and embarrass himself and those inside.

"Coming. Give me just a minute."

Scout recognized Charlie's exasperated response, having heard it on a few other occasions. "Sure thing, Charlie. It's me, Scout. I've got some news for ya."

"I'll be there in a second, kid."

A few minutes passed. *Click.* The door flung open and Hetta emerged wearing a fuchsia suit. "Hey, kid." She ruffled his hair and began making her way down the long hall.

Scout studied her outfit and called out, "Miss Hetta?"

"Yes?" She flipped her blonde curls and batted her eyelashes. "What is it?"

Scout didn't know how to put it into words. He turned around and motioned with his hands to pull something out.

Hetta reached behind her and felt her backside. "Oh, Jesus!" Pressing her back against the wall, she pulled her walking skirt out from her bloomers. Pressing down her skirt, she spun around. "Am I a-okay now?"

"Yes, ma'am."

Sam stepped out of his office, spotting Hetta in the corridor. "Miss Hetta, would you come with me. I need to discuss something of great importance with you."

Hetta tossed Scout a wink and followed Sam into his office while Scout entered Charlie's.

"Whatcha got for me today, kid?" Charlie was lighting up a cigar from behind his desk. He took a seat, kicking up his boots and resting them on his desk.

Scout remained standing; all the chairs were filled with stacks of newspapers. "I won't be staying long, sir. I just returned from a neighborhood in the ward."

"What the devil called you over there?"

"I got a tip that the Secret Service is held up in a rental house over on Sunset."

"Where'd the lead come from?"

"The landlord, himself. Seems that he overheard the agents talking about finding some charred ledger books after the inferno at Burdeshaw's Chemical Manufacturing Plant in the Third Ward back in August."

"Go on." Charlie puffed, blowing out an O-ring.

"Rumor has it that Burdeshaw was actually from Germany and involved in the nation-wide phenol conspiracy."

Charlie rocked back and forth in his chair. "Really?"

"Yup. And, there are a few high-level people in Georgia on his payroll."

Charlie removed his feet and sat up straight. "Who?"

"Dunno. He didn't have any names. The investigation is still underway as they flush out who these people are. He mentioned that they have to break a code that conceals the names in those books first."

Charlie reached inside his desk, pulled out a few coins, and tossed them across the desk at Scout. "Great work. Keep that assignment as priority number one and let me know immediately if you hear of any breaks in the case."

"Will do, boss." Scooping up the money, he left.

**FRIDAY EVENING, SIXTH WARD**

Two men burst through the emergency room doors at Sacred Heart Hospital. One, wearing a brown corduroy overcoat, hollered out, "OH, GOD! I NEED SOME HELP! HELP ME! GIVE HIM SOMETHING FOR THE PAIN!" He struggled to support the weight of the other man who was on the verge of losing consciousness and collapsing, clothes torn, charred, and bloody. Nurse Engel noted the patient's admission on her clipboard while Nurse Jones ran over with a wheelchair. Together, they placed the patient into it as he writhed in pain. Bertie performed a quick assessment. There were second and third-degree burns on his face, chest, and thighs, and full-thickness burns on his hands. Addie learned from the man in the corduroy coat that the injuries were sustained from a grain silo explosion.

"We'll give him something for the pain as soon as I get him into the treatment room." Bertie, unfazed by the farmer's red blistered and peeling skin, ushered him back to be evaluated by the awaiting medical team. Upon returning to the triage area, she remarked to Addie, "I had no idea grain dust was so highly flammable."

"Oh, it is. It's one of the many lessons you learn while growing up on a farm. Did you know that hay is also extremely combustible, too, if it's put away wet?"

"Really?" Bertie took a seat next to Addie.

"It sure is. If the internal temperature of the hay pile gets above 130 degrees, a chemical reaction occurs, and if the gases come into contact with air, they ignite. My Paw, God rest his soul, always told me that if the pile starts to smell musty or develops a sweet caramel scent, it's a quick indicator that the hay is heating up."

"Wow! The things I can learn from you while sitting in the emergency room." Bertie quickly changed the subject. "What time do you and Opal have to meet with Nurse Hartman tonight?"

Addie checked the time. "Not for another hour. My shift ends at seven tonight."

"By the way, how are you doing since Emiline passed away?"

"Some days are better than others. I find myself crying for no apparent reason, and other days I am quick to anger, triggered by the slightest of incident. Dr. Springer shared with me a drawing she did just before she died." Addie patted her uniform pocket. "I carry it with me. I dare not show it to you. I'll break out into a hysterical fit if I do." *I can't believe she came to think of me as her mother. My heart is absolutely breaking.*

"It sounds like your feelings are a bit all over the place."

Addie swallowed hard, choking back welling tears. "They are. I feel like a part of me died with her. I'm still a bit numb to it all. I was relieved to know that an aunt claimed Emiline's body and took her home to Lawrenceville to be buried in a family plot up there." Pausing momentarily, she exhaled through pursed lips. "I'm learning how to compartmentalize my feelings and am finding myself turning to Nurse Hartman for advice on such matters. This is uncharted territory for me."

Bertie grew contemplative and distant, struggling to get out the next sentence.

Addie sensed something was wrong and reached out to touch Bertie on the shoulder. "What is it, Bertie? You know you can tell me anything."

"I've been wrestling with something that happened on one of my shifts a while back. It involves an incident with Deborah and me." Bertie started to weep.

Addie pulled out a handkerchief, handing it to Bertie.

"If I say it out loud, it means it really happened. But the guilt is eating me alive." Bertie blotted her splotchy face. "You know how Nurse Hartman and Nurse Scott always preached to us about the importance of honesty and integrity in the profession?"

Addie nodded her head. "They said it is vital. The physicians, our peers, and the public at large needs to put their complete faith in us and trust that we will provide care to the best of our abilities, administer medications as they are ordered, and deliver treatments adhering to the hospital's policies, procedures, and strict protocols."

Bertie hung her head. "I've completely fudged that all up. I'm a fraud and if I tell the truth, I will be kicked out of nursing school. What am I supposed to do?"

"Oh my stars, Bertie! Whatever did you do?"

"I can't tell you and you're my best friend. I'm so embarrassed and humiliated. Deborah threatened to hurt me if I told anyone."

"Bertie, that's not right. If you can't tell me, then I think you know what the right thing is to do, and that's to tell Nurse Hartman. Don't you?"

Bertie reluctantly agreed.

The sound of an ambulance siren grew closer and then wound down as it pulled in the back driveway. Addie and Bertie jumped up and opened the bay doors to the emergency department.

Brice and Rob pulled out a man on a stretcher in wet coveralls.

"The wife found 'em out in the tobacco field, passed out. During the ride over 'ere, he woke up complainin' of a bad 'eadache and dizziness," Brice said.

Rob adding, "He's droolin' like a fool, too."

Addie directed, "Put him in Room #2. The medical staff is busy with a burn victim in the first room. Let me check in with the doctors to see who can help us with him." Addie quietly entered the first treatment room; doctors and nurses were scrambling about.

"What do you need, Nurse Engel?" one of the doctors asked.

"I've got a patient who collapsed in a tobacco field, now complaining of being dizzy with a headache."

"Is it still raining out?" He looked down, examining the oral and nasal mucosa of the burn victim. "Seems like he's scorched his airway and lungs."

"Yes, it's still raining," Addie replied.

Nurse Owens pulled the stethoscope from her ears. "Doctor, he's getting bradycardic and his blood pressure is dropping."

The patient struggled to breathe.

"Prepare the operating room. We're going to see what we can do to save him," the physician said to the team, pushing the stretcher towards the back treatment room door. Directing his remarks to Addie, he said "Nurse Engel, pull out the *Materia Medica* textbook, look up tobacco poisoning, and follow the treatment protocols. His life will be in your hands while we work to save this one's."

Addie darted from the room, retrieved the book off her triage desk, and burst through the door of Treatment Room #2. Relieved to still see Brice and Rob attending to the patient with Bertie, she took command. "We're on our own while the medical team works to save another man's life. It appears that we're dealing with acute tobacco poisoning." Addie flipped through the pages, stopping to read aloud. "Tobacco is the dried and pressed leaf of *Nicotiana Tabacum*. It contains nicotine, a very poisonous volatile fluid alkaloid. Nicotine is one of the most violent poisons known. It can cause a slow weak pulse, nausea, vomiting, and often diarrhea. Nicotine poisoning can occur from transdermal absorption of nicotine from wet surfaces of the tobacco plant." Addie dropped down a few paragraphs. "Tobacco harvesters are at high risk and should wear protective rain gear and gloves when harvesting while there is dew on the plant or after the rains. Ideally, the farmer should wait until the crop is dry." Addie read on in silence before slamming the book shut. "Okay, y'all. I need for you to strip off his wet clothes. We need to wash all of him with warm soapy water. His symptoms should subside in a day or two. Let's get to work and then transfer him to the med-surg unit for observation. Bertie, since I have to meet Nurse Hartman at seven o'clock, would you mind working on the admission paperwork after we finish here?"

"I sure will," Bertie said, pulling off the boots and socks of the farmer. "And I'll make an appointment to speak with Nurse Hartman, too."

"Good for you, Bertie. I knew you would come around and do the right thing."

An hour later, Addie strolled into Lena's office. Opal and Mr. Waxman were already sitting at the small conference table, pouring over spreadsheets and patient charts with Nurse Hartman.

"Thank you for joining us, Addie. We're finishing reviewing the charts of those patients who passed away on the med-surg unit and are still trying to find a common thread among them."

Addie took a seat, her brow wrinkled with worry. "Nurse Hartman?"

Lena put down the patient file and studied Addie's face. "You look troubled, Addie. What is it?"

"Well, I don't want to sound like some sort of tattle-tale, but you need to know that Bertie just shared with me that she needs to come and talk with you. She said there was an incident that occurred between her and Deborah over a patient and that

Deborah threatened her if she were to say anything about it to anyone."

Alan looked down at his paper and tallied up a few tick marks. "Lena, oh, my God! It's Deborah!"

"Whatever are you talking about Alan?"

"The common thread that we've been looking for is Nurse Owens. That's what all of these patients primarily had in common, dating all the way back to November 1914 with the death of one of Dr. Leventhal's patients, a Mr. Danielson who passed away from stomach cancer." He dropped his pencil and tapped his leg four times. "Fuck me!" Alan jumped up. "I'm so sorry, Lena. I didn't think she was capable of becoming her mother. I had hoped that she could be someone different."

Lena, aware that Addie and Opal had no idea what he was talking about, stood up and grabbed Alan by the shoulders. "Alan, you had no way of knowing."

All of the puzzle pieces fell into place in Addie's head. *Oh my stars! Mr. Waxman is Deborah's uncle and that's why Nurse Hartman said what she said to Deborah the day Nurse Scott was found dead at the bottom of the nursing dorm stairs. She knew his secret!* Addie blurted out, "Do you think Deborah is capable of having killed Nurse Scott?"

"Unfortunately, yes. Yes, I do." Alan felt like he was going to throw up.

Lena grew concerned. "Addie, where is Deborah now?"

"She's in the operating suite."

"Okay. Alan, I need for you to come with me. We're going to handle this situation together." Lena looked over at Addie and Opal. "Ladies, I need your help. Addie, find Bertie and bring her back to my office for a debriefing. Opal, please cover Bertie's shift in the emergency room."

"Yes, ma'am," Addie and Opal replied, rushing out of the office.

Lena called after them, "Walk, ladies. Remain calm." Arm in arm, Lena and Allen hustled toward the operating room suite.

Alan fretted. "How am I going to explain this to Edward?"

"Tell him the truth." Lena peered into the operating room. Bloody rags covered the floor and an array of instrument trays and medication carts were strewn about. The scorched scent of burnt flesh lingered. No one else remained.

The two walked into the room, eventually finding Deborah in the sterilization room cleaning instruments.

Lena opened the door. She and Alan stepped inside. The door immediately closed behind them. "Tough case?" Lena asked.

Deborah set the instruments down in the sink. "Yes, a burned farmer. He died. Dr. Payne just came up and got him to take him back down to the morgue. I'm cleaning up and sterilizing the instruments." Looking over at Alan, she pointed a scalpel at him. "What are you doing in here?"

Alan paled, wondering how to tell her that he was her uncle, saved her from growing up with her murderous mother behind bars at Eastern State Penitentiary, put her in an orphanage in Atlanta, watched her grow up from a distance, and helped fund her education at Sacred Heart Nursing School. "I…I…I…." Stammering, Alan turned to Lena for guidance.

"Deborah, I need for you to stop what you are doing and come to my office. Bertie is waiting for us there. The three of us need to have a little chat."

"What about?" Deborah's eyes darkened. "Did that little bitch tell you what I did?" She shot Alan a look that mirrored one Lily had given him twenty years earlier. Her demeanor became defiant, cold, and demonic. Deborah turned her back, pouring a mixture from two bottles, one marked *chlorine*, the other *ammonia*, into a bucket. She rambled, "I am the best nurse here at Sacred Heart! I save lives and I help usher out those knocking on death's door! I am their angel of mercy! I AM THEIR SAVIOR!" The fumes immediately overwhelmed them all. As Deborah dropped the bucket on the floor, the gas permeated the room while all choked and gasped for air.

Lena grabbed two respirators off a nearby supply shelf, put a gas mask on herself first, and then secured the other one on Alan's face. She pulled him toward the door. "Stand up, Alan. For the love of God, stand up and get up off the floor." Retrieving another mask, she put it on Deborah , dragging her towards the exit. Lena rushed to close off the air vent and broke the window to ventilate the room.

While walking down the hallway from the emergency room to Nurse Hartman's office, Addie and Bertie heard, *Bang! Bang! Bang!* The sound was coming from inside the surgical suite. Once inside, they found Alan kicking the sterilization room door with a gas mask on while holding Deborah in his arms.

"WE'VE BEEN EXPOSED TO CHLORINE GAS!" Alan screamed.

Recalling Nurse Scott's lecture about chlorine gas and that it was heavier than air and hovers low to the ground, Addie remained standing, opening the door so the three could escape. She hastily closed it behind them. Bertie and Addie helped them out of their contaminated clothing and escorted them to be de-contaminated in the nearby showers.

Lena and Alan were placed under medical observation on the med-surg unit for the next two days. On the evening of the first day, Addie thought she saw the two of them reaching out to hold hands while they lay next to each other in their respective hospital beds. When Addie turned to look, their hands recoiled. She recognized a familiar look on Alan's face, one that lingered as he gazed over at Lena. *His eyes smile with light and love, just like Garrett's used to do when he looked at me. No words were needed to convey our feelings about each other. Oh, God! How I grieve for Garrett. I wish he would look at me that way again. He is growing unfamiliar to me these days.* Addie longed for the familiar. *God, how can people change so quickly? I feel like life is moving as swiftly as the Chattahoochee River. Help me keep my head above the waterline.*

Three days passed. Deborah remained unresponsive on the ward after the "unfortunate accident," as it was dubbed by the hospital attorneys after a thorough review of the events. Edward and the leadership team were told by the legal counsel, 'There isn't any hard evidence to suggest Deborah's malicious intent, merely coincidences, and hearsay.' All agreed to squelch rumors in order to avoid scandal. However, after the lawyers heard Bertie's confession about Deborah's strange behavior, the atropine eye drop medication error, and her failure to report the incident immediately to the ward physician, charge nurse, the oncoming shift, or Nurse Hartman, Roberta "Bertie" Jones was immediately expelled from Sacred Heart Hospital. The news sent a shock wave through the entire nursing staff, rocking Addie to the core. On the fourth day, Dr. William's medical examination of Deborah confirmed that she suffered frostbite to the eyes as a consequence of exposure to the chlorine, documenting in her chart, *If she ever awakes, she will be blind.* On the morning of the fifth day, Alan sat in a chair next to Deborah's bed and held her hand. He quietly unveiled the family secrets with promises to visit her mother when he was well enough to travel. Deborah developed breathing complications later that afternoon and succumbed to the pulmonary edema, drowning in her own secretions at eight fifty-six that evening.

# 13

It had been twenty years since Alan had last seen his sister. He wrestled with a twinge of regret, but the feeling immediately passed, replaced by the emotional memories of receiving annual letters, rank-smelling notes written in blood and hair remnants, all saying, *YOU TOOK MY BABY!* He worried about how he would relay the news of Deborah's death. How would Lily take it?

*Click. Creak.* The prison guard unlocked the heavy, white iron gate with the red cross emblem and swung it open, wide enough for Alan to slip into the hospital wing. *Creak. Slam. Click.* The guard remained on the other side while Alan stood alone. Today, the corridor was eerily still, a far different day than he experienced two decades ago.

The door marked *Psychiatric Dept.* slid open. Alan recognized the physician, despite the thinning gray hair, wrinkles, and liver spots on his face and hands. There was something noticeably different about him; it was in the way he walked. His torso listed to the left as he limped over to Alan.

The doctor offered his right hand. "Good to see you, Mr. Waxman."

Alan shook it and then stuffed his hands in his coat jacket, subtly tapping his right thigh four times. "Good to see you too, doc."

Sensing Alan noticed the change in his appearance, he chose to address it as they made their way to Lily's cell. "Yes, I know I look a bit more haggard since the last time I saw you. One of the prison guards got angry with me when he found out that Lilith's infant daughter went missing. He and his boys took their aggressions out on me one afternoon." They stopped in front of a closed door. He lowered his voice. "But, not to worry, I got that son-of-a-bitch back when I found out he got your sister pregnant again."

Confusion washed over Alan's face. "Again?"

"As I was saying, not to worry, it was about ten years ago. I took good care of her and got rid of *it*, making sure she could never conceive again."

Alan struggled to suppress his rage. "You gave her a hysterectomy?"

"I found in my research that by sterilizing our female prisoners, not only are they much calmer and easier to handle, but our rates of illegitimate childbirths have dropped to zero. The warden loves the number zero. No babies mean zero budget dollars to feed and support those urchins. Anyhow, they tried making a few bucks under the table by adopting some kids for a fee but found that parents don't want a prison infant. They were worried about how that kid would turn out. What if that kid grew up to be a murderer or a thief? So, he tasked me to come up with a cost-effective solution. And, I did."

Alan's head swirled with questions that he was too afraid to ask. *Is this what happens inside of prisons?* He had heard of sterilization techniques used in insane asylums and for the mentally deficient. Was this normal practice? Did the physician make sense? Was this his professional opinion or was it that of a mad-man?

The doctor slid the cell door open. Lily, crouched in the far-right corner, was draped in a thick, blue wool blanket. "Don't worry. She won't hurt you. I gave her some sedatives. She's been ranting all of these years that you stole her baby. Was it a coincidence that Deborah went missing right after your visit, Mr. Waxman?" The doctor assessed Alan for a reaction. There wasn't one, so he proceeded, "There was gossip that one of the guards took the baby and smuggled it out of the prison. Another claimed that an inmate on the medical ward snatched it and shoved it down the toilet during the uprising while you were here, a fate not uncommon for unwanted offspring. Regardless, her story is the only one that remains unchanged."

Alan refused to be baited. He stepped over the threshold into the cell. "Lily, it's me." Twenty years was a long time to go by without seeing each other. Would she recognize him? Would he recognize her?

Lilith stood and turned to face the men in the doorway. Alan was taken aback by her gaunt appearance, yellow skin, and bald head. She smiled. She was toothless. The stench of death and decay drifted through the room and became overwhelming.

The physician murmured to Alan. "I forgot to tell you that she suffers from trichotillomania."

Lily held out a dead rat with patches of missing hair. "Do you want to hold my baby?"

Alan gasped, his stomach rolled, and he vomited into the toilet beside him.

The doctor walked over to Lilith and held out his hand, escorting her to take a seat on her bed. She leaned against him. He stroked her bald head. "She's been pulling out her own hair and eating it since she lost her baby. Every month, we have to shave her entire body. In recent years, she's been pulling out the hair of the furry critters she catches and eating that too. We've tried everything to stop her. So, we pulled her teeth."

Alan, repulsed, fled and ran down the hall towards the guard at the gate. The news about Deborah didn't matter anymore. No one here needed to know the truth. Deborah was gone. Lily was gone. Whatever or whoever remained in that cell behind him was not any relation to him. Only darkness and evil dwelled here. Grabbing the bars of the gate, he shook it, ordering, "Get me the fuck out of here this instant!"

*Click. Creak.*

Alan slipped out.

*Creak. Slam. Click.*


### SATURDAY EVENING, SECOND WARD

"Ho, ho, ho! Who wouldn't go? Ho, ho, ho! Who wouldn't go? Up on the housetop, click, click, click. Down thru the chimney with good Saint Nick," the crowd, dressed in their holiday finest, sang out in the Great Room, an expansive area that ran the width of the Alexander mansion on Washington Street. The holiday decorations, more rustic than in years past, consisted of evergreen garland filled with pine cones, cotton, and white silk magnolia blossoms. The grand Christmas tree in the foyer was also decorated in the same manner, complete with copper and gold ornaments and accented with red bows throughout. The tree topper was a crown of deer antlers and pheasant feathers. The string quartet accompanied by the pianist on the Steinway grand piano paused, allowing the applause to subside. They waited for the crowd to turn the page in their programs for the next sing-along song. Following a short introduction in the key of D major, the crowd sang out, "Joy to the world! The Lord is come: Let earth receive her King. Let every heart prepare him room." The men sang out, "And heaven and nature sing." The women responded, "And heaven and nature sing." Together, they concluded the first verse, "And heaven, and heaven, and nature sing."

Lena observed the first-year nursing students, who sat or stood around one of the four celadon couches, dressed in the gowns originally purchased by Edward last year for the first cohort from Rich and Brothers department store, a well-earned tradition she was glad to see continue. It was quite the honor to be invited to the founder's home. Lena knew that many of the young ladies had come from humble beginnings and the opportunity to kick off the holidays with this grand affair was definitely something to write home about. She appreciated the parents' trust that their daughters were well-taken care of, groomed to bloom into exquisite and educated young ladies who all had a servant's heart.

Clyde walked up behind Lena and hissed in her ear, "Where's your boyfriend tonight?"

Lena wanted to elbow him in the gut. Instead, she gave him

a polite reply, "He's out of town visiting family." She excused herself, exiting the room in search of more pleasant company.

Clyde continued to snake his way through the crowd, catching sight of a blonde-haired woman dressed in a white gown. Her appearance, dramatic and overstated, enticed him. There was something familiar about her mannerisms as she sang "Jingle Bells" while huddled in a group of elderly women. *A rose amongst thorns.* He chuckled to himself, making a mental note to introduce himself to her later tonight. He made his way to a group of three men, recognizing one as his father, standing next to the two-story, Georgia granite fireplace. The logs crackled and sparked, sending embers floating up the chimney. His father's face bore a look Clyde was all too familiar with as the congressman poked a larger man in the chest; his white rose boutonniere shook with every jab. Clyde knew the gentleman was being chastised by a driven, bitter, angry, and controlling man who ruled his kingdom with an iron fist.

Congressman Posey spewed a litany of profanity under his breath before adding, "You better make this go away and I'll do my part, you bastard. See that none of this comes to see the light of day. Do what you must. My networks and pockets run deep."

"Yes, Congressman Posey," the man said unflinchingly.

"Everything all right, Father?" Clyde stepped in, commanding the group with complete authority.

"Shut the fuck up and come with me." Clyde shrank and his shoulders slumped as his father grabbed him by the upper arm and escorted him out of the room. Together, they walked across the hall and into Edward's office, known as "The Zoo." Finding the room empty of guests, he closed the door behind him. The zoo was filled with an assortment of wildlife taxidermy, ranging from birds and squirrels to cougars, buffalo, and red foxes, trophies collected over the years by Edward and his father on their hunting expeditions.

"God, how I hate this room!" Clyde shuffled his feet on the zebra-skin rug. "This is where Edward would lecture me for hours on how to be the best leader I could be at Sacred Heart."

"Too bad you didn't heed his lessons. I was hoping he could break you so you would become the man I always hoped you'd be."

Clyde walked over to the far corner of the room, where a thousand-pound Grizzly bear stood on its hind legs with raised claws, mimicking a growl. Baring his own teeth, Clyde growled, "Fuck you too, Mr. Grizzly."

"Would you quit jack-assing around? I need to have a frank discussion with you." Clyde's father walked over to him, pulling out a tiny brown paper bag from inside his tux jacket. He handed it to Clyde.

"You're going to need this after I tell you what I've learned today." He paced back and forth. "I've been told that the Secret Service has uncovered evidence from your friend's chemical factory fire. Evidence that wasn't destroyed as you promised me. Evidence that incriminates you and has the potential to harm me and the family name, a name generations before worked so hard to raise from the depths of this red clay soil."

"Fa-fa-fa...." Clyde stammered, trying to understand what he was referring to.

"Don't 'fa-fa-fa' me!" Mr. Posey stopped pacing and slapped Clyde across the face. "You fu-fu-fucked up, son," he mocked.

"And, now I have to clean up your mess, as always." He turned his back to Clyde, making his way to the door. He turned around. With a tone of resignation in his voice, he added, "I'm done cleaning up your messes."

"But, Father...." Clyde pleaded, taking a step toward the congressman.

His father held out his hand. "Stop...right...there."

Clyde froze in his tracks.

"I want nothing more to do with you. You've been a complete disappointment to me, and you are no longer my son."

Clyde, blindsided, cried out, "But, Father!" Picking up a squirrel perched on a branch and holding an acorn from an end table next to him, he hurled it at his dad. It narrowly missed his head. Instead, it struck the far wall and exploded into pieces. The squirrel ricocheted, taking flight across the room, still clutching the nut.

The congressman left, closing the door behind him.

"Fuck you! Fuck all of you!" Clyde's rant was inaudible, drowned out by the music and singing in the other room. He sunk into one of the leather chairs, opened the tiny sack, and inhaled a healthy amount of white powder.

The door cracked open and a blonde head popped into view. "Hello? Hello?" she sang out.

Clyde recognized the voice but struggled to focus on the appearance of the woman in the puffy white gown who walked over and stood before him—the very same woman he had noticed earlier. The drugs were making his head swim and she appeared blurry. Squinting, he asked, "Do I know you?"

"Of course, you silly fool, you know who I am."

Her image morphed and warped like in carnival's fun-house mirror. "You look like a giant exploding marshmallow."

"I can see you are just as hateful as always." She leaned over him, shaking her bosoms at him. "I used to cradle your head against these many a night." She cackled. "You'll be glad to know that your dad is a fan of them, too. He has been for years." Removing the evidence from Clyde's hands, she walked over to the lit fireplace. "There was a time I'd walk through broken glass for you, you bastard!"

Clyde's vision tunneled before everything went black. "Moira?" Breathless and cyanotic, he reached out, "Moi-ra?" He tried to stand but collapsed to the floor. White foam gurgled from his mouth.

"Moira died when you threw me aside for another. My adoring lovers and fans call me Hetta now!" Tossing the poison into the flames, she sashayed up to him. "Fuck you, Clyde. Welcome to the dead animals club." Moira lifted her arms in the air, as if to pay homage to the trophies on the wall, and twirled around in a circle. She stopped and peered down at Clyde's lifeless form. "I hope you burn in hell. Merry Christmas!" She spat on his head and exited the zoo. Spotting two nefarious-looking men standing at the end of the long hall guarding the side door, Moira blew them a kiss, signaling them to extract and dispose of the fresh kill inside.

# 14

Lena sat next to Alan on his living room couch, both in matching cardinal cotton bathrobes with white piping. Lena curled her legs up under her and reached over to grab her cup of coffee off the end table. "I love the smell of hot coffee and a burning fire on a crisp Christmas morning."

"Me, too. It's one of my favorite scents. What is it about the smell of a fire?"

"It must go back to something primal in us, our hunter-killer instincts." Lena raised the cup to her nose. She took a sip. "Did you know the sense of smell is the most powerful sense associated with memory recall."

"Really? I had no idea. I thought it would be sight." He raised and lowered his eyebrows, causing his spectacles to dance on the bridge of his nose. "My eyes are growing accustomed to waking up with you and seeing you here in the mornings. I must confess that I rather like your company, Lena."

"I must confess that I rather like your company, too, Alan."

Lena sighed gleefully. "Who would have ever guessed that we would get together?"

"What's so surprising about two brilliant-minded people who work endless hours together finding love?"

Lena was taken aback. She never thought she'd hear those words uttered by a man who wasn't her father or brother. "Love?" Did you just say the L-word?" She returned her cup to the saucer and scooted closer to him. She pecked his cheek. "I love you, too, Alan."

"Well, that settles that. We both love each other." He laughed heartily and snapped the morning edition of the *Atlanta Dispatch* open.

"What's going on in Atlanta today?" She rested her head on his shoulder.

"There's a brief article recapping Clyde's death in a tragic car accident. It says here that, 'the Atlanta Police Department has concluded its investigation and that Posey died instantly after his car hit a tree leaving the Alexander Christmas party. According to the police report, officers found a dead deer lying in the gully on the other side of the road and think that Clyde swerved to avoid hitting it. Evidence revealed that he struck the animal. The police found fur and blood on the broken windshield.'"

"I honestly confess that I had mixed emotions when I first learned about his death and have concluded that I won't miss Clyde at all. He pulled the air out of my lungs every time he entered the room and opened his mouth." Lena lifted her head. "I have another confession to make."

"Do tell, my dear."

"There were times during our leadership meetings when I

wanted to punch him in the face for making asinine remarks." She balled up her fists. "God, he was so irritating and cocky. He was so full of himself."

Alan flipped the page. "Clyde and his family come from 'What can you do for me' kind of people. We're different. We're the 'What can I do for you' kind of folks."

"That's what I love about you. You are direct and to the point."

Alan gave her a sideways glance and smiled. "Did you just say the L-word?"

She elbowed him. "I feel like I'm a teenager all over again."

Alan laughed and returned to the paper.

"Hey, would you read the 'Hey, Hetta!' column to me?"

Lena nestled closer to Alan while he turned a few pages.

"Ah, here we go. Hey, Hetta! Uncovering pearls and gems from Atlanta's social scene.

Mr. and Mrs. Henry Maxwell are happy to report that their eldest daughter, Sadie, wedded to Mr. William Bryant from Cordele, Georgia, will be expecting their first grandchild in early Spring."

Lena howled. "Oh, my! I remember reading about their engagement in September. If my math is correct, and it usually is, that baby shouldn't be due until summer. No wonder the young couple opted for a quick courthouse ceremony."

"How scandalous!" Alan read on. "Mrs. Barbara Beach filed for divorce from her husband, Mr. Roscoe Beach, citing that he was an unbearable oaf and a clod of a husband."

"Well, that's descriptive! I'm surprised she didn't leave him sooner."

"Do you want to hear all about the birth announcements, too?"

"No, you can skip that part. What's going on with The 'Peach of a Story' Tellers in the social activities section?"

"City of Atlanta Social Activities. Thursday Evening. The 'Peach of a Story' Tellers will meet at the home of Mr. Gerald Goodrich on Thursday evening. A contest will be held for the best story. All members are urged to attend. Last month's winning story was told by Mrs. Gertrude Deitzer, titled, 'Does your shantyboat have a basement?'"

Both burst out in hysterical laughter until tears ran down their cheeks.

"Oh, God! Their story titles slay me. I think I need a hanky." Lena reached out to Alan.

Alan pulled one from his robe pocket, drying his eyes first before handing it to Lena. He resumed perusing through the contents on the next page. "It looks like the movie premiere of a 'Birth of a Nation' at The Atlanta Theater did well despite protests from the Ku Klux Klan."

Lena patted her cheeks. "I thought that group disbanded."

"They did. According to the article, the group reunited and formally resurrected itself on top of Stone Mountain in a celebratory ceremony on Thanksgiving night."

"What utter nonsense! I think that men covered up in white gowns and wearing pointed hoods is ridiculous. They are small-minded individuals with narrow points of view and are not brave enough to venture out and experience other cultures in this expansive world of ours." Lena preached on, "When it comes right down to it, don't our various faiths teach us to put hate aside and to love one another? How can you have empathy for another if you don't find mutual respect despite race, creed, color, or gender?"

"Well said, my darling." Alan closed the paper, folded it, and set it in his lap. "Did you know that the Klan's name originates from the Greek word, kyklos, meaning circle? Or it can refer to a cycle commonly seen in government called anakyklosis."

"Enlighten me, my sweet scholar."

"Plato, Aristotle, Cicero, and others flushed out their individual concepts, explaining that there are three basic types of government—democracy, aristocracy, and monarchy. Among those three, there are corrupt versions of each, such as mob rule; oligarchy, where power resides among a small group of people; or having an absolute ruler, a tyrant. And then, there is anarchy, where there is no actual or recognized government."

"Interesting. Go on."

"All of the philosophers thought violence would ensue due to protests during times of political evolution and transition. However, Aristotle pointed out ways to slow down or stabilize the cycle by recommending short-term appointments for governmental officials, a large middle class, promotion of peace and unity within your nation, not allowing judges' decisions to be bought, and—the last and most important part of preserving a society's constitution—widespread education. People who are knowledgeable about their country, laws, and constitution will take pride in upholding it and be good citizens."

"My father taught me that an education is vital to society's success. He used to say, 'Knowledge breaks the chains of poverty. Without an education or access to books and facts, one tends to become a victim of sheep-minded thinking and not free-minded thinking.'"

"Your father has a great way with words. He raised you well. I love that you are a free-minded thinker."

"There you go again using the L-word."

"It's easy with you. I can just be myself, no longer a wound-up nervous twit." Alan set the paper on the end table, picked up a small stack of mail, and sorted through the letters.

"You are not a twit."

Alan came to the last letter. The return address read, *Eastern State Penitentiary.* "Damn it! I hoped she'd stop mailing me these letters. It's not even close to Deborah's birthday." He reached for a letter opener lying next to the *Atlanta Dispatch* and carefully slid it through the top of the envelope. Alan extracted and unfolded the note, failing to recognize the handwriting.

"What does it say?"

"Dear Mr. Waxman, I'm sorry to report that your sister Lilith Waxman died...." Aghast, Alan read on, "...on Monday, December 13, 1915 from complications sustained following a surgical procedure to remove a hairball that had caused intestinal blockage. In compliance with her directives, she was cremated and her ashes spread in the garden on the grounds. My deepest sympathies go out to you and your family. Best regards, Richard Saxton, Warden."

Lena reached out to touch Alan's arm. He jerked it away, stood up, and ran upstairs. A few minutes later, he returned, carrying a red box.

Alan walked over to the fireplace. "Darling, would you help me dispose of these?"

Lena stood, joined him, taking the box out of his hands. He

opened it and tossed all of the letters, including the latest one, in the fireplace. Closing the box, he tossed it into the flames, too. Together, they watched his tormented past turn into ashes. Alan turned and took hold of Lena's hands. He looked lovingly into her eyes. "You have healed me, my heart of my troubles, and my body of nervous afflictions. Your love is a powerful drug, Lena."

Tears welled in Lena's eyes.

Alan dropped to one knee. "Will you marry me, Lena Hartman? Will you make me the happiest man in this world?" He pulled out a small red leather box with gold lace borders from his robe pocket and opened it, revealing a five-carat emerald-cut diamond perched on a platinum band filled with alternating sapphires and diamonds on either side. The fire danced in the reflection of the concave clipped facets. The silk-lined box lid read *Cartier* in gold letters.

"Oh, my God!" Lena dropped to her knees. "Yes! Yes! I will marry you, Alan!" She wrapped her arms around him. Together, they toppled over.

Alan rolled out from under her and knelt beside her. Taking the ring out of the box, he placed it on her left ring finger while Lena lay on her back, soaking in the moment. "This ring symbolizes the infinite circle of unwavering love I have for you." He leaned over and gently kissed her, memorizing the small lines and wrinkles around her green eyes and mouth. He carefully opened her robe and did the same with his, appreciating her soft naked form underneath him and the way her dark hair contrasted with her milky white skin. "I can see our future in your eyes." He became aroused.

Lena reached up and traced the lines in his face with her finger. "I can see the love you have for me in yours." She pulled him down on top of her, pressing her warm wet lips and body to his.

## CHRISTMAS EVENING, SIXTH WARD

"Well, me granny told us that we shouldn't throw out our fireplace ashes or coals on Christmas Day for fear of bad luck." Mary Margaret sat cross-legged in front of the fireplace in the dorm library, joined by the remaining seven from the first cohort, including Addie, Opal, Lexie, Alice, Susan, and Belle, who completed the circle.

"My nana said the same thing and she said that we shouldn't sweep dust across our thresholds or carry out the garbage, either," added Belle. "My mother told me that if we heard a cricket chirp from the fireplace, that we'd have good luck in the coming year. So, one year my little brother brought in a handful of crickets and set them loose in the house. Oh my, my mother was livid as we scurried about trying to catch those critters. Thank goodness we had two cats who found them faster than we ever could! I even heard words fall out of my father's mouth that I'd never heard before!"

The group laughed.

It was Opal's turn. "Well, my father used to tell us that if you sat under a pine tree on Christmas Day and heard angels sing that you'd be dead within the year. So, I guess the takeaway message from that one is to not get under a pine tree on Christmas, huh?" Opal turned to Addie. "What old Christmas lore did you grow up hearing in your family?"

Warmed by the fireplace and the loving memories of the early days on the Engel family farm in Hope, Addie shared, "Maw used to say that a single girl who visited the hog pen at midnight on Christmas Eve would find out what kind of guy she would marry. If an old hog squealed first, then her husband would be old. But, if a young pig grunted first, then she'd marry someone good-looking and young."

"We can always count on you for sage rural advice!" Opal joked, slapping Addie on the back.

Addie popped Opal on the back of the head. "Oh my stars! That reminds me of another piece of sound rural advice that I once heard from a friend's granny. She told her that if she didn't want to get pregnant to keep her feet in a bucket."

Alice appeared puzzled. "What? How on earth does that keep you from getting pregnant?"

Addie clarified, "Her granny explained that if you keep your feet in a bucket, you can't spread your legs apart!" She leaned back on her elbows, parting her legs in the middle of the air.

The group doubled over in hysterics.

"That's a vision I can't un-see!" Mary Margaret coughed out. "I can't wait to tell me future daughters that one! Oh, me God! Me stomach hurts!" She wrapped her arms around her belly.

Addie laughed so hard that her belly hurt, too. But the pain gave away to abdominal cramping. She jumped up. "If you'll excuse me, I'll be right back."

"Don't pee your pants, birthday girl!" Opal called out as Addie darted for the bathroom.

Alice nudged Susan. "Since we're Jewish, do you know of any Christmas legends?"

Susan shook her head, shrugging her shoulders. "I sure don't.

I'm only familiar with our traditions and celebration of lights, but it has been most entertaining to learn about all of their grannies' and mothers' wisdom."

Twenty minutes later, Addie emerged from the restroom and passed a few of the new students and Opal in the hallway.

Opal stopped her. "Are you feeling alright, Addie? Was our birthday party this afternoon a bit too much for you to handle?"

Addie feigned a weak laugh. "I'm good." *Did I eat too many sweets? Was it the cake? Was it something I ate? Perhaps it was the shot of apple pie moonshine that Lexie procured from one of the McDaniel brothers?* Addie began feeling clammy and hot. "I'm just going to step outside for a bit of some fresh air."

Opal protested. "But it's freezing out there." She removed her pink cashmere shawl.

Addie had learned a few weeks ago that it was an early Christmas gift from Shelby. Opal shared the secret with her while they were taking a deceased pellagra patient down to the morgue. 'Shelby thought of me when he saw it on a mannequin in a dress shop window on Peachtree Street. Isn't that the sweetest?' she had told her.

"Here, at least wrap this around you." Opal wound the shawl around Addie, covering her head in the process.

Addie walked through the kitchen and out the back door. She proceeded to the large maple tree and leaned against it to survey the sky. The evening was still. A few twinkling white stars emerged as clouds floated overhead, obscuring the rest from view. Addie marveled at God's handiwork. She inhaled the cold air; its scent distinct. *It smells like snow is coming.* She wrapped the shawl tighter around her shoulders, bowing her head to pray.

*God, I miss my family. It's especially hard during the holiday time. I know you have given me a new family and I am forever thankful for my new sisters, but I do look forward to being settled down with a family of my own.* The Bible verse from Jeremiah 29:11-13 came to mind. Addie reminisced about how Maw would sit by the hearth and read the passage to the family at night. She closed her eyes and heard her mother's voice saying, 'For I know the thoughts that I think toward you, saith the Lord, thoughts of peace, and not of evil, to give you an expected end. Then shall ye call upon me, and ye shall go and pray unto me, and I will hearken unto you. And ye shall seek me, and find me, when ye shall search for me with all your heart.'

"Happy Birthday and Merry Christmas, Addie," a voice whispered in her left ear.

Startled, Addie started to scream, but a hand quickly covered her mouth. Garrett stepped out from behind the tree, wrapping her up in his arms.

"Holy moly! Garrett, you scared the ever-living daylights out of me." She swatted at his chest to break free from his embrace. The stale smell of cigars and alcohol escaped from his mouth and seeped out of clothes, evidence that he'd been smoking, drinking, and gambling in the Sacred Heart garage with the McDaniel brothers and the rest. She pulled Garrett to the other side of the large tree, hiding him from any nosey onlookers. "What the hell is wrong with you? You're drunk and you stink to high heaven." Addie, although happy to see him, wasn't pleased to see him in this condition and gave him a disapproving look.

"What? You're not pleased to see me? Don't you miss me?" Garrett tried to step closer to her and kiss her.

Addie pushed him off of her. "Get away from me."

Garrett's smile faded, his mood darkening. "What? Don't you love me anymore? Is there someone else? Is it Randall? Are you dating Randall, now?" Spotting the gold chain around her neck, he reached for it, pulling out the heart pendant he'd given to her last year at the Alexander Christmas party.

Addie, caught off guard, stumbled backward. The chain broke with the pendant still lying in the palm of his hand. Appalled, Addie hollered out, "Oh, my God! You broke my necklace." She shoved him. "How could you?" *Who is this man?* Before she knew it, the words had already tumbled out. "I never want to see you again!" Addie burst into tears and ran back into the house.

Garrett dropped to his knees. He looked up at the clouds. "Oh, dear God! Noooo, what have I done?" he pleaded. "What have I done? I have hurt the only one I have ever loved." Mortified, he stood up and shoved the piece of jewelry in his coat pocket. He stumbled toward the dirt road, straight into the path of oncoming headlights. The ambulance swerved, narrowly missing Garrett, and skidded to a stop.

"Jesus, Mary, and Joseph!" Brice jumped out of the vehicle and ran over to Garrett.

Garrett collapsed into Brice's arms. "I fucked up," he sobbed. "I've lost her for good. Addie never wants to see me again." Pulling out the broken necklace, Garrett held it up and then broke down again. He was inconsolable.

Brice pulled Garrett into an embrace and held him. He hated seeing a grown man cry and searched for the right words to say. "Time will be your best friend, me dear man. This 'ere broken necklace, like ya broken 'eart, can be fixed. But first, we need to

mend ya and remold ya back into the man God created ya to be."
Silhouetted by the ambulance lamp lights, Brice kissed the top
of Garrett's head.

A light snow began to fall.

# 15

*Dear Blue,*

*Today is day #1012, leaving me with only 83 days left of nursing school. Looking back on 1916, it seems like it was a blur of activity. My marks on my monthly report card are continuing to improve. Cleanliness, Work – A-; Cleanliness, Person – A-; Reliability, Patients – B+; Reliability, Records – B; Economy – B; Adaptability – A+; Observation – B+; Industry – B; Disposition – A; Executive Ability – B+.*

*Nurse Hartman is giving me more responsibility to teach and train the freshman class of nurses. Although challenging at times, I'm enjoying that aspect of my role. I don't know if it is the stress of school—the written, practical, or oral exams—that have my nerves out of whack, but there are days when I don't feel good, or that I don't have enough energy to take another step. I have lost thirteen pounds to date. Nurse Hartman and others are expressing their concerns about my health and well-being. I am brushing their remarks aside, letting their worry swirl and eventually dissipate like the smoke from a burned-out candle. I'm just fine and must keep putting one foot in front of the other. I'm a survivor, walking through life, just trying to figure it all out.*

Addie fidgeted in the oversized chair in the nursing dorm library. *Blue, with 1916 drawing to a close, highlights from this past year included the wedding of Nurse Hartman to Alan Waxman on Valentine's Day. While they had a civil ceremony at the courthouse, I believe that our surprise reception for them at the hospital really bowled them over. I'm glad that the two of them found love. Speaking of such matters, I pray to God every night for peace and clarity, because I'm still angry at Garrett. I can't believe he was such an ass and I don't know how to forgive him. On the other hand, I think I have amorous feelings for Randall. We have a lot in common with our work at the hospital. But, I'm not sure if it will amount to anything. Sometimes, I feel like I have a complete handle on my life. And then there are times when I feel like hurling my pencil across the room. I get so tired of trying to make sense of anything anymore. With no one to kiss tonight but my reflection in the mirror, happy New Year's Eve to me!* Addie drew a heart.

Dropping down a few spaces, she drew a line across the page, writing and underlining, *Things to look forward to in 1917.*

*Blue, I'm looking forward to moving into the new Sacred Heart nursing dorm designated for senior students and unmarried nurses. It's located across the street from the main hospital on Spring Street. We've unanimously dubbed it the 'Scott House' in honor of Nurse Clair Scott. Mr. Alexander has commissioned a brass plaque to be made bearing that name and established date, 1917, and it will be hung on the front of the house next week at the ribbon-cutting ceremony. Speaking of new buildings, Alexander Hall will also open later this spring. More importantly, I can't believe I'm embarking on my senior year! Finally!! I am really looking forward to graduating and can't wait to see what's in store for me. Surely to goodness, no further disasters, relationship or otherwise, await me!* Addie drew a smiley face. *With that said, Blue, there are rumors that this country may enter the war. What does that mean for us? Only time will tell.*

# 16

Alan rolled over in bed and put his arm around Lena. She stirred, caught between the blurry worlds of dreaming and awakening. He moved her dark brown braid off her shoulder and kissed her neck softly. "Happy anniversary, my love. It's time to rise and shine."

Lena jabbered nonsense.

Alan continued to caress her body from under the covers before he ran his hand down to the edge of her nightgown and slipped it underneath.

Lena slapped at his hand, pulling the sheets up around her shoulders.

Amused, Alan reattempted to awaken Lena but was met with resistance. She preferred to remain in a state of slumber. Undeterred, he whispered in her ear again, "It's our first anniversary and I have an unwrapped gift for you." He scooted his body closer to hers.

Without opening her eyes, Lena tried to shake the fog. "I still don't know how you do it."

"Do what?"

"You manage to awaken every morning, alert, bright-eyed, and bushy-tailed." Lena rolled on to her back. "I need time to bloom." Lena drifted back into a dream, snoring softly.

Alan watched her chest rise and fall as he wrapped his arms around her. "It's time to get up, my love. If you don't, we're going to be late for work."

"Five more minutes," Lena groaned.

"Alright, then. Stay right where you are. I'm going to rustle up some vittles for us so we can have breakfast in bed."

One eye popped open. "Did you just say 'rustle' and 'vittles' in the same sentence? I must still be dreaming that I married a handsome and rugged cowboy on a vast ranch in Montana."

Alan smacked her bottom as he got out of bed. "Scrambled or over easy?" He picked up his glasses off the bedside table, wrapping the metal temple tips around his ears.

"Over easy with buttered toast, please, my dear." Lena watched him put on his bathrobe and slippers and walk towards the door. "Happy anniversary and happy Valentine's Day to you, too. I can't believe how the year has flown by." Lena grabbed her pillow, placing it behind her back. "How would you like to have dessert after breakfast?"

Alan looked back. "I'd love dessert after breakfast."

### WEDNESDAY NIGHT, SIXTH WARD

"Would anyone like more dessert before I put it away?" Opal inquired throughout the first floor of the Scott House. Heads shook as she went from room to room, from the front porch area to the dining room to the back of the house, finding many of the students buried in their textbooks, studying for finals. She peered into the expansive living room. Addie, dressed in a pale pink kimono, was curled up on the cream-colored sofa and writing in her diary. The white-washed brick fireplace was aglow. "Do you want any more banana pudding?"

Addie waved off the offer. "No, I'm good. No more nanner puddin' for me, thank you."

Opal punched her fists into her hips. "Addie, please don't take offense when I say this to you, but I've been watching you waste away this past year. I've watched a healthy-looking young lady give way to sunken cheeks and a sallow appearance."

"It's none of your business what I look like!" Addie snapped.

"Hey!" Opal tried not to take offense. Addie's demeanor and appearance had changed over their junior year. Struggling and weighing whether or not to say something, Opal finally said, "Addie, I'm your best friend. I know you're heartbroken over your fight with Garrett last year, but you have got to move on." Opal walked over to Addie and sank to her knees in front of her. She placed her hands over Addie's. "I love you as if you were my own sister. If I didn't care about you, I wouldn't have said a word. But I do care about you and you can't let a boy steal your spirit away."

Addie hung her head, embarrassed it had come to this. She let her auburn hair fall over her face, hoping to hide her shame.

Opal brushed the hair from Addie's face. "I'm glad to see you pouring out your soul on these pages. But you also need to know that you can talk to me, anytime, about anything. I feel like you are shutting me out. You've been shutting down and I can't stand by and watch you do this to yourself. We've all noticed a change in you, but when concerns are raised with you, they fall on deaf ears. You refuse to hear the truth. We're all worried about you."

Addie raised her head, and then lowered it again, unable to look Opal in the eyes. *I hate myself for feeling like this. I'm so embarrassed. I try to look for the light, but I feel like I'm drowning in the dark. How could Garrett leave me alone like this? That bastard! I hate him.*

"Look, I know that Nurse Hartman has been keeping you extremely busy and grooming you to become Nurse Scott's replacement. But you've got to take heed to my instructions when I say that you have got to eat and take care of yourself."

Addie protested, "I do eat. I feel like I eat all the time. I can't manage to eat enough and when I do, I feel sick."

Opal took a seat next to Addie and put her arm around her.

Addie rested her head on Opal's shoulder. "I'm exhausted. I feel tired all the time."

"Maybe it's not the stress of school and work, but perhaps you have an underlying physiological condition that is making you feel this way? Have you ever considered that?"

Addie, shocked by the remark, reared back. "What? Like I have a disease or something?"

"I don't know. I just know you don't look or act like the same person that I knew last year and, well, perhaps…."

"Spit it out."

"Perhaps, you need to ask Nurse Hartman about scheduling a physical with Dr. Williams."

"And, when am I supposed to fit that into my schedule? We're in the last weeks of our senior year, cramming for finals, and getting ready to graduate at the end of next month."

"Carve out the time for yourself and make the time, for goodness sake."

Susan walked into the room wearing a camera strapped around her neck. "Hey! I hate to interrupt, but I wanted to snap a few candid photographs for our scrapbook." Raising her camera up to her eyes, she commanded, "Look natural, like you two are busy studying, or finding the cure for smallpox or something important like that."

The two put their heads together, looked up, and smiled. *Click.* The lens captured their image on the negative.

"Perfect. Thanks!"

"Nurse Kessler, you make the perfect historian for our class," Opal praised.

"I love photography and especially like capturing our moments in time." She fiddled with the camera and flipped a silver lever to advance the film. "It will give us something to look back on and cherish when we're old and gray. If anything, I'm documenting and telling our story, not with words, but with pictures."

"Speaking of documenting, and at your convenience, would you sign my autograph book?" Opal pointed at the coffered white ceiling. "My book is sitting on my desk upstairs."

"Sure thing!"

Addie chimed in, "Would you sign mine, too? It's also sitting on my desk on top of my *Principles and Practice of Nursing* textbook."

"Will do. That was such a nice gesture of Nurse Hartman to buy us all books so that we can get everyone's inscriptions before we graduate. I plan on getting some of the physician's signatures tomorrow." Susan turned to leave. "I'll leave my book out on my desk so you can sign mine, too."

"We sure will. Thanks, Susan," they replied.

Susan threw her hand up and waved, disappearing around the corner.

Opal rose to her feet and pulled out a small red envelope from her blue kimono pocket. She handed it to Addie. "A Valentine for my Valentine." She kissed the top of Addie's head. "I'm heading up to bed. Don't dawdle and promise me that you'll make an appointment to see Dr. Williams, sometime soon."

Pained with regret, Addie chided herself for being so self-absorbed. "I'm so sorry. I don't have one to give to you. I completely forgot about today being Valentine's Day. I spent the entire day in Nurse Hartman's office helping her iron out the curriculum for the next cohort of nursing students that will be enrolled at Sacred Heart and Alexander Hall. We kept going around and around about how to incorporate the topic of birth control, a new concept introduced last year by a nurse by the name of Margaret Sanger. Lena wasn't sure if your dad would be receptive to the idea since he's Catholic."

"You mean since *we're* Catholic?"

"Of, course. You know what I meant." Addie scratched her head. "I can't believe I overlooked Valentine's Day. I wondered why Mr. Waxman and Lena were all giddy and glowing every time they saw each other today. I just thought it was because they were celebrating their first-year anniversary."

"Who would have ever predicted that the two of them would get married? I guess tragic events have a way of binding people together." Opal tilted her head to the side, glancing through a part in the sheer curtains at Lena's office window across the street. "But, now that I see them as a couple, they make the perfect pair."

"I guess opposites do attract."

"Perhaps that's what Randall sees in you?"

"What? That I'm pure grit and he's all refined?" Addie's lip curled; a grin emerged. She grabbed a small round yellow pillow off of the couch and threw it at Opal.

Opal caught it and threw it back. "There she is. She's not dead, after all," she joked.

# 17

Edward's proposal and final contract with the Atlanta City Council for Alexander Hall, the Negro hospital, had to meet three criteria: 1) The hospital had to be constructed on a separate street and have a different street address from Sacred Heart Hospital, 2) The "sister" hospital had to operate under an independent name and have its own construction timeline, and 3) Underground tunnels needed to be built, connecting the medical facilities and nursing schools, thereby optimizing operational efficiencies.

Alexander Hall was located around the corner from Sacred Heart on Alexander Street. Brick walls and landscaping gave the property its own unique appearance. The three tunnels, the Greene tunnel that joined Sacred Heart Hospital to its nursing school and the soon-to-be-named and dedicated Gray and Goode tunnels, which connected Sacred Heart to Alexander Hall and the Colored nursing school respectively, completed the underground triangular connection. Medical staff, employees, and nursing students could flow freely between the buildings without mixing with the general population.

One day, Edward knew, the entire medical complex would become integrated. It was just a matter of time. That was his ultimate dream. He looked to his left and smiled. In Clyde's old spot sat a man appointed by Edward last year by the name of Dr. Moses Bishop. He was Dr. William's counterpart, the surgical and medical director for Alexander Hall. Throughout 1916, the leadership team and the board approved Dr. Bishop's appointments, including Dr. Kenneth Hale, originally from New York and a graduate of Meharry Medical College in Nashville, to cover the maternity and pediatric wards. Dr. Abel Wright, a graduate of Howard University, would supervise the general surgical and TB units. Collectively, the new physicians would tend to the needs in the emergency department until such time that additional staff was warranted. Nurse Hartman appointed nurse Cela Hardy to assist her in teaching and governing the new cohort of incoming Colored nurses. Dr. Morgan Payne would continue to oversee the morgue, serving both hospitals' post-mortem needs.

Edward feared the days and months ahead. The City of Atlanta was on the verge of bankruptcy, unable to pay staff salaries. The town's infrastructure was crumbling like the cobblestone roads in desperate need of maintenance. The public schools and Grady, the city's municipal hospital, were falling into a state of disrepair. The unknown kept him awake most nights. Last night wasn't any different as he mulled over how to make some sobering announcements this morning. He wished he would have asked Ms. Maybelle to smuggle in a bottle of champagne to serve with their orange juice. Edward was beginning to regret backing Governor Harris and his decision to pass prohibition throughout the state of Georgia two months earlier. His throat was growing as dry as the alcohol sales. He gulped down his fruit juice. "Oliver, what updates to do you have for us about the grand opening ceremony for Alexander Hall next month?"

Oliver pulled out his notes. "The opening of Alexander Hall will be a beacon of hope for many in this city in light of the uncertainties ahead." He looked at Dr. Bishop and then at Edward. "We contacted the Governor's and Mayor Candler's offices. They have been busy with General Wood and his staff these past few months, scouting for cantonment sites, and my requests in writing and via phone calls to invite them to speak at the grand opening have gone unreturned."

"General Leonard Wood, like the Chief of Staff for the United States Army and former Tech grad, General Wood? The first 'Wrambling Wreck' to cross the goal line in Athens?" Shelby inquired.

"Yes, he's one and the same." Edward held up his hand. "It's alright, Oliver. I'll reach out to our state representative and ward alderman. The governor and mayor have got their hands full with…." He struggled with his next words.

Dr. Bishop reached out and patted Edward on the shoulder. His rich deep baritone voice commanded complete authority. The graying hair around his temples brought years of wisdom with his words. "Edward, it's alright to tell the group what we already suspect to be true."

Lena coaxed, "Go on, Edward. We're healthcare professionals and we're trained to be ready for anything that comes our way."

Tears welled. Edward rested his elbows on the conference table and clasped his hands. "I've been in close contact with my friends at the state and in Washington D.C.. It breaks my heart to tell you in the strictest confidence that our country is on the verge of going to war."

Alan reached under the table and took Lena's hand.

Edward continued, "Georgia is going to play a major role, not only in the preparation and training of troops. If you haven't heard already, Atlanta has been selected as the southeast headquarters for the Red Cross. We're going to have to make the necessary preparations ourselves." Edward pointed at Shelby. "Son, I'm going to need for you to work with Joshua to plot out a vegetable garden in the back of the property. We're going to have to grow enough vegetables to be self-sufficient and keep our staff and patients fed for the next three years. I'm also going to ask you to work with him to triple the size of the medicinal garden so we have enough plants to make medications for both hospitals, too."

Shelby's eyes widened. "Who will help me tend the gardens?"

Lena jumped in. "Cela and I can ask the nurses to help when they can, and we can even ask able-bodied patients for their assistance as they rehab and recover from their maladies."

Alan gestured to the rest of his colleagues. "We'll all pitch in and help."

"You can count on all of us," Dr. Williams said, reassuringly.

Shelby, hit by a wave of nausea, asked, "Edward, what happens if I get drafted?"

"It's my understanding that the first phase of the draft will call for men twenty-one to thirty years of age to register."

Shelby breathed a sigh of relief. "Thank God! I turned thirty-one in November. Talk about dodging a bullet!"

"Literally!" Edward forced a laugh to lighten the mood. "The city's bacteriologist, who is also the chairman of the cabinet committee on crops, has been put in charge of turning private and public parks, abandoned properties, and the like into what they are dubbing, 'Victory Gardens.' Everyone across the country is going to have toe the line and help any way they can, especially if our young men are going to be heading to training camps and our national guard is mobilized. I speculate they will begin to set sail across the Atlantic by June at the earliest."

Dr. Williams did a quick assessment of the ages of his doctors. "Edward, all of the men are over the age of thirty. Dr. Springer, like Dr. Maddox, has recently crossed the threshold of his thirty-first birthday last month."

"Thank you, Dr. Williams. That is a relief, a temporary one for now." Edward turned to Moses. "What about your team?"

"Both Dr. Hale and Dr. Wright are well beyond their thirties."

"Well, now that we have concluded that our medical staff will be stable for the foreseeable future until Uncle Sam raises the age limit and comes calling for them, we're going to have to elevate our levels of nursing training." Edward rubbed his forehead. His thoughts raced. "Dr. Williams, Dr. Bishop, and Lena, I need for the three of you to work together to make sure our nurses can assist you with more procedures so they can provide a higher level of care. There may come a day when I won't have enough doctors in-house. I anticipate that we may encounter patients with a higher level of acuity. I'd rather be proactive and over-prepare than sit idly by and watch us get crushed by an avalanche of issues." Edward penned a note to himself. "I also can't control what I don't know or don't see coming. I need for all of you to keep in close contact with your colleagues across the country. Share with me any new trends or strategies you glean in your conversations. We're going to have to band together with our sister hospitals in the city, across Georgia, and perhaps in the border states." Edward stopped to make another note. "Lena, will you reach out to the other nursing superintendents and develop a communication tree from which we will take point? As a hospital system ,should any one of us become close to maxing out our capacity for patients, resources, or materials, we have the ability to reach out to help each other."

"Will do." Lena scribbled a reminder on her agenda.

"I'll reach out to the other CEOs, too," said Edward.

Alan jotted in his notebook. "Edward, I've made a note to myself to order more supplies that don't have a shelf-life and to have the McDaniel brothers take inventory of everything we have in storage in the garage."

Edward, pleased that he didn't replace Clyde's position in anticipation of conserving expenses, had promoted Alan in January of last year to chief operating officer in addition to his responsibilities maintaining the accounting ledgers. Although Alan was more comfortable relating to numbers than people, he was doing a great job managing the daily operations of the various departments. "Thank you, Alan. I can always count on you to make sure we can account for every penny. Effective immediately, we're really going to have to tighten our belts and be resourceful."

Heads around the table nodded.

Edward clapped his hands together. "Well, we've been invited to the dance and it's our job to put our best foot forward and try our damnedest to not step on each other's toes or fall down. And, as my daddy use to say, 'Let's get to it and just do it!'"

MONDAY AFTERNOON, MARCH 5, 1917, FIRST WARD

"You asked to see me?" Moira sashayed into Charlie Finch's office, wearing a kelly green V-neck dress with a beige lace insert covering her décolleté, and took a seat. Her heavily-teased blonde hair was secured in a bun. Two tightly curled tendrils rested on her heavily blushed cheeks. Worry washed over Charlie's face as he eyed her up and down. "What is it, Charlie?" She patted at her dress. "Is it my dress? I'm choosing to wear more modest apparel now that the city is in a somber place. And, I'm trying not to upstage the ladies at the Junior League. I'm working hard to blend in. In fact, I've got to be uptown for our meeting within the hour. Did you know that I am hob-knobbing with the crème de la crème of Atlanta's social scene?" Moira placed her hand over her heart. "I, Moira, a.k.a. Hetta, have been embraced as one of their own! Can you believe that? I have finally arrived!"

"I hate to burst your bubble, but I regret to inform you that Sam and the *Atlanta Dispatch* board have asked me to pull your 'Hey, Hetta!' column and terminate your services effective immediately."

"WHAT?" Moira, horrified, jumped to her feet. "YOU can't do that." She pointed her finger everywhere—at Charlie, at the wall, at the ceiling. "THEY can't do that!"

"We did. They did. You're done. Your column is getting replaced. We need the extra space in the newspaper for...."

"For what?" *Stomp! Stomp! Stomp!* Moira pounded the heel of her shoe into the floorboards. "For what?" She glared at him. Charlie remained silent. "Oh, for the love of God! Why won't you answer me?" Moira pouted and then shouted, "I'M PACKING MY BAGS! DON'T EXPECT TO SEE ME TONIGHT WHEN YOU GET HOME!"

As she pivoted on her heels, Charlie caught a glimpse of the large, faux jewel encrusted, fan-style comb stuck in her twisted bleached-blonde strands, reminding him of the early days when he thought that particular hairstyle mimicked a headless peacock as her head was buried between his legs. Adding more fuel to the fire, he chuckled softly to himself.

"FUCK YOU, CHARLIE!" Moira's face crimsoned as she exited his office with a slam of the door, as if to put an extra exclamation point on her level of frustration.

Charlie heard Moira's screams and rants through the walls as she made her way down the hall and stormed into Sam's office. Charlie, proud he remained mum, had been sworn to secrecy for fear of losing his own job. He was told, actually threatened, to not to utter the 'war' word yet. "Save that word for the printed paper," said Sam. "War sells papers. We're going to need additional space for announcements about the military's plans, the upcoming draft, community supply drives, and hold space for articles from governmental officials. In the upcoming months, families are going to want to know the play-by-play status of our country's accomplishments, human losses, victories, and defeats. We're going to have to compete for the public's attention. They will get their news by word of mouth, telegraph, letters, and the papers. The *Atlanta Dispatch* is about to play a very vital role.

People will save copies of our papers for posterity. Our paper will be documenting an epic event, one for the history books."

# 18

Addie swallowed hard, fighting off the feeling of being car sick, as she jostled between Opal, Lexie, and Susan in the back seat during the caravan cab ride over to the Sacred Heart graduation and pinning ceremony. The combination of stale air and the building body heat between them—all dressed in their navy capes, starched white caps, and uniforms—made the last half-mile nearly unbearable. Perspiration beaded on her upper lip. The driver talked non-stop, rattling off historical facts about the various buildings they passed en-route to their final destination. As they pulled up to the Gothic-style First Methodist Church on Peachtree Street, he informed them that the church had been constructed out of Stone Mountain granite in 1903 and that the silver and brass bell remained untouched and was not destroyed and melted down like the others during the Civil War during Sherman's burning of the city on his March to the Sea. When the church relocated to this corner from its original location, the square bell tower was erected to house the precious relic.

Addie, anxious to be the first to exit the vehicle, hit her cap on the door frame. Opal, right on the heels of Addie, did the same. Susan laughed, ducking lower to clear the door.

"Look at you applying Nurse Hartman's classroom lessons to be observant and aware of your surroundings," Addie remarked while she and Opal straightened their caps.

The young women thanked the cabbie and joined the others who were filing out onto the side lawn of the church, gathering around Nurse Hartman.

Susan spotted her parents walking from their car. She jumped up and down, waving and hollering, "Hey, Mother! Hey, Father!"

Nurse Hartman snapped her fingers and pointed at Susan. "Nurse Kessler. Please contain yourself and exude the professionalism and poise I demand from you, especially on this very special day." Lena counted caps. Everyone was accounted for. "Ladies, I will ask for your silence from this moment forward. You will form a single file line behind me in alphabetical order, just like we practiced at the Scott House the other day. Printed programs have already been placed in the hymnal racks. A box of candles can be found at the end of the church bench. Go ahead and remove your capes, and hand them to the ladies as you enter this side door." Lena pointed toward the wooden door on her left. "They will take them and hang them up for us. Be sure to retrieve them after the ceremony. Following the service, the taxis will take us back to the nursing dorm, where a reception for you and your families will be hosted on the first floor and in the garden." Appreciating the cloudless blue sky, she lifted her hands to the heavens. "We thank you, God, for this glorious day."

Addie noticed Lena's eyes moisten and she found herself fighting back her own tears, too. Addie was relieved that she no longer felt sick to her stomach, sad that she didn't have any family to celebrate this special day with and yet proud of the accomplishment. *And, then there is the empty hole in my heart left by Garrett.* Addie filed behind Lexie and entered the church.

Once inside, the nurses weaved their way up to the narthex. When the string quartet, the same one that had played at Emiline's birthday party, began "Water Music Suite: Air," by George Frideric Handel, Lena led them down the center aisle to the front pew, where they took their seats. Some pulled out the program, reviewing the order for the service. Others glanced around at the packed room, filled with family, friends, and Sacred Heart staff. When the song concluded, two pipers emerged in the doorway of the narthex, striking up "Amazing Grace," which echoed throughout the chamber. Moved by the nostalgia of the affair, Addie looked back, shocked to see it was the McDaniel twins, Tim and Jim. She nudged Lexie, who elbowed Opal. All three tried to sneak a peek at Sacred Heart's talented ambulance drivers. There wasn't a dry eye to be found following their performance.

"Please stand." The minister gestured.

The pipe organ started the hymn, "There is a Healing Branch that Grows," in the key of B major. The crowd sang all four verses. "There is a healing branch that grows, where every bitter Marah flows; this is our health-renewing tree. 'I am the Lord that healeth thee.'" They concluded with, "Here is a great Physician still, whose hand has all its ancient skill; at His command our pains will flee, 'I am the Lord that healeth thee.'"

The minister motioned for the audience to be seated. His invocation followed.

After a short prayer, the crowd replied, "Amen."

Edward rose from an adjacent pew, taking his place behind the lectern. Wearing his finest black Sunday suit, he tugged at his lapels. "Ladies and gentlemen, this is quite a special occasion. It is the inaugural graduation and pinning ceremony for the first cohort of Sacred Heart nursing students. I am proud to say that my daughter, Opal, is amongst this group." He winked and blew her a kiss. "Your mother and I are very proud of you." He waved his hand over the guests. "As, I imagine, are the rest of you who have entrusted us with your daughters, to educate them to be the best registered nurses this institution has ever seen." A few people laughed, finding the humor in his comment. "Yes, they are the first cohort this hospital has ever turned out, but Nurse Hartman, Dr. John Williams, our medical director, and I are extremely proud of each and every one of them for passing the strictest of tests and oral exams during this three-year program." Edward beamed with pride as he looked at each student. "Today signifies a beginning, a new chapter for each one of them. Only God knows where their paths will take them, but they will go equipped with the necessary skills to handle any kind of situation." The thought of war began to creep into his mind. He dismissed it, afraid that the expression on his face would show his concern and worry. "As the founder and CEO of Sacred Heart and soon-to-be Alexander Hall, it is an honor and a privilege to design a place where we can take care of Georgia citizens at the time in their lives when they need the greatest care, when they are at their most vulnerable, and when they are at their weakest. Patients and their families trust us with their lives. It is my solemn promise to you that we deliver the highest quality medical care. This past year, our medical leadership team even provided services to a few of our community's social settlements." The crowd erupted in applause. "We go where the need is greatest. It is our duty; it is our ca-ca-lling," Edward stammered; his voice cracked. He bit his bottom lip and composed himself. "I would like to conclude with a wonderful Chinese proverb, one that I learned from one of my employees, Mr. Wu. 'If you want happiness for an hour, take a nap. If you want happiness for a day, go fishing. If you want happiness for a month, get married. If you want happiness for a year, inherit a fortune. If you want happiness for a lifetime, help someone else.'" The crowd clapped vigorously as Edward took his seat, passing Lena on her way to the podium.

"Good morning. My name is Lena Hartman." Although legally it was Lena Waxman, she and Allen thought it would create less confusion at the hospital if she continued to use her maiden name. However, while they were out in Atlanta's social scene, she was proud to be introduced as Mrs. Alan Waxman. "Educating and training these lovely ladies was a team undertaking. I would like to thank Mr. Alexander, Dr. Williams, Dr. Springer, Dr. Payne, and Shelby Maddox for assisting me in creating a rigorous curriculum. While these nurses have endured many sleepless nights studying and working, they are being rewarded for their hard work and tenacity today. Their greatest reward will come when they are taking their final breaths in this world, reflecting on a life well-lived, one of service to others." Lena looked over at Allen and smiled. "Life brings the unexpected. As healthcare professionals, it is our job to be prepared to handle anything. It is my job as their instructor to prepare these nurses for life. And, as I have worked with each student, they, in turn, have taught me about myself or have expanded my way of thinking. When we educate another, we both grow through the mutual experience of learning. We can't grow if we aren't courageous. And, before you are seven very courageous women." Lena's remarks were met with hearty applause. "This expansive world of ours is changing and evolving. Why, even in parts of Canada and most recently in Russia, women have been granted the right to vote. Perhaps we'll live to see that opportunity for us in America, too." A few people clapped, some gasped and grumbled. "One can always hope. With that said, I, too, will end my remarks with a lovely Chinese proverb. 'If you are planning for a year, sow rice; if you are planning for a decade, plant trees; if you are planning for a lifetime, educate people.'" A few male and female attendees, the leadership team, and the nursing class gave Lena a standing ovation; the rest remained seated, politely showing their praise. Lena faced the students. "Ladies, please stand and line up over here." Lena pointed to her left.

Edward and Dr. Williams also made their way up front. John carried a stack of graduation certificates while Edward held a silver rectangular platter lined in red velvet containing nursing pins. They took their place on Lena's right.

Lena picked up one of the pins and held it up. "The entire leadership team chose the hospital's colors and the thoughtful design of the Sacred Heart and Alexander Hall nursing pin. It is circular, representing that our quest for knowledge and the pursuit of excellence is endless. The navy outer ring is inscribed with the words, 'Sacred Heart Hospital' at the top and 'School of Nursing' at the bottom. The first cohorts of both nursing schools will be the only ones to have two inlaid diamonds on that outer ring. One sits at three o'clock, which is representative of the time that Jesus took his last breath, dying on the cross for our sins, and the other at nine o'clock, which symbolizes Jesus' passing in the ninth hour in accordance to how time was told in those days. A white cross pattée rests on an18-carat gold background. The arms are convex and curved at the outer edges and narrow toward the center where a red heart is positioned. The year, 1917, is embossed in gold inside it. Two raised gold rays radiate out from the heart on each of the four arms of the cross, signifying Jesus' Sacred Heart, His eternal love for us. The color navy blue represents the healing power of God, as referenced in the Bible. Gold symbolizes courage, compassion, and illumination. White means purity, light, and safety." She lowered her hand.

That was the organist's cue to start, "Balm in Gilead," sung by Dr. Moses Bishop, baritone. His voice resonated throughout the room as he bellowed from the balcony.

Belle spoke in a hushed tone in Addie's ear. "I had no idea Dr. Bishop could sing. Did you?"

Addie marveled at the rich timbre of his voice and shook her head. Goosebumps raised on her forearms when Moses belted out the last refrain. "There is a balm in Gilead, to make the wounded whole. There is a balm in Gilead to heal the sin sick soul."

Lena dabbed her eyes. "I'd like to present to you the Graduating Class of 1917." She called out the first name. "Opal Alexander."

Tears trickled down Edward's face as Lena secured the pin to Opal's uniform.

"I love you, Daddy," Opal mouthed before shaking Nurse Hartman's hand. She walked over to her father and pecked him lightly on the cheek. The silence was broken when Trudy blew her nose into her handkerchief while Pearl appeared uninterested and inconvenienced and Trip doodled on his program with a pencil.

Dr. Williams handed Opal her graduation certificate. "Congratulations, Nurse Alexander, on a job well done!" He, too, shook her hand.

Addie followed Lexie. She scanned the crowd for familiar faces, spotting a few from the hospital, including Randall, Shelby, Mr. and Mrs. Wu, the McDaniel brothers. Even Joshua and Maybelle attended, sitting in the balcony next to Dr. Bishop. Lena affixed Addie's pin. The shadow of a man in the narthex caught Addie's eye, but then vanished.

"Congratulations, Nurse Engel." Lena shook Addie's hand.

Edward added, "We are so proud of you and I look forward to working more closely with you in the coming year."

Addie allowed herself to smile and relish the moment. *I have worked so hard to be right where I am, right now. Maw, Paw, look at me now. Can you believe what your baby girl has accomplished? I feel the warmth of your love in my heart and that of Mrs. Gray, Sissy, and Ben's, too.* Addie wanted to shout out, *I did it!* Instead, she moved down the line to Dr. Williams, who handed Addie her diploma. She returned to the pew and continued to watch and silently cheer on her fellow classmates. She glanced back at Randall and caught him staring at her. He smiled and gave her a low-profile wave. Flustered, Addie faced front, feeling hives breaking out on her chest and neck. *Oh, dear Lord. What the heck is wrong with me? Why can't I return his affections?*

After the last name was called, the minister gave a brief benediction before the organist struck up the last hymn, "O Jesus, I Have Promised." The congregation sang all five verses. During the last verse, the students processed to the front, each picking up a white candle out of a box at the end of the bench. When the song finished, Lena lit her candle from a nearby candelabra, one of a pair positioned on either side of the alter decorated with white lilies, baby's breath, and greenery. The lights were turned off; only the sanctuary candles burned bright. Lena approached Opal, lit her candle, and took her place beside her. Opal lit Lexie's, and Lexie lit Addie's.

After all were illuminated, Lena spoke. "We will be the first Sacred Heart nursing class to recite the Florence Nightingale Pledge together." Nurse Hartman cued the ladies to begin.

All spoke in unison, having memorized and practiced the oath months before the big day. "I solemnly pledge myself before God and in the presence of this assembly to pass my life in purity and to practice my profession faithfully. I shall abstain from whatever is deleterious and mischievous, and shall not take or knowingly administer any harmful drug. I shall do all in my power to maintain and elevate the standard of my profession and will hold in confidence all personal matters committed to my keeping and all family affairs coming to my knowledge in the practice of my calling. I shall be loyal to my work and devoted towards the welfare of those committed to my care."

Together, they lifted their candles in the air and held them there for a count of ten seconds, before slowly lowering them and blowing them out. Syncopated sniffling was heard throughout the sanctuary. Nurse Hartman turned. All filed out behind her cloaked in darkness and in silence. All had heard God's calling. All were ready to serve.

## SATURDAY AFTERNOON, SIXTH WARD

Addie sat on the garden bench in front of the Sacred Heart water fountain, taking a break from the family-filled reception and festivities. Mesmerized by the sound of the falling water, she watched and marveled at the dancing drops cascading down in their own rhythm. All were unique, varying in size and shape, and yet all became one body of liquid once they splashed down in the pool. The sun warmed her face as it started on its westward journey. *I feel the warmth of your love, Maw. It feels like I have my face in your sweet hands.* Overcome with emotion, she stood, turned, and collided with Randall, who was carrying two glasses of fruit punch. The beverage spilled all over the front of Addie's uniform.

"Oh, my heavens!" Randall, apologetic, set the glasses down on the seat of the bench and ripped out his hanky, handing it to her. "I am so sorry. Please accept my sincerest apologies."

Taking it, she blotted and brushed at the damp stains. "Please, don't worry. I'm the one who should apologize. I'm the klutz who ran into you."

"Here, let me help you." He put his hand on hers and slowly slid the hanky out of her hand. Their eyes locked. "I'm so proud of you, Addie. You have achieved something great. An education is something that no one can take away from you. As I sat through the ceremony, I was moved by the power and reverence of it all. I could only imagine that your family and Mrs. Gray were smiling down on you. I know they would be so proud of you, too." He searched her green eyes for a reply, a spark, but they remained unchanged.

"Thank you so much for attending. It meant the world to all of us that some of our doctors were in the audience." *Should I inquire about Garrett? Did he know it was my graduation day? Was he the shadow in the narthex?*

Before Addie could formulate her next words, Randall's next words took her by surprise. "Actually, I was just there for you, Addie. Only for you."

Flustered, Addie was taken aback. She smiled a polite smile, unsure of what to say. *Oh, God! What am I supposed to say to that kind of remark?*

"Have you had a chance to read your autograph book yet?"

"Actually, no. I've been so busy studying for finals, helping Nurse Hartman, or working that I've not had the time or energy to go through it."

"Speaking of energy, how are you feeling? I've been concerned about you."

Addie's smile disappeared. She abruptly let go of his hand and the cloth. Feelings of anger and denial rose as she spewed, "What? Did Opal put you up to this? You two better stay out of my business. I am just fine. I've just been working hard, and this past year has been a bit stressful."

"Whoa! Don't snap at me. I'm simply a concerned friend. I know last year was tough on you and Garrett...."

"Don't mention his name to me ever again." Addie wanted to burst into tears. *Not here. Not now. There is nothing wrong with you.* "If you'll excuse me, I need to go back to the Scott House and change." She flew out of the garden and up the back stairs of the hospital.

"Addie, I'm so sorry," he called out. Afraid he was going to draw attention to himself, he lowered his voice and muttered to himself as he picked up the glasses and walked away. "Opal didn't ask me to talk with you. I'm just worried about you. There is something terribly wrong with you."

Filled with anguish, Addie fled to her second-floor bedroom in Scott House and threw herself down on her twin bed. *What the heck is wrong with me? Why can't I face the simple truth that I have lost weight and look sickly? Do I really look that bad? I am tired all the time. My body aches. Maybe they are right? I need to pull myself together. I feel like I am falling apart. This is supposed to be one of the happiest days of my life. Why can't I allow myself to enjoy it?* Addie rolled over, dried her tears on the backs of her hands, and reached over to pull her five-by-seven autograph book off her desk. She opened the first page and began reading.

> *Evening "Cot" Tales – to my roommate and best friend*
> *Now that you've come to the end of your training days,*
> *You are forever changed, a profession gained,*
> *May it find you happier in every way,*
> *Our friendship in the coming years sustained.*
> *When the time may come when we're apart,*
> *And there'll be no time for our meeting,*
> *Please know you're sitting pretty way down in my heart.*
> *Good luck, and much love and success to you.*
>
> *—Opal Alexander*

Addie turned the page.

*Wishing a star student good health, much happiness, and the best of luck.*

*Here's to all three!*

*—Dr. John Alexander*

On the opposite page, it read,

*To know you is to love you.*

*I loved seeing your smile and positive attitude even when everything was going wrong.*

*I especially loved hearing your "farm tales."*

*Good luck to you, Addie. I will miss you.*

*Lexie Carmichael*

*Addie turned the page.*

*Here's to a choice nurse.*

*—Dr. Morgan Payne*

Below that said,

*I enjoyed our late-night dances in the Bawl Room! I will miss you.*

*—Susan Kessler*

Across the page, the Wus wrote a lovely quote from a Chinese proverb.

*"Teachers open the door, but you must walk through it yourself." Addie, you are taking the next steps through that door and we believe in you.*

*Best wishes from Mr. and Mrs. Wu*

While scanning the entry on the other side of the page, Addie burst into laughter.

*Do you remember that night in OB?*

*I sat at the head and gave the gas.*

*You stood at the knees of the obese lass.*
*Little Miss. Esposito in mild chagrin,*
*Gave another shot of pituitrin.*
*The patient in tones quite wild,*
*Yelled out, twas her last child!*
*The child was born, the danger passed.*
*But, I surely thought we'd have to blast!*
*I will miss you and I wish you much success in your future*
*endeavors.*

—*Alice Fein*

Addie flipped through a few more pages, catching sight of Randall's familiar handwriting.

*Someone is praying for your success,*
*Someone is wishing you love and happiness.*
*Someone is hoping you goodness and cheer.*
*Someone is always here for you, far or near.*
*Someone cares about you until the end of his days.*
*Someone is thinking of you, always.*

—*Anonymous*

Addie shut the book and clutched it to her chest. *Oh my stars! Has Randall fallen in love with me?*

# 19

"I can't believe I have to write an article about a goddamn dead horse," Charlie growled at Sam while the two men conversed in the *Atlanta Dispatch* conference room. "Who really gives a flying flip about the passing of 'Old John'?"

Sam glanced down at the myriad of black and white photographs spread across the table. "He made his selection, picked up the photograph of Old John harnessed to the ambulance accompanied by his long-time driver in front of Grady Hospital. "I learned about that precious animal in a planning meeting for the new Kiwanis Club in Atlanta last month. That horse helped to save many lives in this city, racing up and down the street to carrying the infirmed to either be healed or to heaven. Old John marks the passage of time, now that Grady is getting motorized ambulances." Sam handed the picture to Charlie. "Use this one and have your 500-word article to me by the end of the day. And, don't forget to write a caption for the picture, too."

Charlie glanced down at his wristwatch. "I've got to get over to Alexander Hall's ribbon-cutting ceremony. Don't forget, I've got to cover that event, too."

"I'm aware." Sam was enjoying keeping Charlie on a short leash after learning about his aspirations to take his place one day, a secret shared by Moira during a "pillow talk" session.

"I'll have both pieces on your desk by five o'clock." Charlie excused himself and left. He was a bit grumpier these days, feeling like his days had lost their color, like he was living in a black and white photo like the one in his hand. He missed Moira terribly, knowing she'd broken many hearts when her suiters learned she had left "Gate City" for the "windy city" of Chicago a few weeks ago. "Just another breaking news day here in Atlanta," he grumbled under his breath as he meandered back to his office.

MONDAY EVENING, SECOND WARD

"Thank you for accepting my meeting invitation, Mr. Alexander." Shelby was comfortably seated in the zoo, sipping on a glass of bourbon.

Edward had twenty cases smuggled in from Kentucky by the McDaniel brothers in the Sacred Heart ambulance last month. "Please call me Edward, son." Edward sat back and readied himself.

"Yes, sir, er, Edward. Today was a banner day for you. Congratulations on the opening of Alexander Hall. The ceremony was beautiful, and I thought there was a great turn out." His glass began to shake in his hand. He rested it on his crossed leg. "I especially enjoyed Dr. Bishop's speech, and the brass band from

218

the Whittier social settlement was a lovely touch." He sipped his beverage, hoping to calm his jitters. "There's something to be said about seeing the members in their brass-buttoned crimson uniforms. I think the power of their music makes one's soul happy."

"I do, too. I was glad that we had a good presence from the press and thought our alderman and state rep did a nice job with their speeches, too."

"I don't think that the guests missed the Governor or Mayor's appearance, do you?"

Edward shook his head, knowing full well that those men had their hands full with more pressing matters. The United States had taken a stand. President Wilson had taken a stand, saying, 'The world must be made safe for democracy,' in his plea earlier in the month, officially entering into the war last week, on Tuesday the seventeenth. Atlanta was going to play a major role. Camp McPherson had been chosen as one of fourteen in the country as a military training site.

Shelby weighed his options, unsure whether to continue making small talk, bring up the topic of war, or to get straight to the point, the real reason for this evening's meeting. He chose to be direct. "Well, as you know, I have strong feelings for Opal. And, she has feelings for me, too."

"Does she, now?" As a father, he knew it was a conversation he would eventually have. The day had finally arrived.

"Yes, sir." Shelby sat up straight. "I would like to ask for your permission for her hand in marriage."

There was a noise from behind the door that led to the foyer. Edward had been eager to marry off Pearl first, but no one had stepped up to claim her hand yet. He knew that he and Trudy would have their hands full and Ranzell would have a mess to clean up after Pearl unleashed a tirade when she learned that her younger sister had become betrothed before her. He was just relieved that she was attending a concert sponsored by the Atlanta Music Club and wouldn't be home until later that evening. Perhaps he would put her and Trudy on a train bound for a trip to New York City in the morning. There, the news could be broken with minimal property damage. It would also give her an opportunity to shop, catch a few shows, and more importantly, provide plenty of time to cool down. He saved the idea and would bring it up with Trudy after his meeting with Shelby.

"Son, I am happy to embrace you into our family. Her mother and I gladly give our permission for you to marry our daughter, Opal."

Squeals and claps were again heard from behind the door.

"You can come in now," Edward called out while shaking Shelby's hand.

Opal and Trudy were first to burst through the door. Tears and cheers ensued while Ranzell carried in a tray of Champaign-filled flutes. The four of them took a glass, toasted to their future, and took a sip. Ranzell excused herself.

"Daddy, we are so excited, and we'd like to have a June wedding at the Shrine of the Immaculate Conception, with a reception to follow here at the house." Opal beamed, taking Shelby's hand in hers.

Edward turned to Trudy. "We think next June would...."

Opal interrupted, "No, Daddy. *This* June." She already knew she wanted Addie to be her maid of honor and not her older sister. But, she would ask for her parent's permission about that another day.

Trudy took hold of Edward's hand and squeezed it. That was her signal to him that she already knew that bit of news, and that he'd have to be alright with it. He surmised that the date was probably set, and the colors, music, and flowers chosen. He wasn't used to being railroaded, but today he'd make an exception.

"Okay, this June is fine."

Opal ran over to her parents, hugging them both.

"What date have you both selected?" Edward looked over at Shelby, motioning him to join them in their embrace.

Shelby complied. "I've spoken with my family in Chattanooga. We think that the ninth of June will work with everyone's schedules."

Edward looked at Trudy lovingly. "I take it that it also works with our schedules, darling?"

"Yes, my love. It does."

"Well then, it's settled."

Ranzell reappeared. "Supper is ready."

The group adjourned into the dining room, all discussing and unveiling the plans for the celebration nearly six weeks away. But Edward couldn't shake an ominous feeling. Was it the impending war? Would Shelby eventually get swept up in the draft? Would his daughter's heart get broken if he became a casualty of war? Could her joy-filled dreams be destroyed? These were his worries to bear. It was his role as her father to try and protect her. While he was about ready to give her away, he'd always be there to pick up the pieces if need be. No matter how old she was, she was his precious daughter, his favorite.

## MONDAY NIGHT, SIXTH WARD

"Ahhh." *Why do I feel like I am falling to pieces?* Addie stuck out her tongue in the mirror in the treatment room. She moved the wooden tongue depressor around in her mouth, examining her tonsils and upper palate. *My oral mucosa and gums are pale.* She stared at her reflection. *I look malnourished. My hair is dry and brittle, my cheeks are sallow, and my complexion lacks a glow and a pink pallor.* She palpated the lymph nodes under her jaw bone, down the sides of her neck, and over her clavicular area. *Nothing abnormal here.* Placing the stethoscope in her ears, she listened to her breath in both lungs. *Clear.* She auscultated her heart. *It's beating a bit faster than a normal resting rate.* She counted. *100 beats per minute. There's no murmur.* Moving the bell down to her abdominal region, she listed to all four quadrants for bowel sounds. She heard gurgles and popping noises in every area. *Hyperactive. Really hyperactive.* Addie pulled the stethoscope from her ears and laid down on the exam table. She felt around her tummy. *Tender and distended. Maybe I have a GI bug or parasite?* Addie sorted through all of the possible GI diseases and diagnoses, dismissing them all for one reason or another. She began to think of uterine and ovarian disorders that sometimes mask other issues.

There was a knock on the door. "Excuse me. It's Doctor Randall. Is anyone in there?"

"Holy crap!" Startled, Addie hopped off the table, exiting through the door that led to the adjacent physician's offices. She was doing everything these days to avoid seeing Randall. She wasn't sure how to address his sweet poem in her autograph book. She knew she had feelings for him. But, was it love? Unwilling to deal with it, she chose to ignore him for now. It wasn't the only thing she was ignoring. There was a gnawing feeling and it had been there for quite some time. Opal was right. Randall was right. Everyone was right. She was dodging the obvious. *Something is wrong with me. I'm sick.*

Randall turned the nob and entered, finding no one inside.

# 20

Three days previously, on Friday, the eighteenth of May, the United States Congress had passed the Selective Service Act, requiring all male citizens, white and colored, ages twenty-one to thirty, to register for the draft. According to the *Atlanta Dispatch*, 'applicants need to choose a branch of the military, Army, Navy, or Marine, and sign up at their local office next month. There will be zero tolerance for loafers or slackers as the country raises a national army to service.'

The following day, the city held a grand military parade down Peachtree, Baker, and Mitchell Streets. The newspaper profiled pictures and an accompanying article that listed the parade participants, including the Seventeenth Infantry and 2,000 National Guardsmen from Fort McPherson, who marched to tunes such as "It's a Long Road to Tipperary," and "Dixie." Additional musical performances were provided by the Red Men's and the Eagle's Drum and Bugle Corps. The Greencoats of the Yaarab Temple and their 'Million Dollar' band played 'The Stars and Stripes Forever.' The Governor's Horse Guards, the Boy Scouts, and the Georgia Military Academy Cadets also participated. Women were also represented in the event, marching in the Red Cross and the Ladies of the National League for Women's Service auxiliary units.

Celebrations abounded across America, filling the country with an immense sense of patriotism and pride. Citizens quickly rallied to the cause. As President Wilson so eloquently put it, 'America is privileged to spend her blood and give her might for the principles that gave her birth and happiness, and the peace which she has treasured.' All had a burning desire to demonstrate service and unity.

Today was a beautiful, clear, and sunny day in Atlanta. A southerly warm brisk breeze blew, and Georgia hadn't seen a drop of rain for a while. At eleven-thirty-nine in the morning, the first of soon-to-be four fire alarms throughout the ten-wards sounded over the next hour. A fire had erupted over at the Atlanta Warehouse, located across the railroad tracks in the West End.

Four minutes later, two curious boys set a garbage can on fire behind a home, which destroyed three houses seven blocks from the first alarm location.

At twelve-fifteen, the alarm chimed at firehouse number six. Garrett and his fellow firemen abruptly stopped eating lunch, geared up, and raced to the house fire south of downtown on Washington and Rawson, a clustered working-class neighborhood. A call later went out from their company requesting extra assistance. Flames were rapidly spreading through the residential area. Ladder Company Number Twelve responded. However, while they were en route, at twelve-forty-six, they spotted burning mattresses in Grady's storage shed on Decatur and Fort Streets. The firefighters deduced that the burning embers from the other house fire set these cotton mattresses ablaze. Equipped with only a pump on the truck and with all hoses in use all over the city fighting the other three fires, there was no way for them to extinguish the flames. Telephone operators and the call boxes were overwhelmed, unable to keep up with the volume of calls. Neighbors were alerting neighbors that Atlanta was burning again. Was Atlanta under attack? Could the Germans be to blame?

By one-fifteen, the inferno, accelerated by the wind, had reached Edgewood Avenue. Reinforcements with hoses were promptly dispatched to the area. Residents and business owners poured out of their houses as the flames demolished shanty homes and stores. Men climbed to their rooftops with water bucket brigades and soaked their homes with garden hoses in an effort to save their property. As if mimicking the parade two days before, the fire marched block by block through the Fourth Ward.

By two in the afternoon, Atlanta's Fire Chief summoned all 204 firefighters to report for duty. He even called Mayor Chandler and pleaded for additional help. "Activate every city's fire resources within a 350-mile radius from Chattanooga to Savannah!"

Neighbors helped neighbors by rescuing the infirmed and frail and tried to salvage anything of value, throwing chairs, pictures, and clothing out on the front lawn before the fire ripped through the one and two-story residences. In the blink of an eye, one house after the other crumbled to the ground. Numerous companies all over the city rallied and drove their trucks into the ward, hoping to help evacuate people and their belongings. Women were hysterical and screaming in the streets and alleyways. Families were swiftly severed and separated in the frantic flight to flee. All cried out in search for their missing wives, children, and husbands.

By four o'clock, Grace Methodist, Jackson Avenue Baptist, St. Paul's Episcopal, Westminster Presbyterian, and Wheat Street Baptist Churches were destroyed. While the situation was looking grim, hope emerged and prayers were answered. Additional relief came when Colonel Noyes dispatched all 2,000 officers in training camp and the companies from the Seventeenth Infantry. They were also joined by recruits from the Fifth Regiment and the Georgia Field Hospital. Collectively, the decision was made by the Fire Chief, Mayor, and Colonel Noyes to dynamite homes, creating a fire break. They hoped that the raging Fourth Ward Fire would collide with the burning blasted homes. Lacking the necessary fuel, they would spontaneously extinguish. That was the plan.

A command post was stationed at Peachtree and Baker Street by McPherson's soldiers by four-thirty. Twenty minutes later, Marshall Law was declared. Dynamite was rushed by the car and truck loads from the DuPont Powder Company.

*Ka-boom! Ka-boom! Ka-boom! Ka-boom!* Explosions rocked the city. With news of the impending disaster spreading, people clamored to the rooftops of their businesses and homes or leaned out high-rise windows in the adjacent wards to catch a glimpse of the billowing black smoke and red flames licking the cobalt sky.

Sacred Heart Hospital, like the other infirmaries, was put on high alert, making the necessary preparations to care for the wounded and injured. Edward and Alan dispatched the McDaniel brothers to the Fourth Ward without hesitation.

*Ka-boom! Ka-boom!* One house after another exploded in the Fourth Ward. *Ka-boom! Ka-boom!*

A man covered in soot ran through the first floor of the hospital. His brown trousers singed, he yelled repeatedly, "The Fourth Ward is gone, I tell ya, gone!"

Addie stepped out of the storage closet carrying a tray stacked with gauze bandages.

The man stopped and grabbed her. "The Fourth Ward is gone!" He ran off, continuing to holler up and down the hall. Pandemonium erupted.

Addie dropped everything and ran up the back stairwell to the hospital rooftop. She was soon joined by Lena, Alan, Edward, Randall, Shelby, Opal, and other patients and medical staff. All watched the ghastly sight unfold. People by the hundreds were clogging the streets, frantically running toward them, and to the north and to the south of them. Car and truck horns beeped and blared, police car's sirens wailed, shorts clanged their bells, and horses bucked, whinnied, and reared. Cacophony and chaos reigned. Vehicles zigged and zagged in an attempt to avoid impending collision with each other and the stampeding masses afoot.

Randall saw Addie ashen and sway. "Addie, are you okay?"

Her eyes rolled back and she collapsed. Randall cradled her in his arms. "Nurse Hartman, go and fetch Dr. Williams. There is something terribly wrong with Addie. Prep the operating suite."

Frantic, medical staff helped him take Addie the emergency room to prepare her for surgery.

When Randall rushed out of the ER to retrieve a few supplies from the pharmacy, he nearly collided with Garrett. "What are you doing here? Are you alright? Are you hurt?"

Covered in sweat and soot, Garrett was barely recognizable. "No, we just brought in one of our own. He fell off a ladder and broke his leg. I hopped into Brice's ambulance to help them get through the streets. It's completely crazy out there. People are jumping on any moving vehicle's hood, running board, or roof to escape the madness. There's one more thing. My aunt's house is gone. We've lost everything."

Randall was unable to process the information and confessed, "There's something wrong with Addie. I don't know what it is yet. We're prepping her for surgery."

"What happened?" Garrett got the distinct feeling that the situation was grave.

"She just passed out. Her pulse is rapid and faint." Troubled, he ran his hands through his hair. "I don't know. This past year, she's not been herself. Over the past year, she's lost weight and is pale and sickly."

"Why didn't you do anything for her?"

"I tried. We all tried. But you know how stubborn Addie is, dismissing it as stress and such." Randall stepped aside. "Stay close. You're the closest thing to family that she has. Dr. Williams is going to be taking charge of her case."

The Fourth Ward fire raged on, consuming everything in its path. Somehow, it miraculously avoided Morris Brown University and the Boulevard School. By six o'clock in the evening, it had breached Ponce de Leon Avenue, and an hour and a half later was demolishing everything on Greenwood.

Garrett paced back and forth with Opal and other members of the nursing staff during Addie's exploratory operation. He looked at the clock on the wall. It read seven o'clock.

The door to the operating suite opened. Randall emerged, covered in blood. Grabbing Garrett by the arm, he pulled him inside. "It's bad, it's really bad." Randall started crying.

"What's wrong with her?" Garrett demanded. "What's wrong with Addie?"

Dr. Williams interjected, "It seems that at some point, she contracted a tapeworm. While it has remained dormant for a while, it appears that it has been feeding on her, making her malnourished and severely anemic." He paused.

"Tell him the rest, John," Randall insisted.

"Addie will never be able to have children. The tapeworm perforated the intestines and caused irreparable damage to her ovaries."

"Oh, Jesus!" Garrett's knees buckled. He backed up to the tile wall and slid down it. Burying his head in his hands, he wept.

John continued, remaining focused on the task at hand. "She needs blood. She needs a transfusion if she stands any chance at all to live."

"Give her mine!" Garrett leapt to his feet.

"You must know the risks involved. We've not done that procedure yet, but I've read up on it. I think it will work, it might work, but, I'm not one hundred percent sure."

"She's worth the risk." Garrett was adamant and unwavering.

"Either way, there is the potential that she may die with or without this transfusion."

"Then what does she have to lose, doctor?" Garrett pressed.

"Only time." Dr. Williams turned to Nurse Hartman. "Cross-match him to make sure he is a true match for Addie. Once confirmed, I'll need the necessary supplies to complete the procedure."

"Test my blood," Randall offered. "Just in case."

"Test mine, also," Nurse Kessler added as she monitored Addie's vital signs. Concerned, she said, "Doctor, her blood pressure is starting to fall and heart rate is becoming erratic."

Dr. Williams hustled over and administered more medications to stabilize Addie. "We need to hurry."

Garrett scrambled to wash off and change into a clean patient gown. Randall was pulled away to help with the influx of patients in the emergency room. Within the hour, all blood samples had been examined.

Lena returned with the final verdict. "It appears that Garrett is a true match. The other samples, I'm sorry to say, are incompatible and could cause a life-threatening reaction."

Garrett pulled up a chair next to Addie and put his arm out to be scrubbed and cleaned with iodine. He whispered in her ear, "Addie, I'm so sorry for breaking your heart. That was never my intention. Please forgive me. I don't want you to die. I only want you to be happy and live a long life. You mean the world to me. Now, I'll truly always be a part of you. I love you. I always have. I always will. Come back to me someday, dear Addie."

Dr. Williams made his final preparations. "Is everybody ready?"

Heads nodded.

"Let's begin."

The plan worked. The Fourth Ward conflagration was finally contained and extinguished by ten-forty that night. Fire crews from Augusta, Chattanooga, Decatur, East Point, Gainesville, Greenville, Griffin, Jacksonville, Knoxville, Macon, Marietta, Nashville, Newnan, Rome, and Savannah answered the call for help. Thousands of the homeless refugees made camps in Piedmont Park and in any untouched areas and vacant lots they could find. The Red Cross rallied, setting up shelters and offered food, clothing, and water.

While the city filled with sounds of wailing and woe, Negro spirituals were heard from within their camps. Their songs brought hope and comfort to the distraught and despaired. They sang acapella, "Lord I keep so busy praisin' my Jesus, keep so busy praisin' my Jesus, keep so busy praisin' my Jesus, ain't got time to die, 'cause when I'm helpin' the sick (I'm praisin' my Jesus), when I'm helpin' the sick (I'm praisin' my Jesus), when I'm helpin' the sick (I'm praisin' my Jesus), ain't got time to die."

# 21

Lena sat at the dining room table and signed the bottom of the deed. She blew the wet ink dry. "I'm so glad that we sold Randall my apartment at the Ponce." She folded the paper and stuffed it into an envelope. "Now he'll truly have a place of his own. After all of this travesty, it's important to keep one's sight on the horizon and keep moving forward." She gestured with her hands as if looking out for the horizon and made a slicing motion to mimic a general's command to move forward.

"Yes, ma'am!" Alan saluted as he walked behind her and took the envelope. "I'll put it in my suit pocket and give it him this afternoon at Opal's wedding reception." He tugged on Lena's braided ponytail while kissing the top of her head and took a seat next to her. Setting the envelope down, he picked up the morning paper.

Lena sighed while securing her bathrobe sash. "I really miss reading the 'Hey, Hetta!' column."

"What? I never thought you'd take a liking to reading such

rubbish. I thought you enjoyed more intellectually stimulating subject matter."

"It provided a good escape and a good laugh."

"Yes, but that woman took pot shots at other's expense."

"Touché. You've got me there," Lena said resignedly. "What intellectually stimulating news are you stumbling across today?"

"There are a lot more updates and articles about the Fourth Ward fire. The final property loss estimates are in according to this one."

"Please read it out loud."

He folded the corner of the paper down. "Darling, for the sake of time, knowing how long it takes you to get ready for a party, I'll skim and summarize the important parts. You know I'm a numbers kind of guy, anyway."

Lena stuck her tongue out at him.

Alan laughed and snapped the page back up. "The 'Great Fire' destroyed almost 300 acres. The gas company reported that it lost approximately one million feet of gas the following day due to damaged and leaking lines. Pop-up fires have continued to plague firefighters. Telephone wires are down and water reserves have been exhausted." He stopped. "That means you need to conserve water and take a French bath today."

Lena picked up her fountain pen and threatened to throw it at him.

"1,938 residences were lost and of those 1,682 had wooden shingle roofs. 10,000 people are homeless and only one person died as a result of the fire."

"Wow! I find that really hard to believe. What a miracle after such a tragic disaster!"

"It says here that a lady had a heart attack and died watching her house burn."

Lena raised her right hand in the air. "God rest her soul."

"The story goes on to talk about the momentum to reunite families with each other and with their belongings. Furniture, clothing, and personal effects have been salvaged and taken to the auditorium to be claimed by their owners. The Red Cross has also compiled a 'lost and found' directory to help reconnect separated loved ones." Alan stopped reading and perused the pages.

Lena studied his expression. He raised his eyebrows. "What?" she asked.

"I didn't know that the Mayor declined financial aid from other states and towns. Instead, he organized a committee of Atlanta's prominent citizens and collectively they have raised approximately $50,000 to help provide financial aid to those in need."

"That was extremely generous."

"Knowing Edward, I'm willing to bet you'd find him amongst those mighty men." Alan turned the page and scanned the contents. "This article discusses the catastrophic compounding factors and failures and the lessons learned to prevent such an atrocity again. It recommends making investments to safeguard the city from the possibility of future disasters and that the city should motorize and upgrade the entire fire department. The construction of wooden-shingled businesses and homes should also be prohibited in the future."

"It is always important to assess and make process improvements after a catastrophe. That's what we do in the event of an unforeseen adverse medical outcome."

The levity in Alan's voice disappeared. "My darling, speaking of unforeseen outcomes, what was the name of the nurse you expelled?"

"Her name was Roberta Jones. She preferred to be called 'Bertie.'" Curiosity gave way to dread. "Why do you ask, Alan?"

"Prepare yourself for what I am about to read to you." He reached for Lena's hand. "Suicide by Streetcar. On Monday, a young lady walked in front of a short on Peachtree Street in front of Grover's Bakery. Following an investigation by the Atlanta Police Department, the woman's identity has finally been released after her next of kin were notified. Roberta Jones of…."

"Wha-wha-what?" Lena stammered. "Please wait. Don't tell me that it's our Bertie? It can't be our Bertie!"

Alan patted her hand. "I'm afraid it is. The article goes on to say that she had been suffering from melancholia for over a year according to family members and that her father said she embraced reckless behaviors. Her condition was affecting the family and, as a result, they kicked her out of their home last week. Her whereabouts were unknown until the APD knocked on the Jones family's front door on Tuesday morning. Her identity was revealed and later confirmed when the officers found a crumpled letter from Sacred Heart Hospital School of Nursing in her coat pocket detailing the reasons for her expulsion in December 1915."

"Oh, Jesus! I feel sick to my stomach." Lena released Alan's hand and wrapped her arms around her abdomen. She started rocking. "How am I going to tell Edward today, of all days, about this?"

"Knowing Edward, he's probably already seen it. I'm sure he's already gotten Sam on the phone to run a patient success story or a feature article about Trudy's hospital guild in an upcoming issue to counter this one. And, knowing you, I can probably predict what you are thinking. But, you can't let yourself take the blame for this. You don't know what other underlying circumstances might have played a factor in this. Bottom line, you don't have all the facts and can't presume to speculate how this could have been avoided. You'll drive yourself crazy if you do."

Lena didn't respond.

Alan realized it was too early in the morning to be so pragmatic. Worried that he sounded insensitive, he carefully chose his next words. "What is it, my darling? What's troubling you?"

Lena took in a deep breath and exhaled. "It's Addie. I'm worried about how she'll receive this news. She and Opal were Bertie's best friends in school. I know they lost touch with her after she...."

"Lena, Bertie made poor choices by violating the hospital's rules and jeopardizing a nurse's code of honor when it comes to the care of a patient. You never could have trusted her again. Even if you had put her on probation and given her a second chance, in the back of your mind, you would always question whether she was being truthful or was she being deceitful." Alan, although he spoke the harsh truth, redirected the conversation to something more positive. "Addie has turned a corner and is making strides towards a full recovery, hasn't she?"

"Yes, but Dr. Williams has been keeping Addie so heavily sedated these past weeks so that she can rest and heal that she's not been lucid enough to have a conversation. I don't know if she recalls the fire or even realizes that she lost her house. Randall said that he contacted the insurance carrier on her behalf and explained that she was infirmed. They said they would be assessing the loss and would issue a check to her when they concluded their findings. Thank goodness Doc Gray had taken out a policy on the house long ago and Mrs. Gray made sure it transferred to Addie when she inherited the home."

"Has anyone told Addie what happened to her and what caused her to get so ill?" Alan asked. Lena started crying—Alan immediately regretted asking the question and wanted to kick himself. He hated seeing her cry. He was in uncharted territory. After a year of marriage, he was still trying to learn how to navigate the emotions of women.

"No. Addie should hear it from me." Lena sniffed. "The news must come from me. I'm the closest thing she has to a motherly figure." She wrung her hands. "She's going to be devastated to learn that she's lost a friend to suicide and that she missed her best friend's wedding today. I also don't know how to tell her about her childhood friend, Garrett Darling." Realizing Alan may not be aware of who Garrett was, she clarified. "You remember Mrs. Gray's nephew, the firefighter and Randall's former roommate, don't you? He's the one I told you about who gave Addie his blood and saved her life?" Alan nodded, afraid to interject any more right now. "Well, Randall told me yesterday that Garrett's enrolled in the Army and has already reported to Camp Gordon in Chamblee to help build the cantonment site." She blew her nose on her napkin. "How did it come to this? She's lost her family. She's lost her home, and now she's losing her best friends. And, she's lost the ability to bear children. How is she going to cope when she hears about all this? I'm afraid of how she'll react. I don't want her to feel like she is all alone in this, either."

Alan reached out. "Take my hand, darling."

Lena complied.

"She won't be alone. She'll have you. Actually, she'll have us." Alan watched the worried expression on Lena's face give way to relief. "If my memory serves me correctly, and it usually does, I heard a quote earlier from a very wise and beautiful woman. She said, 'After all of this travesty, it's important to keep one's sight on the horizon and keep moving forward.'" Alan put his hands up, as if searching for the horizon, and sliced one out in a clear command to move forward.

"Yes, sir!" Lena saluted. "You're the best." She lifted his hand to her mouth and kissed it.

Alan reveled having finally found the right words to bring comfort to his wife and dried her tears. He was learning the magic behind a successful marriage where, together, they saw a dark moment give way to the possibilities of hope through mutual understanding, compassion, and love.

### SATURDAY AFTERNOON, SECOND WARD

Dense fog hovered and ash covered the Fourth Ward. Firefighters continued to combat the red devil when it sprang up from breaks in damaged gas lines or from spontaneous combustion. The ravages of the Great Fire may have battered and ripped Atlanta's families apart, but they, like the resilient city, rallied together to mend, heal, and rebuild at a time when the country was banding together for an even bigger mission, a global cause: to fight for democracy abroad. Young men ran to line up and sign up for the draft and couples raced for the altar. Opal and Shelby were among many across the country who exchanged vows in the month of June, opting for an intimate family-only ceremony at the Shrine of the Immaculate Conception.

Opal had no idea that she would have to fight a few battles of her own in the Second Ward as she made final preparations leading up to the big day. Pearl, the reluctant maid of honor, did as little as possible and even locked herself in her room after throwing a tantrum about Opal's understated dress choice for her, a sapphire taffeta dress with a long cream-colored sash. The extra fabric flowed down to the hem of the ankle-length dress. Pearl didn't care that it was a custom piece from Mrs. Wu. Opal had to recruit her father to help mitigate the sibling's war of words. Edward's explanation that fabrics were growing scarce and scrap drives were being held to collect rubber, metal, and any other precious materials to be redirected for the war effort fell on deaf ears. Like with any savvy business negation, Edward used promises and bribes to finally get Pearl to reluctantly comply.

And, the battles, negotiations, and bargaining tactics continued on the Alexander home front. Opal begged her parents to keep the reception small, too, inviting only relatives and close friends. She pleaded, "Please, Daddy, don't invite people that Shelby and I don't know, like politicians, business partners, or want-to-be socialites." She emphasized, "This is our day, Daddy!"

Edward, like Pearl, also reluctantly complied with Opal's whims and wishes. Today, after all, was her day. This afternoon, he took great pleasure in watching Opal. She radiated with happiness. Arm in arm with Shelby, she went from guest to guest, thanking them profusely for attending the quaint garden party. Her strawberry-blonde hair was piled high on her head. A few wayward wisps and curls framed her face now that she had shed the gold crystal tiara and two-tier, cathedral-length lace veil from the wedding ceremony. Donning new teardrop pearl earrings, a gift from her blue-eyed, blonde-haired prince, she kept looking down to admire her simple 18-carate white gold band with tiny rosettes. Shelby's ring complemented hers, although void of any embellishments.

While there were some expense savings with the smaller affair, none were spared when Opal commissioned Mrs. Wu to design her dress to exacting specifications. The elaborate ecru gown had a delicate scoop-necked taffeta bodice complete with a floor-length organza petal skirt. Embracing a Chinese tradition learned from the Wus during a design and fitting session, Opal asked Ying to embroider orange blossoms on the skirt. Small crystals and pearls were added, hand-sewn around the neckline, lace and taffeta bishop sleeves, and along the scalloped-bottomed gown. Opal even chose to carry the symbolic and fragrant flower, representing purity and fertility, in her cascading bouquet filled with gardenias and hydrangeas.

As the afternoon and the festivities drew to a close, Opal and Shelby, hand in hand, walked over to Edward. He stood by a flower planter, filled with lilies, irises, and ivy, at the base of the back-porch stairs and puffed on a cigar.

"Daddy?" Opal batted her eyes at him.

Having surrendered his daughter's hand and entrusting his new son-in-law to protect it, he replied, "Yes, Mrs. Maddox?"

"Oh, that has such a wonderful ring to it," Opal squealed. "I have one more favor to ask of you today."

A flurry of ideas ran through his mind. Nothing was going to spoil her day; he had taken every measure to make it special, including hiding the *Atlanta Dispatch* from her this morning and promising himself to tell her about Bertie on another day, just not today. "Anything. What is it, precious?"

"Would you have a car take the extra food from this reception to one of the local shelters? We don't need it and Shelby and I don't want to see it thrown away."

Edward was genuinely touched by the generosity of the gesture. Having gifted the newlyweds with the deed to an Edwardian-style house a few blocks away, this act of unselfish kindness topped it all and was quite the unexpected gift, one that surpassed all others today. "Consider it done." Edward relished that he had raised this one right. Her heart was always in the right place. Opal was his precious gem and he was truly a proud, blessed, and lucky father.

### SATURDAY NIGHT, SIXTH WARD

Addie wrestled with the bed sheets. *God, I'm so hot. Why can't I think clearly? I feel like I sleep all the time. Why does my abdominal area hurt and cramp so much? Why do my arms and legs feel so heavy? I can barely lift my head off the pillow or find the energy to open my eyes. Why am I having the strangest dreams? I swear I hear Randall talking to me, telling me about how much he loves and cares for me. I can also hear Garrett's voice telling me that he loves me, too. Something about he'll always be with me.* Hallucinating, she reached out to try and touch a pale blue butterfly with iridescent wings fluttering overhead. It disappeared as soon as she touched it. She continued to toss and turn, lost in her visions and random thoughts.

Ying gently knocked on Addie's hospital room door. "Addie? It's Mrs. Wu. I've just come to check in on you." She entered the private room on the second floor of the hospital, carrying a white pitcher filled with orange and magnolia blossoms. She set the arrangement on the bedside table.

"What s-s-smells so heaven-ly?" Addie slurred, a side-effect of the sedative medications. She turned to see the butterfly again. It had floated over and landed on one of the magnolia blooms. She tried to point at it. She said, slowly, "Do you see it? Do you see the beau-tiful b-b-b-lue bu-tter-fly?"

Used to Addie's visual illusions, Mrs. Wu remained unfazed. "Addie, I think you are dreaming, my poor dear girl. Let me help you." While straightening out the bedsheets, she saw Addie lying in a pool of sweat. Following the instructions of Nurse Hartman, she retrieved a fresh gown and stack of linens from the closet and changed the bed while Addie lay in it, turning her from one side to the other as she removed the dirty linens and replaced them with clean ones. Finding a washcloth, she rinsed it under the sink with cool water and wrung it out. Taking a seat next to Addie on the bed, she ran the cloth over Addie's face, neck, and arms while humming her own unique tune to a Chinese lullaby. Translating the Chinese Mother Goose rhyme, she sang, "Away goes the butterfly, To catch it I will never try; The butterfly's about to 'light, I would not have it if I might."

"You're sing-ing a-a-about my butter-fly."

Addie drifted in and out of consciousness while Ying changed her into a clean patient gown. Ying stayed with her until she fell asleep.

*Knock. Knock.*

Ying walked over to the door and opened it.

Randall popped his head inside dressed in his Sunday best. "I just wanted to stop by after the Alexander reception to see how she was doing." Toting a red hard-bound *The Poetical Works of Robert Burns* in his left hand and a small guitar in his right, he entered.

Mrs. Wu nodded and bowed. "She's lucky to have you, Dr. Springer."

"Thank you, Mrs. Wu. I appreciate you looking in on her."

"My pleasure. I brought her some flowers to feed her heart and soul. In my country, magnolias represent beauty and dignity. I thought they were perfect for our dear Addie."

"You are too kind." Randall tucked the book under his arm, grabbed the chair that sat under the window, and set it next to Addie's bed.

"Good-night, Dr. Springer."

"Good-night."

Ying departed, closing the door behind her.

Randall opened the book to page 423 and propped it next to the arrangement. He cleared his throat. "The Sacred Vow." Strumming his guitar to the Scottish tune of "Allen Water," he softly sang, substituting Addie's name in lieu of Annie. "By Allan stream I chanc'd to rove, while Phoebus sank beyond Benledi; the winds are whispering thro' the grove, the yellow corn was waving ready: I listen'd to a lover's sang, an' thought on youthfu' pleasures mony; and aye the wild-wood echoes rang, O, dearly do I love thee, Addie!"

# 22

Addie, dressed in her bathrobe, sat down on the back-porch rocker at the Scott House and opened her diary. Still in a state of disbelief and despair, Addie poured out her heart.

*Dear Blue,*

*I don't even know where to begin. What the hell just happened to me? Nurse Hartman told me to put my feelings and direct all of my rage onto these pages. Well, fine! I keep praying this has all been a bad dream. I feel so foggy-headed still, having lost months of my life in a sedated stupor. "To heal," said the doctors. "To heal?" Are you fucking kidding me? I'm so broken and torn apart after Nurse Hartman told me I can't have children. What did I do to deserve this? I'm still reeling that a transfusion from Garrett saved my life. And, now I have no idea where he is since he's enlisted in the Army. I'm still so bitter that I can't bring myself to ask Randall where he's stationed to thank him. Is that his way to make amends? I feel so conflicted. I'm grateful, and yet there are so many unresolved issues, not to mention other compounding factors. The Great Fire robbed me of my house and mel-*

*ancholia stole one of my best friends from me. I've even missed being a part of Opal's wedding.*

"UGGGGH!" Addie hurled her pencil and it lodged in the window screen. "Fuck me!" She scrambled to retrieve it and continued to vent. *I've woken up and I'm living a nightmare. I jested earlier on my New Year's Eve entry that I hoped that no further disasters awaited. Oh boy, was I ever proven wrong! Dear God in heaven. How do I begin to let go, forgive, and move on? Haven't I had a hard enough life? Why do you test me so? What lessons am I to learn from all of this? Who could ever love me? Who would ever have me? Haven't I endured enough? Is there some silver lining to all of this that escapes me? I feel like a field mouse, being toyed with by a feral cat. Paw at me. Play with me. Put people in my life to love so I can eventually lose them to tragedy. I'm barely keeping it together. I keep having strange dreams where both Garrett and Randall tell me that they love me. What is that all about? Dear God, I don't know how much more I can take. Maw always said to, 'pray when you want to rejoice, pray when you are sad, pray when you want to give thanks, and pray when times are bad.' Dear heavenly Father, I'm on my knees, praying for mercy.*

The sun peaked over the horizon; light dappled through the trees. *Thank goodness Opal returns from her honeymoon next month. I miss confiding in her. I'm hanging on to small bits of happiness so at least I have something good to look forward to.*

# 23

Addie peered through the rain-speckled cab window up at the Maddox's new sage green, three-story home, which sat high on a hill. The sweeping terraced lawn led up to cream-colored ornate plaster banister stairs. Doric columns complemented the two-story wrap around porches and arched windows softened the sharp lines and symmetry of the house. Addie scrunched down in her seat and craned her neck to see that the third floor was complete with a widow's walk. *I feel like I have been transported through time into another world, one that is foreign to me. Everyone and everything has changed so much in these past few months. I am forever changed.* The storm gusts blew leaves from the trees. They fell like red, orange, and yellow confetti to the ground. Struck by a feeling of déjà vu, Addie remembered being overcome by a similar feeling of pain and loneliness when she stood on the Darling's farmhouse porch years earlier, just after learning about the loss of her parents. Struggling to silence the two voices in her head, one telling her to 'pull yourself together and be happy for your best friend' while the darker, self-destructive thoughts filled her with bitterness, resentment, and jealousy. Choosing to embrace the former and not the latter, Addie painted a smile on her face. She stepped out of the cab into the pouring rain, popped open her umbrella, and ran up to the front door framed in stain glass. She twisted the brass doorbell knob. *Ring Ring.*

The door flew open. "Addie!" Opal, wearing a periwinkle dress, quickly ushered Addie inside and took her umbrella.

Addie shed her gloves and raincoat and hung them on the coat rack in the grand foyer. Both embraced, overcome with emotion.

"My goodness!" Opal marveled at the woman standing before her, a far cry from the pale sedated patient she visited three months earlier, prior to leaving for Pensacola for an extended honeymoon. "You look breathtaking in that burgundy suit. I'm so glad you accepted my invitation. Shelby and I just got back from Florida a few weeks ago. He sends his regards. He was called into the hospital earlier this morning by Dr. Williams to help compound some medications for one of his patients, so I've got you all to myself. I've even sent the help home so we can relax and speak freely. I'm still trying to get used to having a maid and a butler. Every time I turn around, I find them standing there, waiting for me to give them orders. I don't know what to do with them exactly. I guess I'll figure it all out in time." Opal grabbed Addie's hand. "Come. We have so much to talk about. Brunch is ready for us in the dining room."

"We're trading cot tales for brunch, I see. My, we're getting so grown up now!"

"We are, aren't we?" Opal glowed, her cheeks fuller and rosier. "I'm so glad that the hurricane from Florida stalled out. Today's weather could have been so much worse."

"Neither wind nor rain could stop me from seeing my best friend today. I would have taken a row-boat over here if I had to!" Addie took a seat at the dining room table. The room was decorated in hues of yellow with damask-patterned wallpaper and thick white crown molding that complemented the dark furniture. A two-tier crystal and gold chandelier hung overhead. Fresh-cut daisies from the backyard garden accented the center of the table. "Speaking of Florida, please tell me all about your wedding and trip to Pensacola. I can't wait to see your pictures."

Opal looked down at her plate filled with eggs, bacon, and a bowl of hot, creamy grits. The smell was off-putting. She swallowed hard. "While I will tell you all about our trip to the sugar-white beaches and our stay at the Hotel San Carlos, I first want to hear all about you. How are you doing? So much has happened between us that...." Opal rubbed her stomach, covered her mouth, and darted out of the room. Finding the nearest restroom, she closed and locked the door.

Addie jumped up and followed her. She grew concerned when she overheard Opal retching. "Are you okay? Do I need to ring Shelby at the hospital?"

"No." A few seconds passed. "I'm alright. Just give me a few minutes. I'll be right out." A few more minutes passed before Opal emerged. "Shelby doesn't need to be called. Actually, Shelby is to blame for my condition." She rubbed her belly, exposing a bit of a bump.

"Oh my stars! You're pregnant! I'm so thrilled for you both!" Addie wrapped her arms around Opal and riddled her with questions. "How far along are you? When are you due? Do you want a boy or a girl? Have you picked out names yet? Are you still going to work at the hospital?"

Opal laughed. "I'm due in April and yes, to your last question. Shelby and I are still trying to figure out the rest. It's all a bit overwhelming, to say the least. Let's go into the parlor and have a seat. If you don't mind, the smell of food is not agreeing with me right now. But, don't worry. I'll be eating like a horse again shortly."

The two walked into the parlor. The room, designed with a feminine touch, was decorated in colors of pink and green. Giant peace lilies in colorful oriental pots accentuated the décor. Taking a seat side by side on the sofa, Opal took Addie's hand in hers. "I am so sorry for everything that's happened to you. Thank the dear Lord for Garrett. He saved your life with his blood. Shelby told me that no one else's was compatible."

"And, thank the good Lord for Lena. She has helped me work through my loss and grief these past few months. There were some really dark days. It was on those days that I felt so alone, it was like I was walking through the valley of the shadow of death. I completely understood how Bertie must have felt when she stepped in front of the streetcar." Addie shook her head sorrowfully. "Opal, I had no idea how sick I was getting. I'm so sorry for dismissing your concerns. When Dr. Williams was investigating the possible causes of my ingestion of the tapeworm, I shared that Deborah had once given me a capsule and not a tablet for a headache. Even though it was a while ago, I always thought it odd and the feeling stuck with me. A capsule she claimed was made by Shelby since she said she couldn't swallow tablets. Dr. Williams questioned Shelby and he refuted the claim. When they decided to rummage through Deborah's old belongings in the storage area in the tunnel, they came across a former patient's tapeworm diet pill bottle that Dr. Williams had asked her to discard."

"Shelby told me that Deborah intentionally did this to you. Addie, I don't know why this happened to the sweetest girl I know, but I thank God every day that you are alive and in my life. You are like a sister to me. I would die if anything were to happen to you. It pained me to see you in such a state after your surgery. You probably don't remember me taking double shifts to take care of you before my wedding. I hated leaving you. But, I knew you were in expert hands and had the best care. Father said he would keep me posted on your status while we were away, and he did."

"Dr. Williams said that the parasite could have remained dormant for years, and it even had the potential to eventually kill me." Unable to hold back any longer, Addie broke down. "I still can't believe Bertie's dead. Garrett's gone. Mrs. Gray's house is destroyed. And, I'll never ever be able to bear children. Who would want a woman like me? I'm broken and incomplete. Who would ever want to marry me?" She became almost inconsolable.

Opal pulled Addie toward her and held her tight. Sobbing, she spoke softly. "I'm always here for you. Always. I love you, Addie. I need you. I need for you to be strong for me. I need you to be this child's godmother."

Addie was taken aback. She pulled away and touched her heart. "Me? Are you sure? Have you and Shelby talked about this?"

Opal nodded and smiled. "There's no one else in this world we'd rather have but you."

"God, I hate it when I get to feeling so sorry for myself that I can't see beyond my own nose. And, here you are. You are the light that shines so brightly at the end of my dark tunnel. I don't know what to say."

"Please say yes!"

"Yes. I am honored you asked and would love to be your child's godmother."

"And, speaking of love, I know there is a man who adores you for exactly who you are. He pined over you while you were ill and I even heard that he serenaded you at night."

"Who are you talking about?"

"Why Randall, of course!"

"No one told me that."

"Everyone was sworn to secrecy, even Mr. and Mrs. Wu."

"You must be joking." Addie could feel her neck and chest flush, embarrassed at the thought and the images of him singing to her at her bedside. "I didn't even know he could sing."

"Did you know he also plays the guitar, quite beautifully I might add?"

"He sang and played the guitar for me? I recall having strange and vivid dreams about Garrett telling me that he loved me and that Randall did the same. I chalked it up to delirium." Addie sat back on the couch. "Opal, remember when we had everyone sign our autograph books before graduation?"

"Yes."

"There was an entry in mine from 'anonymous.' It was a love poem. I recognized the handwriting."

"Who was it from? Dr. Payne?" Opal joked.

"No, silly. Randall."

"Give him a chance, Addie. I know you thought Garrett was the one and only love for you, but he's not here for you now. I don't know what this year will bring us or how the war will affect this country. But, brave young men, like Garrett, are heading overseas to fight. Many will not return home. Have you thought about that? You need to think about yourself for once. You are the only one who can look out for yourself and your best interests. I know you have the nursing school and your new cohort of students to teach and immerse yourself into, but there is a man standing right in front of you declaring his undying love for you. I think you need to sit down and talk to him. Perhaps you will soften and your feelings about Randall will change. I would love for you to give your heart to him. Life is so short and you deserve to be happy. He really wants to be there for you and take care of you, 'for better, for worse, in sickness and in health.' Close and lock the doors to your past, Addie, and choose to open this new door to your future."

*Opal is right. I need to let Garrett go, close that door, and lock it. I need to take a new path, open a new door, and be brave enough to walk through it. Maw, would you tell me the same thing too, if you were still here?*

"I don't know about you, but I'm starving." Opal stood up and reached out to Addie. "Come on. Let's see what's still salvageable to eat."

Taking Opal's hand, Addie rose.

### SUNDAY EVENING, SIXTH WARD

Addie finished her evening rounds on the med-surg unit and made a few notes on her chart, documenting which students were excelling at the bedside and which nurses needed additional coaching from her, the charge nurses, and Lena. Making her way from the 1-A wing to 1-B, she rounded the corner and entered the pediatric corridor. *Take a deep breath, Addie. You know you've been dodging Randall for a while now. Relax and just be yourself. Don't get flustered.* Tucking her clipboard under her arm, she shook out her hands before entering the unit.

A nursing student enrolled in the new May class by the name of Jenny Hoffman from Summerville, Georgia, ran over to Addie. Her black hair had come loose from her bun and rested on her uniform collar. Her cap was askew. "Oh, Nurse Engel, I'm so glad you are here. Dr. Springer had to step out to attend to a toddler with a foreign body up his nose in the emergency room. He asked me to give a gavage feeding to this patient, but I'm still a little nervous about doing it all by myself. She's a bit of a squirmer. When I picked her up, she tried grabbing at my cap and pulled my hair. Would you help me?"

"I'd be happy to. But, first, let's get you straightened up a bit." Addie twirled her index finger in a circle. Jenny turned around. Addie secured her hair and righted her cap. "There, you're good as new."

"Thank you, Nurse Engel." Jenny motioned for Addie to come over to bed number seven, where a frail, malnourished young girl lay in a large crib.

Addie would estimate this child to be about a year old by her appearance, but knew she was much older.

Jenny gave a brief bedside report on the patient's status. "We are giving three-year-old Manelva supplemental nutrition. The APD brought her here after receiving an anonymous tip about abandoned children living in a house. Her parents' whereabouts are unknown. When officers arrived, her baby brother and older sister had already passed. Manelva was the only survivor. I think, as evidenced by my appearance when you first walked in here, you'd agree with me that she's a fighter."

Addie warmed to Jenny's sense of humor as she pulled out a few black hairs from Manelva's grasp. *She's going to make a great nurse. She knows when to reach out for help and she has a good wit about her.*

Anticipating Nurse Engel's next line of questions, Jenny spoke. "I have all of my supplies ready, including a glass funnel, rubber connecting tube, and a 16-French catheter, and all have been boiled for two minutes and been placed on this sterile towel." She pointed to the tray beside her filled with equipment, including warmed formula, a blanket, and safety pins.

"Excellent. As I've demonstrated to you in class, we'll use the blanket and safety pins to make a restraint for her, immobilizing her arms and legs so she can't pull out the feeding tube or cause harm to herself. Are you ready to lower the sides and begin?"

"Yes, ma'am."

The two fashioned the blanket, safely securing Manelva for her nasogastric feeding. Dr. Springer crept into the room as Addie removed the feeding tube and they positioned the patient on her right side to aid in digestion.

"Great job, Nurse Hoffman. I'm going to make a note of your excellent work here tonight. Your workspace was prepped and ready, the instruments were sterilized, and you remained calm and steady-handed during the procedure. Next time, I believe you'll be able to do this all by yourself. However, if the patient is too unruly, then please continue to ask for extra assistance. A patient's safety, as well as your own, should always be top of mind." Addie excused herself and walked over to Randall who sat at the nurse's desk. "Can we talk in private?"

Randall looked all around. "Who me? Are you speaking to me?"

"Yes, you." Addie's insides twisted with jittery nerves.

"Now that you have recovered and are working with the new students, I thought I was becoming invisible to you. Every time I walked into a room, you left. When you saw me from afar, you avoided making eye contact. If you had to speak to me, you were never alone and always had someone in tow."

"You are right. I'm ashamed to admit that I was avoiding you." Addie glanced over at Jenny, who was still cleaning her area. "Nurse Hoffman, Dr. Springer and I are stepping into the hallway. We're just outside these doors if you need us."

"Yes, Nurse Engel."

Randall followed Addie into the hall.

"Yes, Nurse Engel. What exactly did you want to talk about?" Randall folded his arms across his chest.

"I owe you an apology."

Indifferent, he urged, "Go on."

"I've been trying to sort through my feelings about everything in light of all that has happened to me. Nurse Hartman has been helping me process these hardships. I'm in uncharted territory. There isn't a textbook to tell me step by step how to deal with all of this. I'm still wading my way through and trying to forge a new path for me." Addie struggled to find the right words. *I guess I'll just open my mouth, let the words fall out, and speak from the heart.* "I want to thank you for your sweet poem that you wrote in my autograph book before graduation."

"You recognized my handwriting?" Randall lowered his arms and leaned against the wall.

"How could I not, after working with you for all of this time?" *I'm glad to see that his barriers are beginning to break down.* "I also want you to know that I am truly appreciative of you looking in on me while I was so ill." *Should I tell him that I know that he serenaded me? Will he be mad? Will he get defensive? I need to be honest with him if I'm going to have any kind of relationship with him. Don't be afraid, Addie. Speak from the heart.* "I remember having vivid dreams that you sang to me at my bedside and that you told me you loved me." *Oh my stars! I said the L-word. I've put it out there in the universe. I can't take it back. I want to curl up and die right now. What will he say? How is he going to respond?* Addie felt a heat wave rush through her body. She blushed.

Randall placed his hands around her warm cheeks and softly kissed her on the lips.

Before she knew it, Addie had reached up and pulled him into her embrace. Closing her eyes, she passionately returned his kiss. *Everything that seemed upside-down is now right-side-up. Whatever feelings of confusion, heartache, and doubt I had have melted away. Everything has become so clear. I feel safe in his arms and can see a future with this man. Opal was right. I needed to open my*

*heart to Randall. He's been waiting there for me on the other side of
this door. I just had to be brave enough to open it and walk through it.
He wants me for me. He does love me. Oh my stars! Is this what true
love feels like?*

Randall stepped back and smiled. Addie's eyes were still
closed. He dropped to one knee and took her hands in his.

Surprised, Addie's eyes shot open.

"This isn't how I envisioned any of this. I am just following
my heart right now. I know you, Addie, I truly do and I love the
woman you are. I know you have dreams to travel the world and
visit other cultures. I've seen your heart-shaped collage that used
to hang on a blue ribbon on the back of your bedroom door at
Mrs. Gray's house. You wrote at the top, 'Dreams are an aspiration of your heart, so dream big!'" Randall kissed Addie's hands.
"Addie, I want you to be my wife. Will you marry me?"

"Yes! Yes! I will." Addie couldn't believe the words came so
easily to her. As soon as they were uttered, she was pained with
guilt and regret. *Garrett. What will Garrett think? I have just broken his heart. Who's going to tell him? What have I done? Am I doing
the right thing? Randall asked and I said yes. Isn't that supposed to be
the natural order of things? God, Addie, get a hold of yourself. You are
overthinking this. Learn to be happy and quit over complicating this
with more questions.*

Randall hopped back up to his feet. "You have made me so
happy. I'm going upstairs to my office and phone my parents in
New York. They are going to be over the moon for me and they
will learn to love you as I do."

*Learn to love me?*

Randall snatched her up in his arms and kissed her again. "I think we should head to the justice of the peace tomorrow and make it official."

"Really?" Addie began to panic. "I don't have anything to wear."

"Don't worry. I'll phone Dr. Williams and ask for the day off tomorrow. You call Lena and see if she and Alan will serve as our witnesses. Perhaps, she has something you can borrow?"

"I guess so. What about rings?"

"I'll call the local jeweler and have him stop by my apartment in the morning so I can pick a set."

Addie's head spun. It was all happening too fast. "Where are we going to live?"

"You can have your things moved out of the Scott House and into my apartment. We'll get Joshua to help us."

"What about flowers and a honeymoon?"

"I'll get a florist to deliver a boutonniere and bouquet. I can't afford to leave the hospital on vacation with everything going on especially now that we're at war. We're going to have to wait to travel abroad, my dear. But, I promise, you will get to Europe one day."

*Do I want a church wedding instead? I've never really stopped to think about what I wanted my wedding day to be like? 'My dear'? Do I even like that he's calling me 'my dear' already? Do I get a say in the matter?* "You have thought of everything." Addie couldn't bring herself to calling him an affectionate pet name yet.

Randall excused himself and dashed off to his office. Upon seeing a stack of unopened letters on his desk, he sorted through them. One caught his attention. He knew who it was from before he even opened it. The return address read, *Camp Gordon, Chamblee, Georgia.*

*28 September, 1917*

*Dear Randall,*

*I'm sure you have been reading the papers to keep up-to-date on the country's war efforts. Our cantonment site officially opened its doors to the civilian military on September 5ᵗʰ. As you can imagine, it is organized chaos here, with hundreds of groups learning how to march around while having orders barked at them. Builders and brick masons are constructing make-shift barracks and tents are being planted in rows like corn for as far as the eye can see. The air is thick and smells of campfires, dust, urine, and musty puddles.*

*There is a constant caravan of supply wagons pulled by oxen, horses, and mules while men walk behind them with wheel barrels shoveling in loads of manure. The mosquitoes and horse flies are as big as birds. They pester and suck the life and blood out of every man and animal around here. Everyone is on edge, angry, scared, and made irritable by the living conditions. The meals are a far cry from being home-cooked delicacies and tend to be served with a ladle out of a giant kettle every day.*

*We have left our families and the securities of home to fight for democracy abroad. It's my honor and patriotic duty. I am proud to serve our country in this manner. I don't know what my future holds or if I will return from battle. I learned that the first group of American air cadets arrived safely in Foggia, Italy, today for training. I am learning so much about European geography, cities, and towns that were once foreign to me. I find the military strategy fascinating, especially how we are coordinating land, air, and sea attacks with multiple ally nations.*

*I'll be writing my father a note tonight, too. I hate that he is working so hard on the farm to raise crops for the war. But, I learned that he has hired a few men who were not eligible to be enlisted to lend him a hand. While I may not have left things with Addie on the best of terms, I appreciate your letters to keep me abreast of her ever-improving condition and that she has made a full recovery. I know her place is by Nurse Hartman, who is like a mother-figure to Addie. Should she ever decide to ask about me, please give her my best. Share as little or as much information as you feel comfortable doing so. I have one favor to ask of you.*

*I ask that you take good care of Addie and look after her. I pray to God every night that she is protected and loved. I don't want to see her growing old alone. Please make sure she is happy. She deserves to live a joy-filled life.*

*I look forward to reading your next letter. Until then, may God bless you and your work at the hospital.*

*Sincerely, your friend,*
*Garrett*

Randall returned the letter in the envelope, saying, "I promise, Garrett."

# 24

Addie heard Maw's voice say in her head, 'Marriage is about com-
promise, give and take, pick your battles.' That advice had been put
to the test these past few months as Addie began seeing Randall
with a new set of eyes.

"Hurry up, Addie! We don't want to keep my parents waiting
on the train platform." Randall yanked her hand and pulled her
through the throngs of people in the downtown depot.

Breathless from practically running behind him, she snapped,
"Look, Randall. It wasn't my fault that we're running late. I can't
help it if a patient with a bleeding ulcer decided to experience a
cardiac arrest while I was caring for him. What did you want me
to do, just walk away and leave him? I had to stay until the end of
my shift." She yanked her hand free of his and stood still while
the crowd split and moved around her. *Jesus! If anyone should be
empathetic and understanding of the situation, it should be you!* she
wanted to yell out loud but instead picked up the pace to catch
up to him.

December had been one of the coldest months on record

for Georgia. The newspapers had a field day snapping pictures of ice skaters on the lake in Piedmont Park. Once on the platform, Addie exhaled. Her breath hung in the air. She waited for it to dissipate. Spotting Randall carefully hugging and kissing an aristocratic-looking woman in a long black mink coat with matching hat and shaking the hands with a tall stuffy man with a sickly gray pallor, Addie shook out her gloved hands and casually walked toward them.

Randall's mother eyed Addie up and down. Her welcome was as frigid as the weather. "You must be my son's wife."

*I have a name. My name is Addie. I am Randall's wife. I have forfeited everything to be with him: my heart, my financial assets, and my aspirations. What? No hugs or a peck on the cheek for your new daughter-in-law?* Her mother-in-law stuffed her hands in what Addie assumed was a white and brown muff. Then it moved and opened its eyes. "Oh, look! You have the fluffiest dog I have ever seen." Addie reached out, but the canine bared its teeth and growled. She swiftly retracted her hand.

Randall's father stepped forward and extended his leather-gloved hand. He overly punctuated his words. "Good afternoon. We've been waiting for you for five minutes in the blasted cold. I don't want my poor wife or Petunia to endure this air any longer, lest they catch their death out here. May we move things along?"

*Petunia? That mutt is a far cry from being a gentile flower! How could Mrs. Springer possibly catch her death out here, since it appears that she is very well insulated and hasn't missed many meals?* "Yes, sure. Of course." Addie quickly shook his hand and turned to follow Randall, who was already making his way to find a porter to collect his parent's trunks. *Should I make small talk?* "So, how was your trip?"

"How rude!" Mrs. Springer trilled her Rs. "I don't make it a habit to talk and walk at the same time. It's not proper to be conducting a dialogue while on foot." Mrs. Springer shoved her sharp nose in the air and walked past Addie. Mr. Springer marched in lockstep with her.

*Oh my stars! What a piece of work. I'm so glad Randall has put them up at The Georgian Terrace. I don't think my nerves could have handled them had they stayed in our apartment for the next month. What has Randall told them about me? Why didn't he warn me about them? His mother makes me feel like I am from the lowest form of society. Shake it off, Addie. Don't let them get the best of you. Throw your shoulders back and own your place in this world because you breathe in the same air that they do. You are an educated woman, for goodness sake! This is just a test. Pass it with flying colors and earn their approval.*

When Randall saw the number of trunks and suitcases on the porter's trolley, he summoned a cab to transport the baggage to the hotel. His parents insisted on taking a separate cab, opting for a nap before their dinner and choosing to eat their evening meal without Randall or Addie. When they recuperated from their travels and were ready to be entertained, they would summon Randall in the next day or so.

Addie stewed, remaining silent during the car ride uptown to the Sixth Ward. Stepping into their apartment, she unleashed her fury at Randall. Pulling off her gloves, she smacked them across his coat lapels. "What the hell? Why didn't you warn me about them? Why did they treat me so coldly? I'm your wife!"

Randall grabbed her by the upper arms and shook her. "Don't you ever talk to me that way again. My parents are very loving individuals. You might think they are cold, but they only want the best for me. I told them all about you and how much I love you, but...."

Addie twisted out of his grip and took a step back. "But what, Randall?"

"But my mother was hoping I would marry a friend of the family back home. She was disappointed that I didn't and feels like I married someone beneath me."

"Beneath you? Beneath you?" Addie couldn't believe what she was hearing. "I work side by side with you. I am learning how to do operations alongside the rest of our surgeons. I walk beside you, not behind or in front of you. I thought you felt the same way about me. Why didn't you defend me, my character?"

"Addie, I really never thought that I would ever get married. I came to Atlanta hoping to escape their grip, but then I met you and everything changed. However, when I am in their presence, I seem to revert back to their obedient son."

"A son without a backbone," Addie quipped.

Randall reacted instantly, slapping her across the face. "I will not be insulted."

Addie stared at him, horrified that he was even capable of hitting her. She had only seen one side of him before, a caring pediatrician who seemed to have a heart of gold when he worked with the children. *Who is this man standing before me?*

Randall left the apartment, slamming the door on the way out. He exited the building and walked across the street to Hill's Tavern, where they kept a stash of liquor in a hidden room for VIP patrons.

Hours later, Addie awoke to the sound of someone at the front door struggling to unlock it. She glanced at the brass clock on her bedside table. It was three o'clock in the morning. She got up out of bed and slipped into her bathrobe on her way to the front of the apartment. She opened the door, finding Randall staggering in the hallway, staring at a set of keys in his hands.

He slurred his words. "I'm…I'm soooo soooo sorry. Will you ev-er for-give me?"

"Get in here before you wake the neighbors." Addie jerked him inside and helped him out of his cashmere overcoat. She had never seen him in this condition before.

Randall pushed himself on Addie.

"Not tonight, Randall. It's three o'clock in the morning. You're drunk and you need to get some rest."

"We don't ha-ha-have to work to-morrow. I want to make looo-ve to you right now."

"You reek of booze and cigarette smoke." Addie pushed him off of her.

He grabbed her and shoved her to the floor, forcing himself on her.

Unable to maneuver out from under him, she surrendered her body. With every thrust, he wasn't making love to her; he was making her hate him.

"Tell me that you love me," he whispered in her ear.

*I hate you.* "I love you," she replied.

"Tell me that you missed me."

"I missed you." *I hate you.*

Four days, filled with apologies, promises, and presents from

Randall to Addie, passed before they were summoned by his parents to exchange gifts in their hotel suite on Christmas morning. And, celebrations for Addie's birthday were put off for another day. Randall's mother was emphatic, preaching "Jesus' birthday comes first." Addie only spoke when spoken to, keeping the conversation as icy and brief as her recent sexual encounters with Randall. When the room was filled with nothing but silence and the sounds from the crackling fire, Addie excused herself and returned alone to the apartment across the street. *I don't care if this was a life test. I am choosing not to take any part in it. They might be good people, but they aren't my kind of folks. I don't consider them to be my family. I know deep down, they will never embrace me as their own, no matter how hard I try. It's not in my nature to beg people to like me or to conform to another's way of thinking if it's truly not how I genuinely feel. I can't go through life pretending to be someone I'm not. Life lessons are brutal. Like Nurse Hartman says, 'While books can teach us much, life is to be considered the most respected teacher of all.'*

Randall remained with his parents for another hour before departing. He walked a few blocks past the Ponce de Leon apartment building to a small park. Taking a seat under a young pine tree, he pulled out a hand-rolled cigarette and lit it. The nicotine calmed his uneasiness. He wondered if he should have listened to his parents and their marital advice. He wondered if he would have been happier if he remained a bachelor. He wondered if Addie was the right woman for him. "She can't bear you any heirs!" His mother's voice rang in his ears. Randall took one more drag, before flicking the butt on the ground. When he stood, his mother's voice was substituted with the sound of music. He was unfamiliar with the tune. It was difficult to make out. Was it a high-pitched choir or did it sound more like humming harps? Glancing up at the pine limbs hanging overhead, he dismissed the impossible notion that someone was singing in the tree. Weighing his options to either go home or visit a new bordello he had heard about on Hulsey Street from tavern friends, he hailed a cab and directed the driver to Atlanta's notorious red-light district.

### CHRISTMAS NIGHT, CAMP GORDON, CHAMBLEE, GEORGIA

Red and green Christmas lights hung randomly around the camp wherever there were electrical poles. The new recruits gathered around open fires and sang carols. Garrett appreciated the festive atmosphere, although it was fleeting and knew it would all be gone by tomorrow morning. Upon entering his barracks, he spotted a letter lying on his canvas cot. Happy to see it was from Randall, he picked it up and opened it while he stretched out, exhausted from the cold, the marching, and the drills. Minutes later, he wadded up the letter and ran outside, finding the nearest bonfire. He tossed it into the flames. Filled with anger and resentment, he stormed off in search of contraband alcohol.

# 25

Over the course of the day, fierce fighting continued, with heavy attacks from Givenchy to Lys and Avre rivers while enemy destroyers fought along the Belgian coast. Despite President Wilson's efforts to outline a fourteen-point peace treaty in January 1918, Germany pushed forward in a series of two spring offensives on the Western front. By March, Russia eventually signed a treaty with Germany agreeing to exit the war, abdicating a portion of the country's industries and land. As the battles on the various fronts raged on with the Allied troops, the loss of life proved to be catastrophic for the enemy. Their reserves were beginning to wear thin.

### THURSDAY LATE AFTERNOON, SIXTH WARD

"Push, Opal. Push! I can see the top of the baby's head crowning!" Addie directed as Opal grimaced and bore down.

Nurse Hoffman wiped Opal's brow while Lena and Addie delivered the baby.

"Opal, you have a healthy baby boy." Addie attended to the pink screaming infant, administering the necessary ointment to its eyes before wrapping him in a blanket and placing him in Opal's awaiting arms.

Opal glanced down lovingly at him. "He's just perfect, isn't he?"

"He has ten fingers and ten toes." Addie pulled out the ink blotter, imprinting his foot on the birth certificate. "What name did you and Shelby pick out for him?"

"Since it's a boy, we are naming him Edward Shelby Maddox. Shelby wants to call him Eddie."

Lena peered over Opal's shoulder at the baby's sweet blue eyes before attending to Opal's post-delivery care.

"I'm going to step out and notify Shelby and your family of this glorious news. Nurse Hartman is going to get you cleaned up before we transport you and Baby Eddie to the maternity ward," Addie said while gathering instruments and placing them on the tray.

"Will you ask Shelby to come in?" Opal asked, marveling at Eddie, who had already grasped her pinky finger.

Lena emerged from under the drapes at Opal's feet. "My dear Opal, there are some things that need to remain a mystery to men. This is one of those things. You really don't want him to see all of this." Lean waved her hand over the area around her before disappearing behind the sheets again. "Give us a chance to clean you and the baby, change your gown and linens, and make you look as pristine as an angel before he sees the mother of his child."

Opal looked over at Addie, who was washing her hands.

Addie nodded and smiled, knowing the experience was one that would forever be denied to her. *This is God's plan. He has a bigger plan for you. Be at peace with His decision to make you barren. Replace your feelings of envy with love. Be happy for your best friend. Now go and be the messenger of this great news to her family.* She excused herself in search of Shelby, the Alexander, and Maddox families. She finally found all of them gathered in the garden by the fountain. The men were already smoking cigars and taking turns sipping from Edward's silver flask. Addie's announcement was met with cheers, tears, and embraces.

While walking back into the hospital, she looked up. Shielding her eyes from the sun, she saw Randall peering out from his second-story office window. He appeared to be holding a letter in his hand. Addie waved at him and blew him a kiss, giving the illusion that she was still a happily married woman. She could feel her spirit slowly dying every time she lied to herself. While Randall hadn't raised a hand to her again, she almost wished that he would so that he would emotionally reconnect with her. On the nights when he claimed he was at the hospital, she knew deep down that he wasn't and chose not to make inquiries with her colleagues lest she cause unwanted gossip. Randall held all the power, and if she decided to leave him, he would retain all of her assets, which were quite substantial after the insurance check that covered the loss of Mrs. Gray's house was deposited. She was glad they drew up a will; at least she would regain her financial freedom in the event he died before she did.

Randall blew one back before disappearing from view. Taking a seat at his desk, he opened Garrett's letter.

*14 April, 1918*

*Dear Randall,*

*It has taken me a few months to process your last letter from December. At first, I was taken aback by the fact that you married Addie, but I soon realized that as my best friend, you were fulfilling my wishes for her to be loved, cared for, and looked after. I am conveying my congratulations to you both and wish you two the happiest of lives together. I am genuinely glad that she, in turn, loves you, too. You both have so much in common and have shared so many life experiences together at the hospital that I can see how you fell in love. We will have to celebrate when I get home if, God willing, He doesn't claim me first and allows me to return to Georgia.*

*Speaking of such matters, my division, the 82nd "All American Army" will be deployed next week. I will speak vaguely, sharing only that I am going to be stationed in France. I'm not at liberty to reveal any further details with you. Therefore, this will be my last letter to you for quite some time. Please keep me in your prayers. Until we all meet again, either on Earth or in Heaven.*

*Sincerely, your friend,*
*Garrett*

Randall walked over to the window, looked down on Edward and his family, and said, "I doubt that our paths will ever cross again, Garrett. Divine intervention will not have anything to do with it. I have your beautiful girl and I have secured my place in this world. I am seeing things differently now and feel invincible. I have narrowly dodged being enlisted and embrace my new privileged lifestyle amongst men like John and Edward. I consider them to be my equals. Mother was right. I am 'special.'" Randall crumpled up the letter and collected the others from Garrett tucked away in his desk drawer. Taking the elevator down to the basement, he located the coal-fired furnace, opened the iron grate door, and threw them inside. He waited until they all turned to ash before leaving.

# 26

In lieu of Independence Day fireworks, and to remain mindful of the American men fighting abroad, Edward and the leadership team organized a Saturday morning tent revival followed by a Sunday afternoon picnic with Sacred Heart and Alexander Hall staff, patients, and families. "We are all in this together, like our band of brothers across the pond," he said. "We are working side by side to heal the sick, mend the wounded, deliver new life into this world, and grow medicinal herbs and crops to nourish everyone. We will share in the bounty as brothers and sisters in Christ. Let not the color of our skin divide us, but let our character, our hearts, and souls working together define us as Americans. Division within our own borders will only destroy us as a country. Look at what is happening in Europe, where one faction believes they are better than another because of race or religion. If you feel differently, then don't bother to attend!" Many chose to partake in the church evangelism that morning. A few patients were too sick to move outdoors due to their bedridden state. Following the service, staff escorted patients back to their respective wards.

Later that afternoon, at the end of their day shift duties, Addie and Opal changed their clothes to work in the gardens. For the next hour, they toiled under searing sun and oppressive heat. By four-thirty, they found themselves side by side, weeding the vegetable garden. "What did you think of the revival?" Addie asked.

Opal pulled off her wide-brimmed hat and wiped the sweat from her face with the back of her arm. "Preacher Foster did a great job talking about the Devil afoot lurking all around us. I had no idea that the Devil could also be in the form of German agents who are infiltrating this country. I can't believe that they were trying to undermine our economy by attempting to unionize Negro workers in an effort to drive up wages or destroy our resolve by blowing a munitions plant in New Jersey. They sure are sneaky bastards."

"I had no idea, either." Addie scraped at the hard red clay, adding a handful of manure to the soil.

"My goodness! This is the first time in a while where we have a chance to catch up on our cot tales. I hardly see you now that I'm only working three days a week." She put her hands over Addie's gloved ones. "Stop for a minute and talk to me. I can tell that there is something wrong. You are too quiet and serious these days. It's like you're locked away in your head, deep in thought."

Addie ceased digging. "You know me too well, Opal. That's what I love about you. We don't need any words to communicate with each other and can read each other's minds. I really don't want to burden you with the boring details of my life. You have your hands full with work and motherhood." It pained her to say *that* word, *motherhood*.

"I have the sense enough to know when something isn't right with you, Addie. Talk to me."

"Let's get out of the sun and sit under the shade of that tree over there." Addie pointed to a large oak along the back property line.

Grabbing canteens filled with water, the two meandered to the edge of the woods and sat on the cool ground.

Addie poured water down the back of her neck. "Ahh! That feels so much better. What did you think of Preacher Foster's wife? I was mesmerized by how fast she was pushing the pedals on her pump organ. I thought she was going to take off like she was riding a bicycle!"

Opal laughed heartily. "You are impossible, Addie. I love how you try and outsmart me by trying to divert and redirect the conversation."

"I'm as transparent as glass to you, aren't I?" Addie sighed. "So, what do you want to know?"

"How's married life with Randall? I rarely see the two of you these days and you've declined my brunch invitations lately. I know you're working all kinds of crazy hours inside and out-side this place." Opal pointed to the cornfield where Alan and Lena were inspecting the knee-high produce, and then over to the vegetable and herb gardens where staff were assisting pa-tients who were either weeding or harvesting the crops as a part of their rehabilitation and healing process.

*Should I be honest and tell her that while I may love Randall, I have fallen out of love with him? Was I ever really in love with him? Does she need to know that he hit me? Or, that he sleeps in a different bedroom these days? What would she say to me if I told her that I cry myself to sleep after Randall makes love to me? Or, that I envisioned having a different kind of wedding or that every time I look down at my wedding ring, it doesn't feel like I'm wearing the right one. It's supposed to be silver, not gold. What truths should I impart to her so that I'm not burdening her heart with my problems?* "Randall and I are doing just fine." *Truth.* "Randall enrolled into a speaker's bureau called the Four Minute Men. When he's not at the hospital, he takes to the road, traveling all over the state, to disseminate updates about the war and the civilian defense measures. The town folk gather in their local theaters or churches to hear him and others like him." *Truth.*

"I had no idea that he was doing that. What an honorable service he is providing to those people, especially those in our frontier country that may not have access to newspapers, let alone know how to read them."

"That's been the full extent of our lives these days. We're always in service to others in need."

"But, what about to yourself and to each other?" Opal backtracked. "Forgive me. I'm butting my nose into places where I shouldn't be poking around. Now that I'm a mother, I feel fearless and so protective of my loved ones. I feel like I'm a mama bear guarding her cubs."

Opal stopped to take a drink. "Addie, speaking of protecting your loved ones, I need to let you know that Shelby and I made a will now that we have Baby Eddie. We have designated you and Randall to be Baby Eddie's guardians should anything happen to us."

"But I'm already his godmother and nothing is going to happen to either of you." Addie felt conflicted. "I'm not trying to shirk my responsibilities, but what about your sister or family members? How do they feel about your decision?"

"We had a long talk with my father and Shelby's parents. I feel that my sister will not make a suitable parent for our son, and families on both sides are getting up in years enough that they don't want to be burdened with the responsibility of caring for a child. I can't say I blame them. They love to drop everything and travel. Since our country is at war, everything is different. People's personal finances are tight in part because they've invested in war bonds. There are food shortages all over this country, and the cost of living is skyrocketing. Why, even Shelby's barber jacked his prices from fifteen to twenty cents for a haircut last week! Did you know that you can't throw rice anymore at weddings or feed the birds with it?"

Addie sat in silence, soaking in the information.

"Are you alright?"

"Yes, it's difficult to process one's mortality, isn't it? And, to be honest, I was thinking of Garrett and what he's trying to process now that his fate lies in God's hands."

"You're still in love with him, aren't you, Addie?"

*Yes. Yes. I believe I am and always will be. Randall isn't Garrett.* Opting to avoid answering the question, Addie redirected. "I'm touched by the notion that you both would think that much of Randall and me. We're honored. Thank you."

Opal ribbed Addie. "There you go again."

"Come on, we've got some more work to do before the sun goes down."

"At least with this new Daylight Savings plan that President Wilson put into effect back in March, it's giving farmers and us another hour of sunlight to work in the fields." Opal put her hat back on.

"Oh, joy of joys!" Addie yawned. "I am growing weary and tired, Opal."

"It has been a long day. Just think, in a few short hours you'll be back at your apartment, soaking in a hot bubble bath." Opal helped Addie to her feet and the two began walking back to the vegetable garden. "I'm really looking forward to the big family picnic tomorrow." Opal clapped her hands in excitement. "I can't wait for you to see Baby Eddie. He's getting so big! He's got his grandfather wrapped around his little finger. I swear that child can do no wrong in my father's eyes. Why the other day, Baby Eddie spit up all over father's suit. He didn't mind it one bit. He just laughed it off. He is showing us his softer side more and more each day. And, I have the cutest outfit picked out for him. It's a …."

Opal's voice faded. Although she continued to talk, Addie wasn't listening. She had turned up the volume on her internal thoughts and concerns about Garrett, praying that he returned home safely, trading the battlefields for the cornfields…someday.

### SATURDAY NIGHT, TOUL SECTOR IN NORTHEASTERN FRANCE

Garrett looked up at the moon, praying that he'd be able to see the cornfields of home again, as he assisted a medic on the battlefield. Together, they packed a super absorbent cotton bandage into the abdomen of a dying soldier. The enemy sniper had caught their patrol unit off-guard when a few of the men started coughing violently, betraying their position. Soldiers fled and dove for cover behind trees and bushes while pulling the wounded out of harm's way.

"Hand me another Kotex bandage!" The medic held out his hand, keeping a watchful eye on the hemorrhaging man and his immediate surroundings.

Garrett rifled through the medical bag, pulling out another. He thought he had seen it all when he was working for the Atlanta firehouse, but military combat brought to light a whole new level of catastrophic human trauma, anguish, and pain. Compounding these field injuries, many American servicemen were falling victim to the flu or becoming a casualty from engaging in unprotected sex. Because of the United States' anti-contraception laws, the distribution of condoms was banned. As a result, syphilis swept through the units. He was growing weary and tired of sending men on stretchers by the truckloads to Camp Hospital 25, operated by the 43rd Base Hospital, The Emory Medical Unit. Comprised of volunteers organized and recruited by the Atlanta Chapter of the Red Cross, they too trained at Camp Gordon and were a part of the American Expeditionary Forces stationed in Bloise, France, southwest of his troop's current position. Comforted by the fact that there were other Georgians in France, every time he would walk through the hospital tents, he searched to find someone familiar, hoping he'd see Addie's face among the nurses. But, she was not to be found. Instead, he sought companionship with a French civilian nurse named Trinetta. It started with a simple exchange of smiles, which led to lunch dates or breaks to share a cigarette. Trinetta spoke English quite well, having been educated in a pri-

FRIDAY LATE MORNING, OCTOBER II, 1918, FIRST WARD

"Will you excuse me for a minute?" Charlie's voice was growing hoarse. He covered the mouthpiece on his office phone and productively coughed and coughed before finally blowing his nose on an old soft undershirt. He blotted sweat from his forehead and resumed his conversation with a representative from the Georgia Railroad and Power Company. "Sorry about that. I've got a bad cold. Please go over the new restrictions again with me just to be sure I have everything written down correctly."

Annoyed, the gentleman complied. "Per the orders by the War Industries Board and the Georgia Railroad and Power Company, there are new sanctions on electricity usage. Effective immediately, every night will be lightless. No one is allowed to use electricity after 6 pm on weekdays and after 9 pm on the weekends."

Charlie stifled an on-coming cough by swigging some bourbon straight from the bottle and chasing it with a spoonful of honey. "Who were the exceptions, again?" He threw down the spoon and picked up his pencil. His fingers were now sticky from the nectar.

"The exceptions include restaurants, fruit stands, bakeries, and apothecaries."

"Is that it?"

"No, there's more. Further measures are being taken to conserve gas and electricity. A skip-stop system is being implemented across the country for streetcars and such. Sign poles are being erected on the right side of the street. They're going to be highly visible. The 'Car Stop' sign will be painted in white with a red band around it." He expounded. "This is in addition to the City's gas administration's ban of Sunday joy rides. Only essential vehicles are permitted to drive in Georgia, including physicians who have a green cross on the windshield, funeral vehicles, and newspaper and milk trucks."

"My boss will be happy to hear that bit of news." Charlie wheezed while licking his fingers and wiping them on his pant leg.

"And, since money is tight, we feel that fines will go unpaid. Therefore, we have asked police departments statewide to submit the names of the violators to their local papers to be published."

"Jesus! I don't know what's worse, being publicly shamed or being put in jail."

"We're trying to think of how best to mitigate and manage wrong-doers. Jail time will be useless since so many men are needed to fight. Last month's draft recruiting men eighteen to forty-five years old doesn't leave us enough policemen to adequately patrol the streets."

"I understand. I'll get this article submitted in time to make the paper's deadline for the morning edition."

"Thank you for your time, sir. I hope you get over that nasty cold."

"I do, too." Charlie hung up the phone in the nick of time, struck by another violent coughing spell. Reaching for his metal wastepaper basket, he buried his head in it and threw up. "I feel like I'm dying. I've never felt so awful. I feel like my lungs are collapsing on me." His voice echoed from the bottom of the trash can. When the wave finally subsided, he fired up a cigar and chugged more bourbon. He continued to talk out loud to himself, growing delirious from a raging fever. "Fuck me. This country is falling to ruins. We're meatless…" He wheezed and coughed. "We're wheatless, and now were lightless, and the soldiers and civilians are urged to sleep roofless because of this Godforsaken flu epidemic." Charlie tried to take a deep breath but felt like he was drowning in his own fluids. He struggled to get oxygen into his lungs. He gripped the arms of his chair, digging his fingernails into the leather, as he fought and fought to breathe. Blood gurgled from his nose and mouth. Charlie turned cyanotic, and in mere minutes, he was lying dead at his desk.

### FRIDAY EVENING, SIXTH WARD

Inundated with patients, short staffed, and lacking essential supplies, Sacred Heart and Alexander Hall were reaching a critical breaking point. Even the medical personnel and volunteers were falling ill from the flu at rapid rates.

"Do you think the Germans have launched a biological attack on us?" One male patient reached out, touching Addie's arm.

"No, sir. I don't think so. This is due to a new form of a virus," she said from behind her mask.

"Nurse Engel? Nurse Engel?" Dr. Williams waved and called out to her from across the crowded med-surg unit. Patients were stacked in bunk beds, ones pulled from the nursing dorms, while others lay on make-shift palates on the floor. The rank stench of body fluids of every sort saturated the air.

"Yes, Dr. Williams?"

He motioned for her to follow him out into the hallway. She joined him.

"Addie, I need your help. We have encountered an illness that doesn't discriminate. While the flu typically affects the young or the elderly, this one is killing even the healthiest twenty to forty- year-olds. I've never seen anything like it. It is so highly contagious. Edward phoned earlier to tell me that a group of four women belonging to Trudy's hospital guild who had gathered at his house yesterday to sew bandages and socks were already dead."

"Oh my stars!" Addie covered her mouth. Before she could ask about the Alexander family, he directed her to assist him with the unthinkable.

"Addie, I am going to create a medical cocktail to euthanize our dying patients. I need to make sure our supplies hold out. We can't keep up this pace and I can't stop it. But I can prevent our patients from suffering. I will make their final determination. Gather a few volunteers. Once I've marked the patient's right hand with a cross with this red wax marker, have the volunteers transport the patients to the operating suite. I'll get Dr. Payne to assist me with the procedure." He saw Addie's wide-eyed expression. "We're in a crisis. It's an unspoken but not an uncommon practice. I'm merely expediting the inevitable. Organize a few more volunteers to escort the bodies down to the morgue. I'll get Joshua to bless the remains before they are bound and properly marked with their identification so their families can claim them. I need for you to let Lena know and notify the Wus that we'll need extra sheets delivered to the morgue. I'll call Dr. Bishop next door and propose the same for his patients, too."

Overwhelmed and under direct orders, Addie sprinted off to debrief Lena. Together, they implemented and assisted with his plan. As soon as the Sacred Heart and Alexander Hall hospital beds were vacated, new influenza convalescents filled them. The moaning, crying, and the wailing from the ailing and the grieving was dreadful and growing unbearable.

Addie, along with her colleagues, ran from one unit to another, carrying medications, supplies, and linens through the night. Finally reaching a point of complete exhaustion, Addie ran outside through the emergency room doors, still carrying a pillow and towels, tore off her mask, and fell to her knees in the dirt.

She buried her head in the pillow and let loose the most primal guttural scream. "God, I'm in the bowels of hell! What are you doing to your people? What can we do for your people? I can't take this anymore. I've never seen so much pain and suffering." Addie started rocking back and forth. "I can't do this anymore. God, I need your help!" Addie wailed. "I can't take losing another patient." Approaching car lights blinded Addie. She shielded her eyes, trying to make out if it was the McDaniel's brother's ambulance, a police car, or a personal vehicle.

The chauffeur jumped out of the car and opened the door to the back seat. A man emerged carrying something in his arms. Addie recognized the man's hunched silhouette in the darkness. It was Edward. Addie dropped everything and ran to him.

"They're all dead!" he cried out, still clutching a bundled blanket in his arms.

"Who? Mr. Alexander, who is dead?"

He didn't respond.

Addie grabbed the driver and shook him. "Who is dead? Tell me right now!"

He, too, was sobbing. "Mrs. Alexander. Pearl. Trip. Shelby and...."

"NO! NO! Don't you dare say her name! Don't you dare!" Addie beat her fists on his chest.

"Opal."

Addie flew into a rage, hammering her hands against him. He didn't try to stop her. "Take it back! Take everything you said back! It's not true! It can't be true!"

Edward finally spoke. "It's true, Addie. He speaks the truth."

Addie ran back over to him. "Please tell me that's not Baby Eddie."

"It is."

"Oh! Dear God in heaven! I can't breathe." Addie clutched her chest.

"But, he's alive! He's not sick. I've got him here in this quilt." Edward carefully unwrapped him, exposing Baby Eddie's sweet cherubic face. He was asleep, sucking on his fingers.

"He's alright? He's not sick? Are you sure?" Addie palpated his face and arms. He wasn't febrile. She bent over to listen to his heart and breathing. *Ba-dum. Ba-dum. Ba-dum. Ba-dum. His heartbeat is strong and regular, just like little Judson Miller's after I delivered him five years ago. I will never forget that for as long as I live.*

"Here." Edward held the infant out to Addie. "Take him. He's your responsibility now. I know you and Randall will provide for him." He dried his tears. "I know this is what my precious daughter wanted. She knew...somehow she knew that...."

Edward broke down again. Shoving his grandson into Addie's arms, he ducked into the car and slammed the door. A few minutes later, he got back out of the car. "I'm lost. I don't have anywhere to go. I don't know what to do. I don't want to go home. I can't go home right now."

Eddie started to stir. Addie began rocking him.

Edward shoved his hands into his coat pockets. "Can I be of help to you all here?"

"Yes, sir. We could definitely use an extra set of hands. Dr. Williams is in the operating suite with Dr. Payne. And, you'll find Nurse Hartman in the emergency room." Addie pointed toward the double doors.

He shed his overcoat and handed it to his driver. "Here, take this. Please drive my car around back and see if you can help the McDaniel brothers."

"Yes, sir."

Before Edward entered the hospital, he asked, "Addie? Is Joshua working tonight?"

"Yes, sir. He's also down in the morgue."

"What's he doing down there?"

"He was hearing confessions of the infected. Now, he's blessing the bodies of the deceased."

Edward nodded, turned around, and said under his breath, "I have a confession of my own to make to my son."

Addie watched him enter the hospital as the chauffeur turned the car around and drove toward the garage. Cloaked in darkness, she looked to the heavens, saying, "God? What the hell just happened?"

Eddie began to whimper. Tears welled in her eyes as she focused on his angelic face. He opened up his big blue eyes. She studied them for a minute. "God, I see you in everything. Even in the face of disaster, you are here, aren't you?" Tears streamed down her cheeks. Eddie carefully watched her facial expressions, grimaced, and cried with her. "We're going to miss her, aren't we, little one? God, what am I supposed to do now? Where do I even begin?"

Lena walked up to Addie and wrapped her in a blanket, replying, "Let's start by bringing you both in out of the cold and sequestering you in your husband's office. We can pull out one of his credenza drawers and use it for a crib. We'll open the windows and I'll have Mrs. Wu warm a bottle for him and bring up some extra blankets. Right now, you both need your rest. Tonight, I'll gather up diapers and all the necessary supplies you'll need to take care of him. Since Randall is speaking in Athens, Alan and I will drive you back to your apartment in the morning."

Addie exhausted and dazed, looked up at Lena. Words escaped her. *What's Randall going to say when he gets home?*

"I know I'm not your mother, Addie, but I will look after you as if you were my own. And, you will learn to do the same for Baby Eddie." Lena put her arm around Addie's shoulders and escorted them through the garden and into the back entrance of the hospital.

# 28

MONDAY, NOVEMBER 11, 1918, WORLD-WIDE

Enemy and Allied troops continued to battle throughout the European theater while the Spanish flu waged a war of its own across the globe. The day before, a Western Union Cable office in North Sydey, Nova Scotia, a town on eastern coast of Cape Breton Island, had received a top-secret encrypted message from Europe about battle plans that were effective now. Meanwhile, eight-thousand miles away, the virus invaded Western Samoa, a small island county in the Pacific Ocean, and began claiming more lives.

MONDAY MORNING, SIXTH WARD

Addie peered over the crib railings at Eddie. He was wide awake, blowing bubbles and grinning from ear to ear. "Good morning, Baby Eddie!" Addie cooed before hoisting him out and walking over to flip up the window blind. "Let's get you changed and cleaned up before breakfast." In her best baby-talk, she entertained him with the inflections in her voice. "Who's the best baby in the world? Why, you are, aren't you? You don't even make a fuss when you have a dirty diaper, do you?" Addie unpinned and peeled back the cotton cloth. "Holy, mother of God! You are much too little to make such a stinky-winky mess. How do you manage to do this? Phew! Phew!"

Eddie wiggled and giggled while she cleaned and changed him.

"Your daddy should be coming home this morning. He's been gone a lot longer than I expected, but heaven only knows what's detained him this time. I could say a few more things, but I won't speak ill of him in front of you even though you have no idea what I am saying, do you?"

Eddie, mesmerized, squealed, "Mmmmmm! Ooooooo! Na-na-na! Ba-ba-ba!

*Knock. Knock. Knock.*

"Who could that be? Could that be Daddy?" Addie called out, "Coming, dear!" Toting Eddie in one arm, she opened the front door. "Darling, I was expecting you home...."

Edward removed his hat. "Good morning, Addie." Two gentlemen standing beside him dressed in black overcoats did the same. "They're with the Four Minute Men."

"My condolences, ma'am," the shorter and rounder of the two blurted out.

"I'm sorry, I'm a bit confused. Won't y'all come in?" Addie stepped back, opening the door wider.

"Gentlemen, I'll take it from here. Thank you for notifying me of...." Edward hesitated and then entered. "Ah, how's my little grandson doing these days?" He reached out for Eddie and scooped him up, smothering him with kisses. "Is there some-where where we can sit?"

"Sure. Let's go into the living room." The two men vanished as Addie shut the door. She followed Edward into the next room. "What's this all about, Mr. Alexander?"

"Please, call me Edward. I think by now we can be on a first name basis since we're practically family, don't you?" Edward took a seat on the sofa.

Randall and Addie, having retained Lena's furniture, also kept her color palate unchanged. Addie loved the cream-color-ed walls and off-white trim, which provided instant warmth. A small fire crackled and popped in the fireplace, enhancing the quaint homey atmosphere.

"Yes, of course...Edward. What brings you here this morn-ing? Do you need me to come to the hospital today?" Nervous and without waiting for his response, she ploughed on, offering an explanation. "I took the day off to be with Randall. He's been down in the Savannah area these past few weeks and I was ex-pecting him home last night. I figured his train may have been delayed, especially with all of the extra documentation everyone needs to have in order to board these days."

Edward didn't know how to tell her. How would she take the news? He bounced Eddie up and down on his knee a few times before he spoke. "Addie, those two men came to my house this morning at Randall's request to tell me that he died from the flu over the weekend."

"WHAT?"

"Evidently, he fell ill while he was on the road. When he was admitted to the local hospital, his condition was too far gone.

Before he passed, he called his parents to tell them good-bye and they made arrangements to have his body sent back up to New York for a family funeral and burial."

The shock of the news was followed by a whole host of emotions. Sorting through them all, she settled on one. Indignant, Addie balked, "Why didn't he call me? Why am I the last to know? I'm his wife, for goodness sake!" She stomped her foot before collapsing into a nearby armchair. She buried her head in her hands. "They never thought I was good enough for him. Am I supposed to attend the funeral?" She looked up. Edward shook his head. Overcome, she ranted, "Those evil, snobby, uppity, bastards can go burn in hell! Oh, Jesus! I'm a widow!"

Startled by Addie's outburst, Eddie started wailing.

Edward held him out like a sack of potatoes. "Here, take him. He needs his mother."

"I'm not his mother!" Addie snapped, and then immediately regretted it.

Eddie cried harder. His face turned beet red.

Edward, empathetic to Addie's loss and sharing in Eddie's sorrow, wept. "Addie, my daughter knew that deep down you'd make a wonderful mother for him in the event...."

Eddie reached out to Addie.

Addie rushed over and plucked him out of Edward's hands. "Oh, Baby Eddie! I'm so sorry. Edward, I apologize for my behavior. What's to become of all of us now? I can't take any more loss. I've lost everyone I've ever loved. I just can't. I can't...." Addie trembled.

Edward stood and wrapped his arms around the two of them while they sobbed. "We need to pray, Addie. We need to pray right now for God's help. We must surrender to Him because we can't do this all by ourselves. We are never alone in our heartache."

Addie sniffed and nodded.

"Dear God, we ask that you comfort our broken hearts right now. We've endured so much loss and death over these past few months, not only personally but all over the world. Please be with Addie and my grandchild in their time of sorrow. We pray for her dearly departed husband, Randall and his family..."

*Sons of bitches! Sorry, God. I'm really, really angry and hurt right now.*

"...as we mourn his passing. We take solace in knowing that you are aware of the greater plans already in place and awaiting us. You are our hope and our future. We thank you for blessing us with gifts, gifts to lead, teach, and care for others. We are your humble servants, Lord. Please protect and strengthen us so that we can go forth and do your work in Your name, we pray. Amen."

"Amen." Addie pulled away. "What in heaven's name are we supposed to do now?"

Suddenly, there was a loud popping noise off in the distance.

"Those were gun shots." Edward grew concerned as he strained to listen.

Footsteps could be heard moving rapidly up and down the hall.

Addie picked up on a new noise. "Do you hear that? Doesn't that sound like pots and pans clanging through the walls?" A ruckus broke loose in the streets below. Addie and Edward bolted for the curved windows overlooking the square on Peachtree Street. Streetcars and automobiles had come to a complete stop.

Drivers honked their horns while some got out and started dancing on their hoods or in the middle of the street. Shop owners and customers flooded into the road. Hats flew up in the air. Windows opened on every floor of the Georgian Terrace. Guests leaned out, shouting and waving their scarves. Some even tore up paper and threw it like confetti. "Edward, what on earth is going on out there? Would you please open the window?"

Edward ran over to a side window, parted the curtains, unlatched and opened it. He put his hand to his ear. "Do you hear that? It's church bells! Lots and lots of them! Do you hear them?"

*Ding! Ding! Dong! Ding! Ding! Dong! Ding! Dong! Ding! Dong!*

"Hot diggity dog!" he said while swinging his arms and skipping over to Addie, planting a big kiss on her forehead. He was beaming, for the first time in a long while.

"What was that for?"

He cradled her face in his hands. "Our prayers have been answered, Addie. Everything is going to be okay. The war is over!"

"The war is over?" Addie stared at him in disbelief.

"The war is over!"

"The war is over!" Addie hugged Eddie and kissed him softly on his head. "Oh my stars! Baby Eddie, the war is over!!" *Oh, my God! Could Garrett still be alive?*

What began as an ordinary day became one of the most memorable in history. At 5:15 am, Germany had signed an armistice. As per the encrypted telegrams received the day prior, the world was notified that all fighting on the Western front was to cease on the eleventh month of the eleventh day at eleven o'clock in the morning.

Georgia Governor Dorsey closed city offices and superintendents of schools informed their principals to suspend classes for the rest of the day. Businesses shut their doors and hung "Closed" signs while jubilant citizens celebrated in the streets.

Mayor Chandler issued a proclamation, saying, "To the people of Atlanta: This is a great joy! The most terrible war in history has come to an end! Peace is again to reign throughout the world and freedom universally prevail!

"Let us not forget the sacrifices of those who have made our present happiness possible. There is much yet to be done. Our soldiers and sailors across the sea and at home must be cared for. Let this day be one when our gladness will take a substantial form, and funds needed by the United War Work be freely given…On tomorrow, Tuesday, the 12th, a victory parade will be held. The parade will form at 1:30 o'clock and be under the direction of Major-General Cameron, commander at Camp Gordon, who has just returned from the European front…

"The city hall and all city works in so far as practicable will be discontinued at 12 o'clock Tuesday, and it is hoped that the day will be generally observed by all our citizens as a half holiday."

# 29

Addie tucked Eddie into his crib and turned out the bedroom lights. Settling into the candlelit living room, she picked up her diary. She dated her entry, scribing,

*Blue,*

*Where do I even begin? So much has happened over this past year. Last year, this country went to war. The Great Fire claimed my home and destroyed much of the Fourth Ward. This year, the Spanish flu has taken its toll, not only in this town but all over the world. Like so many hundreds of thousands of others, I've lost my husband, my best friend Opal, most of her family, and hundreds of patients to this pandemic outbreak. I wanted to reach out to Mr. Darling to make sure he was okay, but I've been afraid to. During one of our many arguments, Randall told me that he and Garrett had been exchanging letters and that Garrett was aware that I married him. I cringed inside when he told me. A part of me felt like I betrayed Garrett somehow. But then I remembered our argument and that he broke my necklace. How do you learn to let go of the bitterness when that very person that hurt you can give his blood to heal you? I became despondent last*

299

*month when Randall read Garrett's most recent correspondence. He wrote to say that he had married a French woman, a nurse, by the name of Trina, who had two children, twins. She had lost her husband in a battle at sea and that they met earlier this year at a base hospital. Sensing that the war would soon be coming to an end, he plans on bringing his family back to the states when his division returns next year. I'll be honest, my soul was crushed when he said, "his family." But then I looked over at Baby Eddie. He's my family now, my responsibility, and I was overwhelmed with God's grace. I resent myself, knowing I can't be jealous of Garrett's life just because I made a bad decision to marry Randall. I have resigned myself to the fact that Garrett and I were never meant to be and that he still could be lost to the war or to the flu. But, right now, I have lost him to another. Blue, I must confess, he continues to haunt me in my dreams. I hear his voice calling out, "Come back to me, Addie. I love you, Addie." I can't shake it.*

Addie stopped and went into the kitchen to make a cup of hot tea. She returned and resumed writing. *I can't change anything now. I was lost and now I'm ready to reclaim my place in this world, not as Mrs. Randall Springer (God rest his soul), but as Addie Rose Engel. I felt like I disappeared for a while, but I'm slowly finding my way back. Life can turn on a dime when you least expect it. How I choose to react to that change is what defines me. I must admit, I'm a work in progress. I need to listen to my gut more and not ignore those feelings. When I didn't trust myself, I gave my heart to the wrong man. And, life taught me the difference between loving someone and being in love with someone. I hated myself for deceiving my heart and true feelings. But I'm learning how to forgive myself for making such a foolish mistake. I'm a different person now, having grown from the experience. I've learned to make peace, forgive, let go of my anger and resentment.*

*I tried calling Randall's parents, but they wouldn't accept "the widow's" phone calls, and I was told by the condescending female voice on the other end of the receiver to never call the house again. Instead, I wrote them a lovely letter, sent flowers to his funeral, and have donated his clothes to charity. I'm learning that there are elements in life that one can do little about. And, there are moments in life where I am blinded by the dark and I can't find my way. Or, that I can't move because I'm so tired, too exhausted to even take my next breath. But I do because I'm still alive and I'm Baby Eddie's mother.*

*Tonight, freedom reigns throughout the land and I, too, am free! Free to be me. Maw often told me about two thieves that can rob life from you: fear and regret. I choose to not live in their shadows anymore.*

### DECEMBER 28, 1918, JOURNAL OF THE AMERICAN MEDICAL ASSOCIATION

"...1918 has gone: a year momentous as the termination of the most cruel was in the annals of the human race; a year which marked, the end at least for a time, of man's destruction of man; unfortunately a year in which developed a most fatal infectious disease causing the death of hundreds of thousands of human beings. Medical science for four and one-half years devoted itself to putting men on the firing line and keeping them there. Now it must turn with its whole might to combating the greatest enemy of all—infectious disease."

# 30

Post-war, Atlanta's social scene awoke with a new vigor. Calendars filled as clubs and organizations returned to hosting grand galas and gatherings. And in true Southern fashion, debutantes bloomed and reemerged like the vibrant colored azaleas in spring to make their first introductions at an array of community events and tea parties.

While the city's economy was on the mend, the Fourth Ward, like Europe, was also in a period of reconstruction and renewal. Communities and families, once broken and torn apart by the savages and losses of the war and flu pandemic, were finally on the road to healing and recovery.

## TUESDAY MORNING, SIXTH WARD

*I will find beauty in this day,* Addie said to herself as she stepped off the Ponce apartment elevator pushing a blue baby buggy. She adopted the new mantra after reading a Mark Twain quote a few months ago in the *Atlanta Dispatch*: "Give every day the chance to become the most beautiful day of your life."

Struck by the notion to dress up today, she did, trusting her feelings to do just that. She felt a bit self-conscious about wearing her burgundy Edwardian suit, the same outfit she wore to Opal's brunch last year, and knew she was overdressed to shop at the local fruit stand as she secured a new hat with coiled fabric flowers and pink ostrich feathers in place. Ever since Opal's death, one of her best dresses hung in her closet. She couldn't bring herself to wear it again, until this morning. Something had changed in her when she awoke. While the sun still rose from the east and hung in a cloudless blue sky, the wind blew in from a different direction today, from the east and not the west like it typically did.

Suppressing any negative internal comments, she strutted through the lobby, her head held high. Stopping in front of the wall of mail boxes, she retrieved her key from her purse and unlocked her box. She pulled out a worn and dirty letter postmarked from France, February 1919. Addressed to Randall Springer at the hospital, it was hand-marked to forward it to his home address. Flipping it over, she saw there wasn't a return address. She opened it and then stuffed it into her purse. Lifting the blanket to check on Eddie, she found him napping. Addie rushed out of the side door, pushing the stroller as fast as she could, dodging pedestrians on the sidewalk as she made her way to the park a few blocks away. Finding an empty bench under a Dogwood tree, she sat down, and pulled out the letter. Breathless, her pulse raced.

*26 February, 1919*

*Dear Randall,*

*I hope this letter finds you and Addie doing well. The 82ⁿᵈ Division is relocating to Bordeaux and setting sail across the Atlantic early in May. We anticipate making it to New York by the end of the month. From there, I'll travel by train back to Hope, where I'll join my awaiting family. Trina, Albert, and Desiree will depart from France to America ahead of me. They are leaving the country at the end of this week. I am looking forward to seeing familiar faces and long to return to the comforts of Father's home-cooked meals. While I enjoyed being a firefighter, this city mouse is going back to being a country mouse (Addie will get the joke). I have decided to resume working with corn and vegetables, especially now after working alongside our medics in combat. I've seen the unthinkable and the atrocities haunt me at night.*

*Since father still hasn't invested in a telephone, please write back to me at my Hope address. Father will keep your letter waiting for me to open until my return. I look forward to your reply and have prayed nightly that God has kept you both safe. Over here, the flu claimed as many soldiers as bullets and bombs did, with our unit suffering over 7,500 battlefield-related casualties alone.*

*Until we meet again under the golden summer sun with the Georgia red clay under our boots, God willing.*

*Sincerely, your friend,*

*Garrett*

"Oh my stars! Garrett has no idea that Randall died. I need to tell him. Should I tell him? Baby Eddie, what do you think?"

Addie lifted the blanket. This time, Eddie was wide awake and smiling. "Are you smiling because you have just pooped or are you smiling at me because we need to drive up to Hope?"

Eddie wiggled his arms and legs in excitement, giggling and gurgling while making "m" sounds.

Addie handed him his rattle. "I guess that settles it. Let's take a road trip. I'm going to show you my hometown and introduce you to a childhood friend and his family. I'll show you where I went to school and where my family is buried on the old family farm in a place called Guardian Angel Cemetery. But first, we need to run back up to the apartment to pack a few things for our excursion and ring Lena to explain to her that I need the night off tonight for personal reasons."

### TUESDAY LATE AFTERNOON, HOPE, GEORGIA

As the sun was beginning its descent in the western sky, Addie had already stopped by the family cemetery and was driving down the dirt road toward the Darling farm. Distant memories, fond and tragic, flooded back. As she steered the car, off in the distance she saw a man chasing two children in the side yard of the Darling property. Addie was relieved to see that Mr. Darling hadn't fallen victim to the flu. Brown, yellow, and white chickens flew up in the air and flapped their wings to avoid being caught up in the fray. The cotton was already in the ground and the cornfields were well on their way to being knee-high by the fourth of July as the green stalks swayed in the humid summer breeze. She rolled down her window and stuck her hand out, feeling the wind pass over her white-gloved fingers. As she approached the driveway, exhilaration suddenly gave way to fear. *I can't do it. I can't stop. I can't bring myself to slow down this car. How do I even begin to make small talk with Garrett? I'm still mad that he hurt me. Or, perhaps, I should start by thanking him for saving my life, or should I just bust out with, 'Hey! I'm so glad you made it back home. Thank you for your service to this country. By the way, your best friend is dead and I'm a widow now.'* Addie kept her foot on the accelerator, passing the white shiplap farmhouse with green shutters and white wicker furniture on the front porch. *I can't do it. I don't know what to say.*

Eddie, lying in the bassinet in the front seat, started to fuss.

"Oh, don't cry, little one. I'll drive into town and see if we can't find us a place to stop so I can feed you. I'm a bit parched myself and would love to drink an icy cold Coca-Cola right now."

Addie drove into the downtown area of Hope. She couldn't believe how much it had changed. There was a new men's hat shop, a women's dress store, a bakery, and even a new gas station. Finding a parking spot, she fed Eddie in the car. When he returned to a state of slumber, she placed him in the baby carriage and strolled down the town sidewalks in search of the familiar among the many faces on the street, but too much time had passed, and no one recognized her. She was a stranger in their eyes. Spotting the local drug store, she stepped inside.

*Ding. Ding.* The bell on the door rang out.

Eager to quench her thirst with the dark refreshing fountain soda, Addie placed her order and took a seat at a bistro table in the bay window. She rocked the buggy back and forth, watching the people pass by as Eddie slept. Addie spotted two middle-aged women a few doors down, each dressed in a white blouse and brown full skirts with matching straw hats. Addie assumed they were either be best friends or sisters by the looks of them. They even clutched their purses in the same manner as they waltzed into the store.

*Ding. Ding.*

"Good afternoon, ladies!" the soda jerk said from behind the counter.

"Good afternoon, Thaddeus," they replied as they started browsing.

The taller of the two spoke. "Ida Mae, I think it is a great idea to introduce your daughter to that new farm boy."

"Thelma, don't you think it's too soon? After all, it's only been four months since they buried his wife."

"Why Ida Mae, I do not. Every good and viable man needs a good woman." Thelma tossed a wink over at Thaddeus, who busied himself wiping the granite counters over and over again, trying to soak in every word of their conversation, just like Addie was doing.

"He needs an *American* woman that can drive a car on the right side of the road and not the left-hand side. Did you know she nearly killed my brother's cousin's wife, Tilly, who was walking on the dirt road? Poor Tilly dove into a ditch when the woman nearly hit her and swerved and flipped her truck in the opposite ditch."

"It burst into flames. I know. I know. We've all heard the story over and over again, Ida Mae. It was a tragic end to that foreigner's short life here. Now all that man has is those two kids to take care of."

Picking up a can of peaches, she studied the label before returning it to the shelf. "It ain't natural for two men to be raising kids. I told the preacher that very same thing last Sunday. It ain't natural, I say."

*Ding. Ding.*

Addie darted from the store and was making her way back to the Darling farm as fast as she could. *Be calm. Don't speed. Be yourself. Act natural. Don't get nervous. Don't get flustered. You are still Mrs. Randall Maddox to him.* She talked to herself the entire way until she turned into the driveway of the Darling residence. Then the silence was deafening. She took a deep breath, lifted Eddie out of his carrier, and exited the car. The children and Mr. Darling weren't in the side yard anymore. They were nowhere to be seen, but Addie heard them off in the distance in the cotton field. The children's laughter complemented the rolling rhythmic songs of the cicada and the chirps and tweets of the birds in the magnolia trees overhead.

*Screech. Slam.*

Addie recognized the sound. It was the back screen door opening and closing. She approached, passing a row of newly planted rose bushes. *They're just like the ones Maw use to plant in our backyard. That's so weird.* She adjusted Eddie on her right hip and turned the corner of the house. *Garrett!* He was a bit thinner, wearing his old coveralls and white cotton button down shirt under it, bent over a basket filled with laundry. He was hanging the wet clothes and sheets on the line, securing them in place with wooden clothespins. The linens danced in the breeze. She just stood there, watching him.

Sensing her eyes on him, Garrett turned around. He dropped

the clothes to the ground. Covering his mouth, he stifled his sobs as they walked toward each other. He stopped, remembering she was Mrs. Randall Springer and not Addie Engel any more. And she had a baby? He didn't think she was able to have children. Maybe all of it was a bad dream. He worried that she was still angry with him. He didn't know what to say, and yet there was so much to say to Addie, but he couldn't find the right words for Mrs. Springer. He just stood there.

"Hey!" Her hair caught the sunlight just like the pebble filled with Fools Gold that he had given her before she left for the city years ago.

"You always knew how to kick off a conversation." He laughed nervously, running his hands through his copper hair.

*The wrinkles around his forehead and eyes tell a story of stress, worry, and of things he can't unsee. I recognize the look.* Realizing that the last time she saw him, it ended in a fight, Addie motioned for him that it was okay to approach her. "Well, don't just stand there. Come give me a hug."

Garrett awkwardly patted her on the back. "Where's Randall and by the way, are you babysitting someone's child? Who is this?"

"This is Eddie." Overcome by a rush of heat and emotions, Addie swayed.

Garrett caught her before she fell and swiftly removed Eddie from her arms while she steadied herself against his body.

"I think the heat is getting to me." Addie pulled off her gloves and hat, rolled up her sleeves, and sat down on the ground to remove her boots and socks. She stood up, grounding herself in the green grass with the cool red clay under her bare feet. "Oh, that feels so much better."

Garrett walked over to the laundry basket and laid Eddie amongst the clean laundry. Grabbing a bucket of fresh drawn water from the pump well, Garrett offered her a wooden ladle filled with cool water.

She took it from him and drank. "Thank you." She handed it back to him. "Can we walk and talk. I've got so much to tell you, and I don't know where to begin."

"Sure." They started to stroll around the property, mindful to stay close to Eddie.

She shook out her hands, her cheeks flushed. "I'm a bundle of nerves. I actually drove past this place and stopped in town before I got up enough nerve to come back here."

"Why? Why would you be nervous?"

Addie scanned her surroundings. "Where's your wife?"

Garrett pointed in the direction of the cemetery.

Still unsure if the two women had been talking about Garrett's wife, Addie asked, "Is she putting flowers on your mother's grave?"

He spoke with sorrow in his voice, but there weren't any tears. "No, Dad buried her back in March before I got home. Trina got into an accident. She took the truck and was heading to the market, but she realized she was driving on the wrong side of the road and to avoid hitting a woman, overcorrected and flipped it into a ditch. The truck burst into flames. The sheriff said she broke her back and died instantly."

"Oh, I'm so sorry to hear that, Garrett. I truly am."

"Thank you. I never thought I'd be a widower when I got home. I'm so numb, Addie. I've lost so many friends in battle or to the flu that I learned to compartmentalize my feelings about mortality. I'm almost callous to it, now. I've simply accepted it as a part of life. We inhale, we bring life into the world. We exhale, we embrace death. It's the last thing our bodies do before our souls depart this world."

Addie stopped in front of a rose bush. She studied the blooming red roses.

"I planted these last month."

"They're just like Maw's."

"You're right. They're from her rose garden. I took a few that were growing up by the cemetery and transplanted them here. I don't know why I did it. I thought of you every time I saw them. Maybe, I just wanted a piece of something familiar again."

"I know exactly what you mean." A glint of gold caught her eye from one of the branches. Addie carefully parted the thorny stems and removed the heart-shaped pendant necklace hanging from it. She stared at it in disbelief.

"I am so sorry for everything that happened between us. Would you please forgive me? I was such a horse's ass. The alcohol and gambling got the better of me. I repaired your necklace and carried it into battle with me." He pressed his hand to his heart. "I kept it in my right breast pocket and would touch it before I entered combat. It was my good-luck charm. And, here you are, standing right here in front of me. I've traveled to Europe and back and all I know is that I am home. This is my home." He wanted to say, 'You are my home, Addie. I planted these rose bushes hoping to bring you back to me. I was calling you home.' But he knew she wasn't his any longer. He watched her green eyes spark back to life and begin to water. The wind blew pieces of her auburn hair around her face. He ached for her. He wanted to hold her in his arms, but the invisible wall between them was impenetrable. She belonged to Randall.

Addie knew exactly how Garrett was feeling. They never needed words to know what the other was thinking. *I need to break down this barrier between us.* She held up the necklace. "I forgive you. I forgave you a long time ago, Garrett. I was just too proud to tell you, and by the time I learned that you saved my life, you were already gone. I didn't know where to find you to tell you. Randall never told me where you were stationed. And, to be honest, I never probed him further. But I prayed every night in silence that God and his angels protected you from harm. Your blood courses through my veins. Garrett, you have always been with me. You never left me." Movement from the basket caught Addie's eye. "Please, excuse me." Addie lifted her skirt and ran over to pick up Eddie. As she hoisted him up, he gave her the biggest grin and blew a few bubbles. "Do you have gas, little one?"

Eddie mouthed *ma-ma-ma* before he finally discovered his voice. "Mama. Mama. Mama."

"Oh my God! You spoke, Baby Eddie! You spoke!" Addie spun around. "You said *mama*! You called me Mama!" She turned to Garrett. "He called me Mama!"

Garrett remained cool and unaffected, having sequestered his rising feelings and squashing any chance of hope that remained. He couldn't bear being hurt anymore. He walled up his heart. "It's getting late. I need to get supper on the table. Shouldn't you be getting back to the city? I bet Randall will be pleased to hear that Eddie said his first words today. By the way, when did you adopt?"

*Now there's that awkwardness between us again. It's like we're stepping all over each other's toes at a barn dance. We aren't in sync with each other anymore. I am getting the feeling that my presence here is irritating him. Perhaps the war changed him? He just lost his wife. I don't need to burden him with any more loss. I need to go.* Addie heard the sound of children's laughter approaching. She couldn't bring herself to meeting them, let alone see Mr. Darling. She quickly gathered her clothes, returned the necklace to Garrett as she said polite good-byes in haste, and raced back to the car. Once Eddie was secured, she threw the car into reverse and peeled out onto the country road, leaving behind a cloud of ochre dust. Through the tears, she forbade herself from looking back all the way home to Atlanta.

# 31

Nurse Hartman counted the paper medication cups. "Everything here seems to be in order," Lena said as she double-checked the medication tray before handing it off to the student nurse. "Please make sure Nurse O'Malley rounds with you and together, check each patient's chart to make sure the right medicine, the right dosage, is administered to the right patient."

"Yes, Nurse Hartman," the student confirmed.

Lena stepped out of the med-surg unit and returned to her desk.

*Ring. Ring.*

Lena picked up the phone, "Hello? Sacred Heart Hospital, this is Nurse Hartman speaking. How may I help you?"

"Nurse Hartman, this is Garrett Darling. I'm not sure if you remember me but...."

"Of course, I remember who you are. How wonderful it is to hear your voice. I must tell you how proud I am of your service to this country."

"Well, thank you, ma'am. It's good to be back home."

"I'm sure that it is. I'm a bit confused as to why you want to talk with me. What can I do for you, Garrett?"

"I'm calling because…." Garrett was regretting making the call. But there was something odd about Addie's behavior yesterday that he couldn't put his finger on. The feeling gnawed at him throughout the night. After discussing it over with his father earlier that morning over coffee, he drove into Hope to place the call. "I'm calling because I wanted to reconnect with Dr. Randall Springer now that I've returned from the war. When I spoke with hospital concierge, asking to speak to him, she patched my call through to you. So, naturally, I'm a bit confused, too. Can you please tell me where I can find him?"

### WEDNESDAY LATE NIGHT, SIXTH WARD

Addie, exhausted from picking up an extra shift in the emergency room, bathed and changed into her nightgown, slipping on her purple silk bathrobe. She checked in on Eddie, who was sleeping peacefully. Grateful for the babysitting services of Mrs. Swanson—her next-door neighbor, also a widow, who was in her late 50s—Addie knew she was able to call on her at a moment's notice when the hospital required her services. Taking a seat on the edge of the couch, she retrieved her diary off the coffee table. From between the back pages, she pulled out Emiline's drawing and studied it before tucking it away again. Wound tight like the pin curls in her hair, Addie was hoping that work would take her mind off the debacle that was her reunion with Garrett, but it didn't. She kept playing the events over and over in her mind.

*What is wrong with me? Why couldn't I have been honest with Garrett and come right out to tell him the truth? God, I'm such an idiot!*

*Knock. Knock.*

Startled, she set her diary down and shot up off the sofa, glancing over at the clock on the wall. *Ten-thirty! I wonder who it could be. Maybe Mrs. Swanson needs to borrow an egg or a cup of sugar. She is famous for baking and cooking concoctions late into the night.* Addie unlocked the door and opened it. "Yes?"

Garrett stood there, dressed in his Sunday best, his hair slicked back. He held a bouquet of red roses in his hand.

Caught completely off guard, unsure if she should be ecstatic or angry, she peppered him with questions. "How do you know where I live? What are you doing here at this late hour? How did you find me? Oh, God! Have you been drinking, again?"

"No, Addie, I'm not drunk. I need to talk to you."

"I think we've said everything we need to say to each other, don't you?" She started to close the door.

He stuck out his shiny black boot in the door, preventing her from closing it. "I don't think you have, Addie."

Addie opened the door again and rolled her eyes. "Get in here before the neighbors think I've turned into a Lady of the Evening." She pointed toward the living room. "Come in. Can I get you something to drink?"

"No. I'm good. I'm really good right now." Garrett presented her with the hand-cut flowers. "Here, these are for you."

"Thank you. Make yourself comfortable and I'll put these in water. I'll be right back." *Oh my God! How did he know where I lived? Why is he here at such a late hour? Why is he dressed up? What are the flowers for?* Finding a glass pitcher half-filled with water on the kitchen counter, she stuck them in it. Catching her reflection in the glass framed picture in the hall, a watercolor painting of a country landscape, she removed the bobby pins from her spit curls and raked her fingers through her hair. *Am I a sight, or what? I wonder if he can tell that I've been crying.* She straightened her robe and pinched her cheeks. Primped and ready, she rejoined him for a split second. Overwhelmed by nerves, she excused herself again. "Sorry, I need to check on my son. I'll be right back."

Garrett took a seat on the far end of the couch, moving her diary to the coffee table. "Don't you mean Opal's son?"

Addie froze and slowly backtracked. "How do you know that?"

"I drove into Hope today and called the hospital."

"Uhhh, who did you speak to?"

"I spoke with Nurse Hartman. I wanted to reconnect with Randall."

Addie fiddled with her robe sash.

"I didn't know...."

"Didn't know what?"

"I didn't know that Randall died."

"Well, he did. He up and died on me. Let me guess, Lena told you all about that, too?"

"Yes, she did."

"I guess that catches you up on every tragic thing that has happened since we last saw each other." Addie folded her arms across her chest.

Garrett could tell she was a bundle of nerves. She wasn't one that took too keenly to surprises. Silence passed between them before he spoke again. "After you left in such a hurry yesterday, I was bothered by your behavior. I hated how we left things. You avoided answering any of my questions and you didn't even stay to see my dad or my kids. I think there is still a cloud of dust lingering outside our house from where you spun out of the drive. It was so large it engulfed everything in sight. Dad and I may have to repaint the house. It's orange now."

Addie started to giggle before lowering her arms and giving way to a full belly laugh. "Oh my stars! I haven't laughed like that in so long." She sat down on the opposite end of the sofa, facing him. "I'm so sorry about that. I did leave your house like a maniac, didn't I? I bet you thought my cheese was slipping off my cracker and I had gone mental, didn't you?"

"I did."

"Hey! Is that very nice?" She threw a decorative pillow at him.

He caught it. "I'm glad to see that you still have a sense of humor."

"It's the only thing that is keeping me sane these days, Garrett. I swear, if I didn't have Eddie, you'd find me wandering the halls wearing a white patient gown over in the insane asylum in Milledgeville."

"There's my Addie." Garrett inched closer to her.

"On a more serious note and you are going to think I am the most awful person for saying this, but I must tell you that when Randall died, the burden of being called Mrs. Randall Springer lifted." She looked down at her gold band and removed it, placing it on the coffee table on top of her diary. "I never belonged to him."

"It doesn't come as a big surprise to me, Addie. After all, I was his roommate. I always thought it was odd that he never mentioned you in his letters. He always wrote that he was becoming an important man with high aspirations, discussing his invaluable work either at Sacred Heart or with the Four Minute Men."

"I should have known better. I got caught up in a whirlwind of emotions. I married the part of him that I grew to admire and respect at the hospital and came to despise the narcissistic side that devalued my worth in the relationship." Addie watched Garrett scoot closer. He reached out and touched her hand. She wrapped her other hand around his. "Don't ever leave me again, Garrett. I don't ever want to let go of you." She started to cry.

Scooping her up into his embrace, she buried her head in his shoulder and sobbed. The familiar all came rushing back – her lilac scented hair, her touch, and her love for him overflowed. "You asked me about the rose bushes?" Addie nodded. "Well, I planted them and never gave up hope that you'd come back to me someday."

"That day is today." Addie grabbed him tighter. "I prayed so hard that you'd come back to me, too. I was such a fool to not see that what we had was so special. Why didn't I accept your proposal so long ago? Why did I arrogantly gamble away the sands of time in our precious friendship?"

"It wasn't our time then."

"I felt like we were so out of sync yesterday."

"We were because I was visited by Mrs. Randall Springer. Tonight, I'm calling on Ms. Addie Engel and asking her to be my wife." Garrett pulled out the necklace and placed it around her neck. She melted into him as he tenderly kissed her cheeks, pressing his lips and body to hers. "Let's reset our hourglass, start over, and begin anew. I love you completely, my dear Addie."

"I love you in this world and beyond, Garrett Darling." Addie reached into her bathrobe pocket and pulled out the pebble he had given to her. She handed it to him. "I've carried this with me everywhere. I've never let you go. I've always been yours and I'd be honored to be your wife, to walk hand in hand with you, until I take my last breath on this earth. I am forever yours." She kissed him passionately.

Garrett stopped briefly, adding, "You do realize that we have three kids between us, right?"

Addie laughed. "Isn't that crazy? There were days when I thought that none of this could have been possible. I can't wait to meet Albert and Desiree."

"I love them as my own. And, you will, too. They are the best parts of their mother. They bring me so much joy."

"When would you like me to meet them?" Addie caressed the lines in his face.

"Tomorrow. Tonight, the stars shine for us, my dear." Garrett picked her up. Realizing he didn't know which direction to go, Addie stifled her giggles while pointing the way to the bedroom. They took their time to rediscover one another before their bodies moved in unison once again.

# 32

*Ding! Dong! Ding! Dong!* The church bells rang out from the small white Methodist church in Hope. A few school-aged children took turns pulling on the rope in the narthex, all dressed in their best clothes.

"That's enough, kids." Mr. Darling shooed them along. "Don't want to alarm some town folk into thinkin' we got some kind of emergency or somethin'. Better go find your parents and take a seat. The weddin' is 'bout ready to start."

"Psst! Psst!" Addie peered around the front door of the church, motioning for Mr. Darling to come and join her outside.

He obliged. Addie was dressed in Mrs. Darling's scoop-necked white lace wedding gown with sheer butterfly sleeves. He wiped away tears. "Well, don't you just look like an angel! Wait until my son sees you in a few minutes. You're gonna take his breath away, I tell ya."

"Mrs. Wu did a great job bringing this beautiful gown back to life, didn't she?"

Mr. Darling nodded. "You look radiant."

"It's time," a female voice said from inside.

"Best I go take my place next to my son." He pecked her cheek. "I'll see you in there." He turned to walk away and then returned. "I almost forgot to give you this." He handed her a blue handkerchief embroidered with white flowers. "It was my wife's, too. Thought it might come in handy."

"Oh! Thank you. That was so sweet of you to do." Addie tucked it in her white glove, lifted her veil over Opal's tiara, and lowered it over her face. She stepped into the church, finding Edward clad in his morning suit and carrying Eddie, who wore a matching suit, custom made by Mr. and Mrs. Wu.

Addie's lower lip quivered; she bit it.

"Don't you dare start crying, young lady. If you start wailing, then I'm going to have to join you, and then Eddie and the rest of that congregation in there are going to be bawling their heads off right along with you. And, you don't want to do that, do you?"

Addie smiled and shook her head. "No, sir. Thank you for being here for me, to give *us* away."

"I was honored that you asked, knowing that my family is smiling down on all of us today. I'm always going to be here for you and Eddie."

"By the way, where are Albert and Desiree?"

"Lena and Alan are taking care of them and they are already inside with the other members of our Sacred Heart family." Edward offered his arm and Addie slipped her arm through his as they waited for two teenage boys to open the sanctuary doors. When they did, Addie reached up and touched her heart pendant.

The pianist placed her fingers on the keys and played Mendelssohn's "*Wedding March*" in C major. Garrett's knees buckled when he saw Addie coming down the aisle. He grabbed his father's arm and broke down. He couldn't believe this day had finally arrived.

As Addie processed, she felt the warmth and love overflowing in her heart, from Maw, Paw, Sissy, Ben, Mrs. Gray, Opal and Emiline. She envisioned them all walking with her. *I'm not alone. I know you all are a part of me. I carry your love for me with me everywhere I go. I can feel your presence with me now and I thank you for being here. Today, I am marrying my best friend, the love of my life, for richer or for poorer, in sickness and in health, until death us do part. I do love you so, Garrett Darling. I've finally come home, finding my home with you amongst the high cotton and magnolias.*

# 33

*Dear Blue,*

*What a year 1919 has been! I'm looking forward to celebrating our first Christmas as the Darling family. Garrett and I have been wrapping presents throughout the evening and placing them under the Christmas tree, filled with hand-made ornaments from Albert and Desiree. I can't wait to see the expressions on the kids' faces in the morning. I never knew my heart could overflow with such love and joy.*

Addie flipped the pages back and reviewed her very first entry. *Name: Addie Rose Engel…Life goals: 1) Make a difference in this world by being the best nurse and person I can be; 2) Help others; 3) Travel the world; 4) Find a place that I can call "home" amongst the high cotton and magnolias; and 5) Marry the love of my life and have a family of my own. Favorite Bible quote: Again, Jesus spoke to them saying, "I am the light of the world; he who follows me will not walk in darkness, but will have the light of life." (John 8:12). (It reminds me of what Maw used to tell me, to walk in the light and shy away from the temptations of the demons in the dark). Favorite quote: "The two most important days in your life are the day you are born and the day you find out why." – Mark Twain. Dear Lord above, I'm still trying to figure all that out....*

She smiled and resumed writing, *As I reflect over the years, I never understood until now that all of life's trials and tribulations are purposeful, to bring us to a higher level of appreciation and gratefulness. Together, Garrett and I look forward to finding the beauty in each day in the years to come.*

# 34

Desiree held her father's hand as they studied the brand new "History of Sacred Heart and Alexander Hall Hospitals" exhibit on the first floor of Sacred Heart Medical Center.

"I still am amazed how the founder, Mr. Alexander, had the foresight to build these hospitals and design them knowing one day it would become a large incorporated medical complex and teaching campus."

Garrett, now grey and in his mid-sixties, squeezed his daughter's hand. "When the tornados hit Georgia in the early 50s, those storms and high winds caused major damage throughout the city and to the hospitals. Alexander Hall had a few large trees land on the building. When they were rebuilding, found that there was travertine tile underneath the red brick façade. The board chose to reveal Edward's construction secrets and re-design the entire medical center into what it is today."

"I hate that they had to tear down the old Scott House." Desiree examined vintage photos and then pointed. "Oh! Look at

Mom's nursing uniform, cap, and cape. That was a very honorable thing for you to do on her behalf, Dad. Did you see how they displayed her pin in this lighted box?"

Garrett squinted, adjusting his glasses to get a better look at it. "I saw your mom graduate and receive this pin. Your mom wore that on her collar when she returned to teach down here a few days a week when you kids got older. Wore it nearly every day up until the time she got sick." He directed Desiree's attention to a vintage black and white photo. "I love this picture of her when she was a student, sitting next to Ed's mom on the couch."

"They were so young."

Garrett laughed. "You were once that young, too, if I recall."

"Once, before I went to med school and became a mom of two children."

"Two lovely grandchildren, I might add."

"Your mother and I are so proud of you, of all of our children. You're an up and coming obstetrician, Albert is a police officer, and Ed is following in the footsteps of his grandfather, learning how to manage this place."

Garrett looked at his wristwatch. "It's time. We need to get back to the room."

Weaving their way through the hospital corridors to the elevators, passing the Edward Alexander II Auditorium, they rode up to the ninth floor, the Waxman Cancer Unit. The medical staff bustled behind the nursing desk, answering call lights, while machines beeped and buzzed from inside the patient rooms as they walked by them.

"What's your favorite memory, Dad?"

"Gosh, there are so many. What's yours?"

"I loved our family trips abroad, like to France to see where my birth parents grew up. Oh, remember that ride on the prop plane to Hawaii when Ed threw up on the stewardess?" Desiree howled with laughter.

"How could I forget, Dr. Miller!" Ed, wearing a *Director of Emergency Services* badge, emerged from the next room and kissed his sister on the cheek. "Hey, Dad."

Garrett embraced his son. "How's she doing?"

"Dr. Miller told me that she is transitioning and moving on to the Elysian Fields of heroic souls."

"Is she in any more pain?" Desiree asked as the three entered the room to find the rest of the family, children, and grandchildren huddled around the bed where Addie lay.

Garrett walked over to her and took her hand, running his fingers over her white gold wedding band while Addie slowly opened her eyes. "Hey! How's my girl doing?" He hated that the pancreatic cancer had metastasized and was stealing his love from him.

She tugged at the oxygen mask and removed it. "I've…had… better days. I'm…tired, Garrett."

He nodded, fighting back tears.

"I loved…I've lived."

Dr. Judson Miller watched the telemetry monitor. Her heartbeat was bradycardic and irregular. He picked up her other hand. "My mother used to tell me the story over and over again how you helped deliver me into this world. I believe that you willed for me to be a doctor that very day so that I could be here to take care of you and return the favor. I thank the good Lord for bringing us together."

Breathless, Addie panted, "God…is…always…good…all… the…time."

Albert wandered over to the window and raised the blinds. "Dad, y'all need to come see this." He cranked the window open. "There's a group of people gathering below lighting candles and singing."

Desiree reached out to take Judson's hand and walked over to join them. "We organized a candlelight vigil for Mom." She reached in her purse and pulled out a candle and holder and lit it, placing it in the window. "She has touched so many lives."

"Who are all those people?" Garrett asked.

Ed replied, "They are nurses, our medical staff, former patients, and their families."

"Can you hear them singing?" Albert cupped his hand to his ear.

A guitarist led the crowd in song. "Softly and tenderly Jesus is calling, calling for you and for me." The group went on to sing all four verses. They followed it with "O Jesus, I Have Promised."

Then, an elderly piper dressed in McDaniel clan colors emerged.

"That's Tim. His twin brother, Jim, passed away a few years ago, right after Brice did," Judson explained before he turned his attention back to Addie and silenced the machine alarms.

Tim played "Amazing Grace" and the people lifted their candles high in the air while Judson asked the family to rejoin him around the bedside.

Addie reached out to Garrett. He leaned over her and embraced her for the last time. "Come…back…to…me…someday. I'll…be…waiting …." Unable to find the strength to speak, she mouthed to her family, "I love you, all." She closed her eyes and exhaled.

Judson placed his stethoscope on his mother-in-law's chest. *Ba….dum. Ba….dum. Ba….*

A few moments later, Garrett, joined by his children and grandchildren, walked over to the window, raised the candle, and blew it out.

The following year, the Darling family gathered together again at Sacred Heart Medical Center in celebration and to participate in the ribbon-cutting ceremony for the new Addie Darling Learning and Resource Library with the Reverend Dr. Joshua Goode, Jr. delivering the invocation to the hundreds of guests in attendance. The facility was designed to promote continuous education, impart knowledge, and inspire the next generation of nurses and healthcare workers. Inscribed above the front doors, it read, *Shine your light brightly so that others may see your path. In loving memory of Addie Rose Darling, RN (1895 – 1960).*

# About the Author

Katie Hart Smith, a columnist and published author for 25 years, loved writing as a child, creating her own story and picture books at a very early age. Smith has a wide array of work ranging from medical and academic, to historical fiction, non-fiction, and children's stories. She served on the editorial board and was a manuscript reviewer for the *Orthopaedic Nursing Journal* and was a former member of the advisory board for *Atlanta Sports & Fitness Magazine*. Her monthly column, "From the Heart," is featured in the Gwinnett Citizen newspaper.

As a young adult, she pursued a nursing career and obtained a B.S. in Nursing from Georgia State University and later received a MBA from Troy State University. Throughout her professional career, Smith continued to write and lecture for the medical community, including Emory University's Nell Hodgson Woodruff School of Nursing. In 1995, Smith published, "In the Face of

Disaster: Personal Reflections" in the *Orthopaedic Nursing Journal*, recounting her work assisting with the Flint River Flood recovery efforts.

Inspirational people, places, and social issues are the driving forces for Smith's work. She published *Couch Time with Carolyn*, a memoir, in 2014. This novel was followed by the Sacred Heart (historical fiction) series that focused on the medical community in 1900s Atlanta. The first two books, *Aspirations of the Heart* and *Hope Never Rests*, have been placed in the Georgia Governor's Mansion Library. Katie has been nominated for the *Georgia Author of the Year* award in multiple categories in 2015, 2017, and 2018.

She and her husband, Jeff, reside in Lawrenceville. She is an active civic leader in the Gwinnett community to include her service on the City of Lawrenceville City Council and she was even the first recipient of the Gwinnett Chamber of Commerce's *Healthcare Professional of the Year* award in 2011, recognized for her clinical, literary, and community contributions. Katie has been a featured author at numerous Georgia literary festivals and libraries, and is a member of the National League of American Pen Women and the Atlanta Writers Club. She is a sought out speaker on a local and national level.

For more information, visit: www.katiehartsmith.com.

For more information about Deeds Publishing, visit: www.deedspublishing.com.

CPSIA information can be obtained
at www.ICGtesting.com
Printed in the USA
FSHW021509170619
59128FS

9 781947 309791